LIFE IS SHORT BUT WIDE

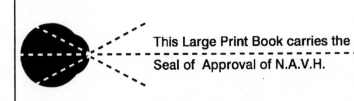

This Large Print Book carries the
Seal of Approval of N.A.V.H.

LIFE IS SHORT
BUT WIDE

J. CALIFORNIA COOPER

THORNDIKE PRESS

A part of Gale, Cengage Learning

GALE
CENGAGE Learning·

Detroit • New York • San Francisco • New Haven, Conn • Waterville, Maine • London

GALE
CENGAGE Learning

Copyright © 2009 by J. California Cooper.
Thorndike Press, a part of Gale, Cengage Learning.

Thorndike Press® Large Print African-American.
The text of this Large Print edition is unabridged.
Other aspects of the book may vary from the original edition
Set in 16 pt. Plantin.
Printed on permanent paper.

LIBRARY OF CONGRESS CATALOGING-IN-PUBLICATION DATA

Cooper, J. California.
    Life is short but wide / by J. California Cooper.
      p. cm. — (Thorndike Press large print African-American)
    ISBN-13: 978-1-4104-1923-1 (alk. paper)
    ISBN-10: 1-4104-1923-1 (alk. paper)
    1. African Americans—Fiction. 2. Oklahoma—History—20th century—Fiction. 3. Domestic fiction. 4. Large type books. I. Title.
PS3553.O5874L54 2009b
813'.54—dc22   2009019414

Published in 2009 by arrangement with Doubleday, an imprint of Knopf Doubleday Publishing Group, a division of Random House, Inc.

Printed in Mexico
2 3 4 5 6 7 13 12 11 10 09

DEDICATED WITH LOVE

Joseph C. and Maxine R. Cooper, my
parents
Paris W. Williams, my chile

PEOPLE IMPORTANT TO ME

Mrs. Velda Berkly of Berkeley, a kind friend,
Dr. Vincent Harding, Alycia Pitts, niece, Dr.
Martin L. King, Jr., Shooty & Becki Fer-
mon, Bette Midler, Yvonne Westmorland of
Oakland, Dr. Richardson of Marcus Books,
Oakland, Danny Glover, Thespian, Senator
Paul, and Sheila, Wellstone, Eartha Kitt,
Dentrus Clay of Southern Café
(Mmmmm), Oakland, Ca., Kim J. Johnson,
of Oklahoma Library.

BookClub members of Seattle, Wa.: Jackie
Roberts, Harriet Slye, Sylvia Bushnell, Edna
C. Nunn, Vanetta Arnold, Liz Causby-
Miles, Pat Coleman, Doris Hill, Nancy
Palmer and Trish Tanner, to name a few.

I cannot tell you how much I love, admire

& applaud Barack Obama and his fantastic, wonderful wife, Michelle Obama.

OTHER VERY IMPORTANT PEOPLE

The people of Iraq, and all other Peoples on this earth that are suffering from the manipulations of great iniquities of inhuman Mankind. May God have mercy on all of us.

ACKNOWLEDGMENTS

I wish to express my gratitude for the opportunity to have worked with Janet Hill on my last several books. I trusted her. She was indispensable. Always generous with her skillful knowledge, she was of great importance to this book. Her caring, no less than her patience, was of great importance to me. I have been very fortunate to have her working with me. I will sorely miss her, from the heart.

I welcome my new editor, Christian Nwachukwu, Jr. I have already benefited from his sharp, but cool, efficiency. I thank him for his extreme kindness'es in the past. Always.

I must thank Russell Perreault for all his kindness'es. He is always a wonderful, agile thinker, and a pleasure to work with.

I do thank Ray & Susan Glend of Chicago for keeping me well with their very effective products.

Curtis Bunn of the National Book Club Conferences of Atlanta, Ga.

Doris Rush for welcoming me to Portland, Oregon.

I thank all my readers for reading. I really love all of you. I thank everyone at Doubleday for everything they do. I really appreciate everything anyone may do for me.

My name is Mrs. Hattie B. Brown, and I am ninety-one years old. My mother, Mrs. Mary Lee Brown, is 105 years old and she has almost all her own teeth. She eats very well, and is still living; so I'm probably going to have a long life.

Now, me and my mother talk bout life all the time, that's ninety-one years' worth, and I have found out that life is sure full of lessons. I have seen most people just skip through their life and don't pay no attention to what they are missing in life: the lessons!

The lessons that tell you it's better to be right, and do right instead of wrong. That will save you from a whole lot of troubles as you go along your way. God runs my life so I don't have to worry bout it.

I'm old, but I'm not too old for everything, and I've made some mistakes, but they were my mistakes and my business.

I have seen so much, right alongside of my

mother, with her teaching me about life and pointing things out to me.

Where we live, Wideland, was once a rural village, and still is a small town. When I was born there were mostly Whites, a few Blacks and Native Americans, even a few Chinese. People was too poor to own anybody, so it was mostly a free, live-where-you-want-to state, but it was still Oklahoma.

Same things happen in Wideland just like everywhere else; they just not as slick and smart about it here. But everybody has their way, and that's why I want to tell you about it. I have to tell this story in the shape of a "Y." Two lives move down into one life. I will tell you one side (hers) first, then the other side (his) next, then these lives will meet and move on through life together. I will tell you when they meet, or you'll just know.

There was a family here who lived such things, it could have taught me, or anybody who needed to know, how to live. What got me, as my mother told me this story, was how some people depend on "good luck" to get them through life. For me, I believe good luck is opportunity met with action.

But, again, as the story grew on my watch, I saw that these lives, all in one family, had many, many different turns. Ain't that interesting though?

One person I thought would never have a life because her body was broken, in a way; she couldn't move much through her life, but I think, in the end, she might have had the most successful life. So you can't tell about life just from looking.

The one I thought was the prettiest and the smartest has the least successful living, and the emptiest life, far as I could see.

Now, let me tell you about my mother and me; neither is too good at counting these many people's ages. So they will not be perfect in order. There are some people in my own family and I don't know their ages, so don't expect me to remember everybody else.

I want to be clear about this, though. When I was watching their lives being lived, I was most drawn to Herman and Myine. I do know their ages. When Rose married that man, Leroy, I saw Herman hanging on the gate, wanting to come to the little wedding. He was bout nine or ten years old. Myine was born the next year, I think, so Herman and Myine are bout ten years apart in age.

The rest of all these different people in the story, I'm gonna tell you, I'm not sure bout so many of them, so don't hold me accountable, cause I'm not. They are just there, part of this interesting life.

My mother is better at counting than I am,

but she don't always remember my age now. She sure does remember her own though. But if you are counting ages, you ain't paying enough attention to the story no way.

The day comes when you look out over this world, and see things you want to do, but now . . . you can only wish you had done them. You get too old to do the things you once dreamed of doing, or just things you want to do even now.

Now . . . it's another thing I really want you to know, it's this. We were created by Jehovah God, and He is a God of Love, and no matter how long we live, we never lose the need to love, and for love. Love runs, and ruins, many lives.

My mama has told me many things about when there were slaves in our family. I didn't know them, but I love them. I ain't shamed of them. Cause they was down, and they got up cause they believed in God. Because of them, I feel God in my blood.

Now, my mama is saying, go ahead and tell you this story, and stop wasting time. So . . . I will begin.

CHAPTER 1

Occasionally, actually quite often, someone will refer to a family or person as dysfunctional. Which, I believe, is a sign of ignorance, for the obvious reason that 70 or 80 percent of all the people who have ever lived were dysfunctional. The other 20 or 30 percent tried to be, or had sense enough to be, a little wiser. Among them, the greatest were disliked, hated, killed, or crucified. And they weren't even perfect, except one.

For instance they crucified Jesus of Nazareth, and all his disciples, Martin Luther King, Jr., Mahatma Gandhi, and others. People who thought as much or more of others than they did of themselves. People killed the people who seemed to wish good things for mankind.

Throughout the history of mankind the struggle for survival on this earth has been extremely, horribly intense and never ending. Wars have been fought, almost continually, when there were enough people to pick sides and fight; and enough dispensable men to be called on to die for their leader, country, or the current god. Then there was slavery; every country or body wanted a slave. Someone to do their work or make money for them. Sometimes slaves were all a war was about. And, if not a whole war, then groups, communities, families, and friends would fight and kill each other. Ain't that interesting?

Not just African slaves; every nationality alive has been a slave, at some time, for some other nation. Believe me. It would seem most of mankind likes killing. For Greed of something, for Gold or financial reward. They doing it now!

You probably know all about history so let us skip, for my purpose, to the twentieth century. People are still fighting slavery in one form or another. In many parts of the world women are fighting for food or medicine, a roof for their children, or some way to keep from being raped, while some other females fight to be able to show their naked behinds, breasts, and everything else they can get out in front of somebody.

In several other parts of the world people are being denied their life, or stolen from their life to be sold. Children are being stolen, every day, killed or given away. Everything I can think of, you already know.

I believe all anyone wants is to be "happy." Everyone just wants to be happy. Why are they not happy? Other people.

Black people, Brown people, Native Americans are treated abominably. White races are not excluded. Poor white people have a struggle to survive also, no matter what they may think. Poor is the operative word. And yet . . . No one wants to leave this earth. Hate to die or scared to die.

I am trying to say too much, and don't know how to say it. But I have often wondered at the Cain and Abel murder. I have wondered who Cain's progeny are. He and the wife he took to the land of Nod had children; and so on and so on, until today. There must be millions of them now. Sometime I think I recognize one on television; they would be the ones trying to run the world.

When you look at history and life, you know the rich, and most anyone in high places, did not get there by being honest or good . . . a few, maybe. If not they, then an ancestor lied and deceived, even murdered.

You may believe me or not. I don't mind. The truth is not popular.

I truly marvel at the struggle for Love.

Parents, children, relatives, all people are part of it. I'm leaving out the insane or mindless; but they, too, usually respond to love and kindness.

Some people think this struggle for love makes the doing of all mean, petty, even evil things necessary. Why? Stupid and mindless is my guess. Because it ain't going to turn out right for them.

Sometimes it's a struggle to get over self-love first. Sometimes in this struggle for love, we give up, or lose, everything, and we still don't achieve love. Some people don't even recognize real love when it comes without being called or sought.

Well, I want to tell you this story: this strange, sad, kind'a beautiful, life story. I want to speak about Love, chile.

CHAPTER 2

In the early twentieth century Wideland was an ordinary, small town in Oklahoma where the ordinary people were beginning to prosper a bit, and the town was expanding. The railroad came in 1907, and by 1910, the steady building-up, all the activity and prosperity, had drawn people of many backgrounds to Wideland. Local calamities, diseases, floods, hurricanes, famine, also sent many people out of their lands, or homes, to seek something better.

In a restless, young country there are many poor people seeking a place where they might find riches, if possible, labor, surely, and pursue some happiness. As usual, there were small investors seeking a better start where everything was needed; items and services were bought and traded briskly. The mentally crooked always follow, bringing hurt and pain for someone.

Wideland was a nice little town grown up

from a village with a good reputation. People came seeking to make a home for their family and future. Large enough to have several churches, two pharmacies, and two doctors, one good one; they both served the small hospital that was for emergencies. A variety of small clothing stores for men and women; working clothes, nothing too grand. Small secondhand shops for everyone.

Wideland even had two small banks, whose owners created the Society, those that considered themselves the elite. There were lumberyards, a hardware store, and a few good-sized stores for buying food and necessities. Farmers and others provided a place for people to bring things to sell or barter; things someone else invariably needed, for most all the people were the striving poor.

A small police station, a small shack for the post office, and a new courthouse to be proud of were built near a large creek diverted off the Long River that ran alongside Wideland. There were many whites, some Blacks and Native Americans, a few Asians. For a long time there was one lawyer, now there were two. More people meant more problems, so the attorneys made a living.

Wideland had good weather and bad weather, none was extreme except occasionally. It was an easy town to live in.

An African American cowboy, Val Strong, and his Native American Cherokee brother-friend, Wings, came to town to find, or build, a house for the pretty young woman Val had recently married, Irene Lowell. They rode in on horses they had caught, broken, and trained themselves. That was their way of life.

Val's mother was a strong, lovely Native American. His father, an African, Black and roundly muscled, strong. He had escaped from his slave-master and lived with the Indians for years. He had been killed in one of the wars or skirmishes the U.S. fought against the Indians. For the land the Indian was born in, and the land the white man had sailed into.

Val had been raised with the Native Americans and in his heart he was a young, strong Brave. Wings had been his friend of his youth, and indeed, he was a young strong Brave.

They wore cowboy hats, and leather pants and boots, even with spurs on their boots. They were handsome, indeed! They worked together running cattle for anyone who had cattle to run from one destination to another. Sometimes they crossed several states: New Mexico, Texas, Kansas, Arizona, even New Jersey, and farther. They had driven cattle as far east as they cared to go. They were leery about people who were too strange. They were quiet and kept themselves apart, except from the men they worked with whom they liked.

Herding cattle paid good money. Val had saved all his working life, about fifteen years. Now he had a sizable sum to purchase a house for his new wife; she did not want to live on a reservation. He was eager to start his new life. He was in love.

As he had passed through Wideland many times, he observed the town and the people. The sky was deep blue and stretched to far, far yonder, and was full of enchanting voluptuous clouds. Plenty of pretty birds, fish, and animals lived there. He loved all the natural beauty of God's creations. He also wanted to stay near the reservation.

He didn't know how deep the little town was, but he knew it was long; it stretched a long, long way to the north and south, following the river. He decided his wife, and later, children, would be safe when he was away on a cattle drive. It seemed a town where a family could live in contentment.

The handsome dark-brown sunburnt

man, Val, was around thirty years old when he married Irene. Irene was from a little town near Wideland. She had learned to read, write, and cipher, and shared her knowledge in a little shack with a sign nailed over the door saying "School." She had no teaching certificate, but taught all ages and colors. She dearly needed the money for she meant to be independent, and had no help.

There weren't many students in her classes at a time; who had the money? Older people knew the advantages of being able to read and count; they came, and brought their children and grandchildren. She charged a pittance, and that was all her living.

She helped serve two meals a day at Mz. Shaw's rooming house, where she lived. Irene also helped clean the other guest rooms in exchange for her own tiny room, and the small shack she used for a teaching classroom.

Mz. Shaw owned the room and boarding-house. There weren't many boarders at Mz. Shaw's, and they were most all men. Irene kept her eyes down in the dining room as she did her duties. But when Val came through the town on a cattle drive and stayed overnight at Mz. Shaw's, she had noticed him.

She saw that whenever she raised her eyes, he was always looking at her. After the first time he saw her, he returned about every two weeks. He changed; he did not sleep out in the fields under the stars with his herding partner, Wings *(sometime called just "Wing")*, as had been his habit. He slept at Mz. Shaw's when in Wideland.

Mz. Shaw's was not the best place to stay in Wideland, but colored people were not allowed to stay everywhere, and Val would not spend his hard-earned money just for a place to sleep. He was used to sleeping outdoors under the stars until winter moved over the land. Mz. Shaw's was honest, clean, and cheap, and the food, cooked by Mz. Shaw, was good, better than that at the "best" houses.

Irene had tried to pay as little attention to Val as necessary, except a few quick glances across the table. She thought he was handsome, but she was looking for a better job or way to make a living. She would rather have a good job than a poor husband. "He probably already married anyway," she thought, and put him out of her mind. "No time for that foolishness!"

She thought a lot about a husband; someone to help her, protect her. She prayed a lot at night, asking, "Lord, please direct my

22

feet cause how can I know what to do?" But Irene had good sense, and the Lord probably let her lead her own self; because how else is a person going to learn?

Val had asked Mz. Shaw if Miss Lowell was married, and when he found out she was not, he thought of her even more often. After he had that information, on his next trip he brought her an ocean-colored turquoise flower. He gave it to her, saying, "That's what color the ocean look like." She could only sigh, "Ohhhhhhhhh," with a smile.

Irene loved the lovely little jewel. It was her first real gift from a man she did not think could be expecting anything from her. She looked into his face, still smiling as she thanked him, and walked away. She had not had so many experiences that she knew exactly what a person did in "courting," she had learned mostly what not to do. But she remembered to smile at him again as she placed his gift gently and firmly in her apron pocket.

Irene was a medium-sized woman, bright and healthy. She had smooth brown-gold skin and clear, hazel eyes like dusky sunshine. Even though they were sad eyes, they were bright and honest, seeking some happiness, yet reserved and subdued. Irene was twenty-two years old. She had been struggling to survive ever since she could remember. She had run away from a motherless home, at last, five years ago. Running from her father, brothers, uncles, and white men pulling after her body.

Irene, clean, mannerable, and presenting herself well, had found work as a servant to a family with three children. It was a fairly wealthy house, and they spent good money on the children's education and tutors. Irene always sat in on all their classes for the five years she was there.

She had learned to read and write and more, along with the children. She was alert to life's demands. Her learning was her tool for her living. Now she taught what she had learned. She still had her same books, loved, worn, but very well cared for. She taught from them, sometimes copied from them for her students, but seldom let anyone touch them. No, sir!

Now, Val thought of her very, very often. He loved his mother and his Indian family, but sometimes he had looked at American houses in passing. He wondered at the privacy and quiet inside those rooms. Native Americans lived in many types of structures. Some even built low, flat houses similar to the white man's before the white man came. But those were Indians who worked the land, not migrating with the seasons and animals.

Val, being a young healthy man, looked at all women, their clothes, their ways. He was handsome, and they looked at him, too. He did not like the white women because of his family's history with white men, but he knew there were Brown women, and women who were Black, like his father. And now, he had met one. He liked the women on his reservation, but felt like they were sisters. "Oh, Irene, Irene."

It had taken a few months, though he asked often, before Irene allowed him to take walks with her. She knew about men and how they could be. She had a healthy and wise fear of them.

Val, with good sense, was patient. He was a thoughtful man, and discovered she liked books and learning. He could not read, but he had brought her a few books here and there, wherever he could find them. Spelling books, simple reading books, and even one from Europe he had found in a bartering shop. The books pleased her; that made him happy.

When she found he could not read, she decided to teach him. He had already begun to fall in love with her, and now, slowly she began to love him, not too much, but a little. They did not see each other often because of his work schedule, but it was at least twice a month.

Soon, very soon, that was not enough for him. He wanted her as his wife. He decided to ask her to marry him. She had to decide whether she loved him a little or liked him a lot. She decided to ask Mz. Shaw, the landlady, for some advice.

Mz. Shaw had thoughts. "Chile, that man is a working man. He don' seem to be no gambler or liar. He always pay me what he owe me, and don't make no fuss bout it. That Indian friend of his, he ain't no thief, cause I done tried him. And, usually, if a Indian like you, you a pretty good person. How do ya feel bout him? You gonna have to sleep with him! I don blive you done done that already, has you?" She smiled and gave Irene a sly, sidelong inquiring look.

Irene gave a little gasp, "No, ma'am! The last thing I need is a baby sittin on my hip!"

Mz. Shaw nodded her head, wisely, as she said, "That's right, chile, keep that dress down over yo knees. Cause once they get that juney-puney, mens be gone." She moved a pan on the hot stove, stirred another one as she shook her head dolefully. "Chile, this here world is a wilderness, and you out here struggling on yo own, all by yo'self. This a hard world sometime. Specially for womens. I ain't crazy bout that ole husband of mine, but he's mine, and he work hard WITH me, not on me. He younger 'en me, but I watches him."

Irene, though serious, smiled in understanding.

Mz. Shaw continued, as she stirred her pots. "Ya got to think bout some things! Where you gonna live? Is he gonna take you to live on some Indian reservation? Live in the wilds? Ya betta ask him bout that. Do he save his money? Ya need a home if you gonna leave this'un here. Ya can't walk out into the streets and hope for the best; ya betta check on that best first. Why, you a lady what can read and write! See what he have in store for ya. If ya ain't sure you loves him, ya can wait for a little. You a nice-lookin woman. Be somebody else comin right along." She gave Irene that sidelong look again. "Less'en ya done already give him some, and liked it ya own self."

As Irene left for her class, she waved the last words away and started hoping her students were there waiting in the shack. She needed even those few nickels and dimes, and even pennies.

Later, Irene took Mz. Shaw's words and,

as she lay in her small, but clean and neat bed in her small, but clean room that night she thought about Val. "I don't like poor. I don't want to be poor. And if I have children I want them to do better'n me. Be something besides born. But I do like him, Val. He kind of old, I think. Thirty-three or something. He way older than me. But, still, he is working. Oh, Lord, don't you forget to direct my feet. Cause I'm scared. Scared to do it, and scared not to."

CHAPTER 3

Val and Irene continued their courtship, such as it was, and it bloomed slowly. She still didn't know if she loved him when she agreed to marry him.

She looked in his eyes, seriously, and told him, "I don't want to be no farmer's wife, Val. I ain't diggin and picking round in no dirt under no hot sun. I don't want to cry cause I don't have no food either. I don't want no babies standing out under no hot sun with their eyes full of tears and their stomach full of empty air."

His heart was full of love, so he assured her, "I'll take care of you. I make a good livin, and I ain't no farmer, though I do know how to plant things to grow; every Indian does."

"You a Indian?"

"They are men, and I am a man."

Val had been referred to a Jewish man who

dealt in land and such, Mr. Meyer, who lived in the Wideland area. Val rode over to see him one day. Mr. Meyer told him, "I believe there is something coming up pretty quick. There is a lady, an old lady, whose children have moved east and their mother is out here all alone. She is the last white person on that street. They want to move her back east with them. She don't want to go, but I blive she is going. Give me a couple of weeks, then stop back by and perhaps I will have it to show you. It's gonna cost round bout two hundred dollars, though. It's worth it. Don't know if you can owe them or not, but they got banks here. You got credit?"

Val shook his head, "No, ain't never needed none."

Mr. Meyer shook his head, understanding. "Well, it's time to think of all these things now you're gonna get married. Young man, when you get married many things change." He laughed softly. "For the better, though, I must say. It's usually for the better. She a nice woman?"

Val grinned and nodded his head. "She is very nice. A good woman. A teacher."

Mr. Meyer liked that. "Well, we'll just work on getting a good house for her."

So now Val was back to look at the house.

Val liked the house and was even surprised it was as nice as it was. It was two stories, large and well built. The original owner had used good materials for this home for his family, and it was well planned out and built.

The house was about thirty-five years old, it had been white but was yellowing from age. It sat on five acres of land with neighboring houses, usually with the same degree of land, clustered in that area. The house had a large front porch with most windows looking out to the trees and yard.

The owner, a calculating builder, balanced the house. A lawn and a once blooming garden, now dying. Ventilation, drainage, and water service. All prime quality. Iron clamps and girders, fireproof. He had also built a three-room shotgun house far off to the side of the front acreage, for a laborer, or a guest, if needed.

There were four large bedrooms upstairs: a parlor room, dining room, and kitchen downstairs. The carpets were worn thin from many years of children, cleanings, and now neglect, as children left home and the widowed mother aged. The curtains, left behind, lifting in the breeze, were a bit ragged. The paint in all the rooms was old and yellowed with age.

The kitchen had a good wood stove for cooking and heat, and the sink had a water pump bringing water from the well. Stairs with a solid banister led upstairs to the bedrooms. The movers had left an upright piano in the living room; it just sat there looking lonely, but slightly grand.

Val thought all in all it was a good house for his young bride, who had never had a home of her own. "It will be mine. And my children will have a home. All this land, and these trees, the birds in them and the bugs beneath them will be mine. Ours."

He paid one hundred and fifty dollars for the house. A goodly sum at that time. That money stood for years of sleeping on the ground, and sweat running down his face and back, smelling of horses and cattle.

The house sat on the acreage with a good number of trees. Fine beautiful oaks, a good-sized pecan tree, many willows and other types. Plus several fruit trees, peach, apple, plum, full grown. They all needed some attention, but Val knew how to do that too.

Family name of Smith rented the house across the road. Joseph and Bertha, recently married. Clean and poor. Joe worked at the lumberyard, and did odd handyman jobs for a thin living.

Bertha stayed home to care for her husband, running off now and again to do domestic work to help with the money they sorely needed. She mostly sat in a narrow front window to watch life go slowly by. She loved flowers and horses. Actually she loved anything live.

Val hired Bertha to clean his new house for his new wife. Wash the curtains, polish the banister and floors, clean the fireplaces, polish up the kitchen, and all the things a woman would see needed to be done. He smiled proudly. "I want my wife to like this here house, Mz. Bertha! This my first and only wife and this our first house!"

Proud, he nearly flew back to Irene, wrapped his arms around her, saying, "Better start getting ready to move, sweetheart, into your own house. I done . . . I have bought it. It's ours! I blive you are going to like it!"

CHAPTER 4

Perhaps only someone who has never had a home can imagine the feeling that possessed Irene's heart. Her eyes filled with tears that rolled down her happy face. She was very happy, and grateful to Val. She thought to herself as she looked at him, "My husband. I am beginning a new life! A good life."

Then, immediately, she said aloud to him, "There is that one thing I want you to remember, Val. I am not going to be no farmer. I mean that, Val."

He smiled and pressed her warm, firm body to his as he said, "You will have a little kitchen garden, won't you?"

"A 'little' kitchen garden is fine, but no big un!" She stepped back from his arms. "I can't hardly believe that house is nice as you said it is. And you had the money for all that?"

He smiled and pulled her back to his hungry arms, saying nothing.

She sighed. "Well, I'm just happy to have a house to ourself."

On the day they moved, Val had driven the wagon for what seemed to Irene a long time before they reached Wideland. She was frowning, looking the town over when Val turned off a busy street and proceeded up a small hill. At last Val pointed, and Irene finally did see the house. Then Val turned the wagon, filled with her few things and many secondhand gifts from Mz. Shaw, into the yard. She was more than pleased. "A house! My own house! Two stories!" In her thoughts she said, "At last, mine!"

Wings was there to help Val, of course. They happily emptied the wagon, and became at home in their new house. Irene ran her hand, lovingly, over the piano. Tears formed for the hundredth time as she thought, "My mind is at rest, my heart is at rest, because my man has provided. Our home. Thank You, God."

Val was surprised later that night. He knew his wife was tired; they all were. But Irene opened her heart and body up to him as never before. Their new bedroom, a thin mattress on the floor, was filled with shining joy, pleasure, and bliss. Even for Irene, for the first time. At last, she understood why everyone wanted to do this thing called loving. It was loving; something to be shared only with your husband, not a father, uncle, or brother, or strange white man.

When Val and Irene had their first child, a baby girl, Irene named her Rose, because Irene loved roses. She had planted a few and they came up! Another few years, and the second, and last, child was born. They let Wings name her. He named her Tante. Irene liked the sound of the name so it remained.

Bertha and Joseph had their first child somewhere around that time; my mother was having her own children, so she didn't keep up with everybody over there so much at that time.

Anyway, having listened to Irene teach about literature, Bertha had learned some odd bits; she named her daughter Juliet. It took about a year to discover that child, Juliet, was born with a problem with her legs. She always fell when she tried to walk. People said she could crawl very well, and did. But she had to be watched closely so she wouldn't crawl on or into the wrong things.

By that time, Wings had married a lovely maiden named Spring Feather. But he did not move off the reservation. "Spring wants to be close to her mother," Wings said.

"Until she learns to cook better, I am happy to be where both our mothers do the cooking." He looked down at his hands as he smiled, saying, "I'll never move away from there anyway. I like being free. I don't want five or six trees, I want a forest! I want a range. I want to see all the animals and birds every day." Val leaned back in his chair, smiled in agreement, but he loved his Irene and his home.

They slowly settled into the neighborhood. In time they bought some chickens for the hen house. Several colors, several kinds. Eggs were a main staple; they wouldn't have to buy them. Then he started turning the earth for planting food. Irene watched him; it wouldn't be a farm. For the moment, their start in life was complete.

Except for the times Irene brought little Rose to Bertha's house, and later, Tante, so she could talk with Bertha, there was no company for either woman. Bertha's family lived too far away; in any event she never mentioned them, and none came to visit. As Juliet grew, she waited, sitting every day looking through a front window at the door across the street . . . and life.

Juliet was glad to have a family near even if they weren't big enough to come through that door yet. In her young mind she thought, like her mama told her, "They comin one day!"

Over the years, Wings, always observant, had noticed the little girl sitting lonely in the window across the street from his friends. The next time he came to visit Val, Wings brought some material with him, and showed Juliet how to make simple baskets. "You can make em out of anything, once you learn the way it goes. But use these reeds for now. I'll bring you some more when I remember."

Young Juliet possessed a strong mind, and was given to much thinking in her quiet, lonely life. She was almost overwhelmed when she saw he had also brought a small container which would hold about four pounds of rich soil. He put the container close to the window where the sunshine would reach it, and said, "Here are some seeds. You plant em in this here dirt, water em every day accordin to how hot it is and how dry they are. When they grow, you can eat em. I'm not tellin you what they are. I'll let you be surprised."

When he left, Juliet's heart was about to burst! He had no idea how much that meant to the little disabled girl who was beginning to feel so useless to herself and her mother around the house.

As time went by, when Irene had a little extra time, she took little scraps of material and made a doll for Juliet. Then she would give Juliet little pieces of material, left over from her own sewing for her family, so Juliet could learn to sew, and make things for her doll. In this way Irene and Bertha became friends. Bertha was so glad to have someone showing interest, caring about her child.

CHAPTER 5

Sometimes Bertha did small domestic jobs for a few ladies, and Irene would keep an eye on Juliet to see she was still sitting in the window where Bertha sat her every day.

Irene's kitchen garden was larger now, but not too large. She laughed as she told Val, "I got help, and company now. I can work long as I want to, and stop when I want to. I like gardening now." She quickly added, "I don't want any larger garden though." Years passed that way. Time passes quickly when life is smooth and you are busy.

Rose and Tante were good-mannered, lovely little girls. Their mother insisted on good manners. "Makes a huge difference in this here world!" They both wore their full heads of hair braided, one braid on each shoulder with bright little ribbons or knitting yarn tied neatly on them. Their cheeks rosy in smooth, healthy skin, Rose's rich brown, and Tante's golden-pecan.

Their mother insisted that they care for their teeth morning and night. "We don't have no dentist money to waste round here! We can keep our teeth long as we live if we just keep them clean."

She started early teaching them to read, write, and count. "There isn't any room for fools in this world, ladies! You never know when you gonna have to take care your own self!"

Val brought them books, whatever kind, whenever he saw one for sale that he could afford. When he couldn't afford it, he paid down, asking the seller to hold it for just a little while.

Rose was a gentle and caring child, moving without haste, but steadily through her chores. She was always trying to help her mother even when she didn't know exactly how. Tante was zesty, full of energy, life, and laughter. She was also very smart; she learned quickly. She preferred being out of the house, always finding something to do in the yard. She begged Val for a dog.

Val brought them a healthy, frisky German shepherd dog to grow up with them, to protect them. Everyone loved the dog they named Brave, except the neighbors. He didn't like to "do his business" in his own yard; he went far down the road in the neighbors' yards. Keeping up with, and cleaning up after, Brave was one of Tante's jobs. She liked the job, it gave her a chance to talk to all the other people in her neighborhood.

The girls took Brave to visit Juliet all the time. Juliet loved holding, petting Brave. "He is so fluffy soft, and so pretty, Mama. Why cain't we have one, Mama?" She never wanted to let them leave and take Brave away. Bertha often had to put them out because they found it hard to leave the crying little girl.

When they would leave, Juliet would cry to her mother, "How come I can't have a puppy-dog too, Mama?" Bertha, who believed the truth was always best, would answer, "Cause we ain't hardly feed yourself, chile. We can't give no good food to a dog. Jes play with that 'un when you can."

So they lived life, and they all grew.

Irene loved her children equally, but was closer to Rose. Rose was always underfoot, sewing, cleaning, working with her mother. Tante got up heading outside with the free, clear air, birds, bugs, and Brave. Brave would always be waiting for her. She seemed a laughing, happy child, but inside her mind . . . some feeling, just out of the reach of her mind, was that feeling that something was missing. She didn't know what it was, or even why she thought it was, but . . . it was.

Tante adored her father and Wings. The three of them were a separate family in her mind. She called Wings "Uncle," and Wings liked her best. He didn't like Rose less, he just paid less attention to her because she was always in the house doing woman things.

Wings would remark, "That little roughneck, Tante, is always trying to get up on a horse! You watch her, Val, one day she will ride away from here!" When she was seven years old they found a small horse in a herd of wild horses caught for Wings' friends and family. Wings decided it should be for Tante. They broke in the gloriously free and beautiful little horse, cleaned it up, and named the horse Windy.

Rose was content to sit on the veranda and watch Tante ride; she wasn't interested. She liked to smooth or brush Windy's lustrous coat, but she was content to sit on the porch with the dog, Brave, and watch her sister ride through the wind with her braids flying.

When her father was away herding cattle, Tante had to keep Windy clean, feed him, and keep the yard clean all by herself with just a little help from her mother and sister. She did it all. That gave her more to talk about with her father when he returned.

Val loved to herd cattle, but he loved to come home. He loved to look at the house as his horse trotted toward it. He would ride up the street and, suddenly, there it was! His life!

The wars and rumors of wars in Europe had not really touched their personal world.

The years passed pleasantly for the family. The girls grew in health, and were schooled at home. The home in which they lived was warm and cozy, filled with love. Rose was now ten years old; she was not lazy, but she was not excited about anything.

CHAPTER 6

Tante . . . I guess that chile was round eight or nine years old then. I'm not sure about that, but I do know she was begging for knowledge and loved books. She had made a friend, Bill Evans, at the newspaper office where she went to get a weekly Wideland newspaper sometimes.

Bill Evans was a news reporter. A kind man, he was from the East, and was supposed to be passing through Wideland. He got broke gambling one night, and had to stay to work awhile. He was good at his work, so the Wideland news service was glad to employ him.

He had sold Tante a newspaper over the counter, once or twice. He smiled, and was nice, so Tante gathered her courage to talk to him. You never knew in Oklahoma in those days. But being from the East, and knowing more about life, he was different. He liked Tante as she turned her bright, fresh face up to him to ask, "Do you all have anything else I can read?"

Books were still hard to get. Her friend Bill, the newspaperman, helped by ordering books for her even though he had been chided about her. "It might not be so good that little negra gal comin in here talkin to you, Bill! Sor'da spoils the office. Folks might not like it." But Bill didn't stop. He liked Tante because she had spunk. He laughed to himself as he thought, "and a brain. She likes books. She even reads this little weekly newspaper we publish."

Tante had dreams. Some books taught her what few choices she might have. What few choices any woman might have, especially a Negro or an Indian. She wanted to go to New York, the place she read so much about. The place Mr. Evans talked so much about.

Throughout that year he told her about the "Jazz Age" they were both missing. About women getting the vote at last. One day he told her about prohibition of liquor, about the rise of organized crime. He shook his head as he smiled, saying, "I have a master's degree in philosophy as well as other good things!" They talked a lot, outside, leaning against the side of the newspaper office.

Once he told her, "You're an awfully friendly young lady, Tante. You got to be careful making friends with grown men. They are not all nice men . . . nor ladies either, I guess." But mostly he talked about New York, and even England and Paris.

Everything seemed to come out of New York. Clothes, politics, the riches, the beauty. After heavy thinking, Tante would say to herself, "The only way I'll ever get outta Wideland is to study hard enough to get into some college!"

Irene read the newspapers Tante brought her. She had told her family of the war with Germany in 1917. She made them mindful of washing their hands by telling them about the pandemic of Spanish Influenza of 1918 killing from ten to sixty million people of the world.

She talked often of college to Rose and Tante. She had never allowed her own self to think of college. Sadly, she knew she couldn't ever go. "But they got colored colleges now, even in Oklahoma." Tante paid no mind to that news.

Rose didn't worry about college. She was happy just cooking or cleaning beside her mother, or sitting on the porch with Brave beside her or at her feet. Windy, the horse, was kept on the reservation with Wings now.

"He needs more room," Daddy had said.

Val was gone most of the time, but Irene took her children to the small Negro church a short distance from the house. "You need to learn about God in this Godless world. Because if I know anything about life, you are going to need Him." So they went to church.

Irene always asked her girls, "What did you learn about God this Sunday?" The answers from Rose were usually "He's mean. He going to put us in a burning place!" And, just as usual, Tante, with her fast, studious self, would say, "You need to read for yourself, Rose. The Bible doesn't say everything that preacher says. In fact, it doesn't hardly say anything that minister says. You have to read it for yourself. Tricky people make the Bible tricky. I study it for myself!"

Life had been moving slowly, comfortably in most of the world. But slowly, almost imperceptibly, it began to move a little faster.

CHAPTER 7

Irene had reached out to teach the small colored community, starting with Bertha, and sometimes Joe. She didn't charge them because she knew they had no money for extras. But a few others began to come to the classroom in the little shotgun house she taught in. The class grew slowly. Most had no money. They bartered food or work.

Times were hard, as usual. So she didn't charge everybody. But every cent counted so she charged those who could pay a little. You had to bring your own pencil and paper, but she provided that sometimes, also. "Well," she told herself, "you have made some progress. At least you are teaching in a shack on your own land, not someone else's."

A few years passed, and everything held steady, but Irene had been slowing down some, lying down for short periods during the day. She was taking little packets of powders the pharmacist sold her for her aching head. But, still, she always got up to do whatever chores her home needed. Little Rose was a good help to her. Irene would lie down thinking, "I am not that old to be getting sick. What is the matter with me? I'm too tired, too early. I'm so glad this child is here, Lord. Thank you."

A few more years, and Irene began to remain in bed most of every day, against her will. She directed the order of her house, but her strength was ebbing away each day. The doctor did not know what to do except keep giving her the same packets of powder, hardly more than bicarbonate of soda.

He resented having to come to her house, but he had not studied long, and was not a rich doctor. "You can jes send one of your gals down for these next time. You got something I don't know what to do with. Pro'bly something that comes with being a Negra."

Good, knowledgeable doctors were difficult, if not impossible, to get in country towns, and sometimes even in big cities, and sometimes your color decided the time and medicine you received.

Irene would gather her small strength, and say to him, "Doctor, I don't have any 'gals.'

My daughters are girls or young ladies." He never gave any sign of hearing her. She was too weak to say more, and she needed him for what little he could do. "Lord, help me and my daughters, please."

Over the years, they had been going to the little church that was of no particular denomination anymore. Sometimes the traveling minister was Baptist, sometimes Methodist. But it was a sermon, and that was what the small congregation wanted.

Lately, their regular minister lived in Wideland. He was a reddish-looking, plump, apparently nice, ineffectual minister who traveled a wide area for pay and food. He was unconsciously hypocritical, even malicious and mean. He was tolerant of nothing that was not his idea. He had great reverence for money, and he was not very intelligent. He leaned heavily on the Bible he did not understand; he always carried it wherever he went. Even to the corner if that was as far as he was going.

Bertha wasn't sure about him; Tante apparently didn't like him; Val was unconscious of him. Rose worshipped him when he spoke with fire and brimstone in his voice at funerals. Irene just shook her head, saying nothing, but thinking, "I am not going to speak against any man of the church."

But, after all, he spoke of God. Whether he was right or wrong didn't matter, because no one ever asked to see if what he said was in the Bible. Just to have someone speak of God in hallowed tones was enough for most of the congregation.

They were just glad to have a church, a regular preacher, and a place to go, and gossip, on their day of rest. Most didn't like the new minister; he was too glib and grasping. He passed the "plate" so many times in one day, it often returned to him empty.

He had no wife nor children with him. His eyes always glittered at the ladies, and, every once in a while, a few smelled liquor on his breath when he had been invited for Sunday dinner. Those who really wanted to know God's word read their own Bibles at home, like Tante did.

Tante liked to talk to everybody, most of all she liked to hear Wings talk about his history. The trail of tears, the sorrows of his people. She was interested in everything.

She always picked up her newspaper, which she, now, got free for delivering a few extras to special customers. She wanted to make that a paying job. "I can pick up an old newspaper off the street for myself. I don't need to work to get a newspaper; I need some money!" She was making plans.

"I got to pay for my college."

Tante was always making new friends on her few newspaper deliveries. Some she was able to borrow books from. Some liked the "little clean colored girl" who liked to read. One man even loaned her books on higher mathematics, English, geography, and a book titled *The Natural Wonders of the World.* Tante hungrily devoured them. She was fascinated with Europe. The man, he wasn't from Oklahoma, talked to her about college and scholarships.

Some white people didn't like Tante at all. Said, "Get off my porch!" or "Get away from round here!" It confused and hurt her. "What's wrong with them? Why? I wasn't doing anything wrong!" But she knew. Coloreds weren't liked everywhere. She just couldn't understand why. She liked all the Negro people she knew.

More important to her, the thought of New York buried itself in her fertile mind, and college became even more of an obsession for her. She didn't hate Wideland, but she didn't want to stay, nor live, there.

CHAPTER 8

There were more Negro people in Wideland then. Coloreds lived just about everywhere. Except for the "elite" property, money was such that if you wanted to sell your house, you took whoever had enough money, so the colored population was moving up.

Of the young men that Rose and Tante met in church, at a wedding, or at a funeral, Tante smiled at them all. Rose looked at them, then quietly looked down into her lap. If they had dreams, or liked books, Tante would become quite friendly. "Do you have any books?" was one of her first, and most important, questions.

Rose just smiled at them, and might ask, "Are you in Wideland to stay? Do you go to school? My mother teaches school." She was impressed by one young man, Leroy. He was not very handsome, but he made up for that by being a very engaging, nice young man. They parted friends, but she really didn't pay special attention to any of the boys. Probably because she was very shy.

Irene was very glad that Tante liked books and had dreams of going to college. There were not many Negro colleges in their area, if any, as far as she knew. She told Tante, "I know right after freedom came there was several schools and colleges that were started. We'll find some information on those in Oklahoma. Just give me a little time." Tante wasn't thinking about staying in Oklahoma. New York was where she dreamed of going.

Irene was still growing steadily weaker, daily. The medicine the doctor had been giving her did her no good at all. Bertha now came by to see Irene every day. She knew of the lump Irene had discovered at the base of her neck. Irene kept a scarf or towel around her neck so her children and Val would not notice it. The lump gave her pain only occasionally; it just sat in its place, worrying her, sapping the strength from her body. Growing.

CHAPTER 9

At this time, I believe it was around 1928. I'm not sure, but it was after the wars in Europe; Ford Motor Company was mass-producing cars. There were, at least, thirteen million cars on the roads. Traffic lights were in existence, the radio was being sold. There were transcontinental telephones. They had even put the first airplane in a war. Times and things were forging ahead in supposed progress.

Life began to move with more speed. Just a little, but you could feel it. You could see it, if you were watching Life.

Irene's doctor still did not know what to do with her malady. He really hadn't worried, he still thought it must be just a Negro thing. He didn't keep up with any medical journals, they were cast aside as he continued to prescribe, and sell, *his* powders. Other doctors might be knowledgeable, but they cost more. Irene didn't want to take any money away from her family.

Val couldn't ask his Indian doctor for help in the matter because he didn't know there was a matter yet. He wouldn't have cared about the money. He knew there was something wrong, but Irene had been especially careful in keeping the growing lump hidden from him. Earlier in her illness, loving Val as she did, and being a passionate woman, she was able to cover her pain from him. Sometime the moans were stifled cries of pain.

She always forced herself to gather enough strength when he was home to cook at least one meal with Rose's help. But Val lived many nights on the cold ground, dreaming of making love to his wife when he returned home from a long drive; his wife was in no condition to make love to him as she wanted. She told him it was just a woman's problem. He would ask no more questions . . . for a while.

Just lately, in the last few months after Tante's graduation from high school, Irene had taken to staying in the bed later in the mornings. She would hug Val as tight as she could, then push him away, saying, "It's just a ladies' problem, honey. Don't you worry, I'll be fine pretty soon." But her voice was getting weaker. Val felt so helpless, and he thought he should not ask his young daughters.

It had taken several hard, long, painful years, but it had to come. One morning Rose went upstairs with a cup of tea for her mother, made from leaves Wings had brought. She had baked a fresh loaf of bread, so there was a thick piece of toast with homemade apple jam on the tray. She planned to coax her mother into eating, but Irene did not answer.

On her mother's face was a frowning smile, and her hands were closed tightly in fists. Irene had died during the night, quietly, like she did everything else in her life.

Rose set the tray down, and thought she would see her mother raise her head with her loving, grateful smile, as usual. But her mother did not raise her head, as usual. Her dear mother was dead. Irene was dead. Gone.

Rose ran from the room screaming for Tante. She kept running until, across the street, she reached Bertha's tired, decaying house, screaming for Bertha. Bertha came running through her door to the porch, passing Rose, heading toward Irene's house. Rose followed her crying, "She dead, Mz. Smith! She died! Oh, my Lord, my Lord.

My mama's gone. What are we gonna do now?!"

Bertha ran up the stairs to the bedroom. Without turning her head, she said to Rose, "Hush, chile, hush. You still got God. You got your daddy; you gonna be alright! You gotta be stronger than you ever been. Your mama may be gone, but your daddy is due home. Go get the minister, any minister, and bring Mr. Gipson from the funeral parlor. Where is Tante?"

Bertha had washed, prepared, and laid out Irene's body for her burial and the funeral when Val reached his home. Most funeral services were held in the parlor of the deceased's home; hence the term "funeral parlor" when burying the dead became a business. Money, place, and facilities decided, as things became more modern, the type of funeral a person would have.

The death of his lovely wife hit Val very hard. He had always been able to count on her being there with his children. He hadn't even known she was really that sick, that close to death. Now . . . she was gone. And . . . he loved her.

He had bought her another little pretty turquoise jewel. He had always brought her something when he returned home. She had hundreds of the lovely turquoise pieces. Her oceans. They were given to her to lift her spirit. "But my own soul is gone," Val thought. "She has left me. I ain't got nobody no more."

He lay across the bed Irene had died in and cried, deep, harsh sounds that men make when they are in pain. Sounds of feelings that came from the bottom of his heart and body. He couldn't stop crying. He finally fell asleep, drained. When he woke during the night his daughters were lying close, one on each side. He placed his arms around them, and fell asleep again, a little comforted. "These are our children. Our flesh."

In the morning he found his daughters had quietly crawled out of the bed, covering him with a blanket. He went, slowly, downstairs, and putting his arms around his daughters, he thanked God they had their mother until they were almost grown. They cried, again, together.

Juliet cried at home, in her mother's arms. She had truly loved her "Aunt" Irene.

CHAPTER 10

Everyone knew Rose would take her mother's death hard, but they were not as sure about Tante. Tante seemed to keep it inside of herself. They only saw her cry, helplessly, a few times. But they could tell by her swollen face in the mornings that she cried during the nights. The two sisters stood holding hands around their father's back, as he held them close under his arms.

Val was tired, and showing his age also. The blow of Irene's death had struck him mightily. He had always made sure to hide his weariness from his wife. He didn't like her to worry that he was getting too old to work such long stretches as he did. There was less cattle herding now, and he thought he had two daughters who expected to go to college. He thanked God the house was paid for.

It was a quiet funeral, many people came from all around the countryside. They brought all types of beautiful wildflowers or blossoming branches of trees. Val didn't know the little school-shack's reputation had reached so many people. He was proud. Some people in Wings's family had come to Irene to learn to read and write also. They came bringing beautiful mementos, flowers, and foods.

No one knew any of Irene's people to let them know she had passed on. But her husband and daughters grieved very hard. She was buried in a beautifully serene wooded area near Wings's people. "Rest in Peace, dear Wife and Mother" was carved on her small tombstone by Val.

Then the little family of three went home to plan how to face the future. Val felt he had no future; and he was indeed breaking down. Tante's grief went into her plans; they became more urgent. She must get away before something happened to make her remain in Wideland. Rose would go to speak with the minister, now and then, to ask him to tell her about the heavenly place where her mother was waiting.

He told her, her mother was waiting in heaven for her family. Tante thought that was untrue. "How does she know where we will go?" She decided her mother was resting and waiting in her grave until the resurrection, as the Bible said she would.

Tante had somehow managed to get a small scholarship, and she had a little money her family and friends had contributed to her education. She was now preparing to leave for college. She kept her mind directed toward the East. She mulled over Hampton and Howard universities. She finally chose Howard University, smaller then, but already showing evidence of the greatness it would acquire. She was accepted. She had very good scholastic records. She never made less than a B+ in any subject; she worked hard to accomplish that.

There was no college wardrobe for Tante. She, Rose, Juliet, and Mz. Bertha Smith sewed feverishly, looking at the few magazines Bertha brought from her domestic job for a wealthy mistress. The ladies in the church reached deeply into already empty pockets; they donated several yards of fabric and a good navy-blue, secondhand coat.

But Tante's looks were clean, fresh, and good enough that the few things she had were the right colors to switch and change around enough to be satisfied. She had to be satisfied. She didn't want to leave her family sad and more broke than they were already.

Juliet watched from her window, wishing and dreaming that it was herself going off to college, or off to . . . anywhere.

The young sisters held each other and their father tightly when Tante was leaving for college. Tante was thinking, "I am going to make my own future!" as the train pulled away from the station and the only people in the world she knew who loved her.

Val and Rose watched the train pull farther and farther away, until, and even after, it was long out of sight. Then they walked, slowly, away, holding hands. They were silent for awhile, then Rose said to her father, "One by one our family is disappearing from our life, huh, Daddy?"

He put his arm around her, and patted her shoulder. "There has only been one, Rosie, but such a big empty place she left behind. Life is like that. People go, and some of them come back. Tante will come back, and we still got each other anyhow." He smiled down at her, but he didn't feel that smile in his heart. He still missed Irene, terribly. The only time he felt comforted was on the reservation, where she was buried.

He didn't leave his daughter alone that night, but early the next morning, after breakfast, he gave Rose some money, and said he would be back in "a little." "You'll be alright. Mz. Smith is right across the way, and I'll be here checkin on you. I'm not gone." Then he was gone . . . to seek his comfort in the forest, near his wife's grave, with the huge sky full of plump clouds, slowly drifting along like his life.

His life fell easily back into its old shape. With Wings's family, he was comforted. He walked a long path to Irene's grave every morning, and just sat there awhile. He came back and sat by Wings's door, looking into the multitude of trees, and the vast, unending sky, just thinking. Wings could see his friend was not going home soon. They built him a place of his own and, without anybody realizing it, the new place became Val's home. It cost nothing, and it meant so much comfort. Looking into the sky one day, he thought, "I'm still home."

With Wings's help he gradually went back to herding cattle, less now than before. There was another depression coming on. But he worked. "I have two daughters; one tryin to go to college, one tryin to keep a house for me. I got to keep makin money. They need money." He didn't realize that what Rose needed was him.

I sure remember those times; I was old

enough then to see for myself once my mother got me really interested.

CHAPTER 11

Rose took over the housecleaning, separating her mother's clothes, crying as she held each piece to give to the poor, and to Mz. Smith to cut down for Juliet. Slowly she settled into the big house as the sole occupant. "Daddy is gonna be here sometime soon. Sometime." She was surrounded with the remnants of her family, but . . . they were gone. Only the tears remained.

She cooked every day. So she always had something cooking for her father when he stopped to see her to give her some money. At first he stayed overnight, but waking in the morning to the sight of the empty bed, and of the closed-in walls, seemed to start his day off wrong. Walls seemed to break his mind down. To be close to life he needed to be out in the open air.

He always ate something to please Rose, but, soon, he seldom stayed overnight. She complained (she didn't mean to) that he was wasting food she would have to throw out.

"Give it to the Smiths, Rose. Don't throw nothin away!" He bought her one of the new iceboxes, and signed her up to receive a block of ice once a week. Three cents a block. "Now, save some food for yourself, baby." He thought she didn't really know how hard times were; but she did know. She thought he didn't know how lonely times were.

Then, when a few wealthy people of the town put in electricity, she didn't. She still used kerosene lamps and candles. Her water was free. There was always someone to cut wood for her stove and fireplaces, from her own trees. A neighbor passing by in his wagon or Joe Smith.

As time went by Rose was making her way in life with the help of her father, and a little help from Irene's students. She liked teaching others to read and write. She liked having people near during the day. Sometimes she even thought of marrying, vaguely.

She had gone back into Tante's room and began to read some of the books there. She would end up lying across Tante's bed reading an afternoon away. She learned things to add to her lessons. She wished now she had shared more of Tante's activities. She would close a book, thinking, "My, my, my! This world is really something!"

Val had spoken to her about fixing the shotgun house up to rent it out, and had even done some work on it. It really didn't need much now. But Rose was slow to make up her mind. "I use that little house for teaching when I have students. I don't know if I want somebody that close to my house. I like it quiet and peaceful. Whoever I rent it to will probably have children, and I don't want them mixing up in the yard with me. Stealing my eggs, running all over my garden, or killing and frying my chickens for their own self."

During the depression Joe Smith's job was paying less and less. What could a colored man say? He was struggling to pay his small rent, and was eyeing the shotgun house, thinking, "Could I maybe fix it up and Bertha clean it up? Miss Rose might jes let us move in it, then she won't be out here by herself. I can do nough work round here to even us up on the rent." But he was a shy man, and didn't mention it to Rose or Bertha.

Joe just continued on his weary, worried way to the lumberyard, with his dull brown eyes set in their reddened whites, staring ahead of him looking at everything, seeing

69

nothing. He was looking for something he could find, fix, and sell.

He hung around the lumberyard waiting for some work. For a long time now, since the depression had come, his hours were fewer, and his pay much less. He thought, "Depression sposed to be over, but it sho ain't gone from round heah yet."

The depression years were slow, and hard on everyone. Farmers, laborers, electricians, auto makers, everyone suffered because no one had any money. Harder on some coloreds because when it came to hiring, other colors came first.

Even liquor bootleggers were barely getting by. Since the Wall Street crash in 1929, even the rich were having a harder time of life, but most of them were going to make it out all right. The poor people thanked God for Roosevelt's New Deal that helped them survive. Sometimes you had to travel to get to the New Deal, and Joe Smith was almost an old man. "I cain't leave my Bertha and Juliet with jes nothin, even if I'm goin somewhere's to try to get somethin!"

Val, who had been a sad man a long time, finally gave up trying to live on, and died. It was an unexpected hard blow to Rose; she was miserable. She cried a vale of tears; wretched despair was her daily misery. At

70

night she screamed aloud at God in her grief, in that empty, empty house.

Wings could not help her; he was in despair, agonized and sickened by Val's death. To focus his mind he wanted to carve the headstone and dig the grave. He wanted to bury Val right next to Irene in the same wooded sanctuary that was full of birds and other live things that Val had loved. He wanted Val near his own grave. He was not superstitious, he was just used to his friend being near him.

Wings had found Val's savings in a can in the feather case Val had used for a pillow. He took it to Rose, gladly, for his brother-friend.

Rose didn't know how Tante found out because in her personal grief she had forgotten Tante. Tante sent a message through the Wideland newspaper office that she was coming home for the funeral. That helped Rose so much she was able to stop crying all through the days and nights.

She knew Tante could not afford the trip, and it would take at least two or three days on the bus. She informed the minister the funeral would be held in Val's own parlor. "His body can lie there as long as it has to. This is his home."

People came by to view the body as Rose

sat at Val's feet. When the body began to smell slightly, Rose still sat there, unworried, unfazed.

Rose cleaned Tante's room and the rest of the house, then sat back down to wait. "I must think of what to feed Tante while she is home." Rose knew her father had been sending Tante some money each month to help her. "That's what must'a killed him, all the strain of looking after us!"

She would be ashamed of such thoughts for a while, then the thoughts would break through again, "She must be through with college now! She can come on home and help me with this place!" A little light flickered in her brain. "We can have two grades in school! I'll get that shotgun house ready for a real school for us to teach in!"

Rose had not forgotten her father had just died. She was no less grieved, stressed, depressed, and miserable. She just realized there was still a future, that life was not over, it goes on. With her arms resting on the kitchen table, she rested her head on them and cried again, dry sobs. She felt, almost, all alone in the world.

Tante finally arrived amid all the doings, and Reverend Smoke preached the funeral of Val. He kept his little greedy eyes on the front-row chairs where the bereaved daughters of Val sat. After he got them crying real hard, and everybody moaning and sniffling, he quieted his preaching down. They laid Val's coffin in the wagon that Wings had brought to fetch him. Val's daughters climbed onto the wagon and rode away with Wings, to bury their beloved father next to their dearly beloved mother.

Later, after they returned to their house, Tante began to pack to go back to university and to work. Rose was outdone, feeling abandoned. She cried and begged and pleaded for Tante to stay home with her.

Tante sat Rose in a chair, and put her arm around her. She leaned close to her sister, whom she loved, and said, "Rose, I am not you. I am not through doing what I have to do for myself. I have a master's degree. I want a doctorate. I know what I am doing with my life.

"Wideland is not my life. Now, you? You must decide for yourself. You can sell whatever property is here. I don't care. It's yours. I give you my half. I will get my own for myself. I wouldn't sell it right now though; prices are too low. Prices are not going to stay low as they are now; I'm watching the stock market, and every day I read several newspapers.

"Hold this land awhile, while you decide just what you want to do with your life. Then do whatever that is! Because that is what I am going to do." Tante stood up to finish packing, saying, "I am going to try to get the money to have a telephone put in this house for you so you can reach me and I can reach you whenever there is an emergency."

Rose's eyes were wide open. She couldn't believe her ears, that her sister was saying these things. She couldn't believe her sister was leaving her again. Her heart sobbed, "Here, alone; all by myself."

Tante pulled her sister to her breast, saying, "You have to be an adult about your life now. You are a grown woman. If you have a dream, try to work toward that dream; if you don't have a dream, you need to look around you, see what you do have, then work to keep it in the best way possible. You must like it here, you've never tried to leave. Rent that little house out, and keep teaching. I'll do what I can for you, but the facts are I am working on my dreams. I won't have much to send. Life takes everything you have to keep going on. And I mean to keep going with my life."

They walked together to the train station, and Rose waited for the train to come take her sister away. She watched her sister leaving her. Life's pain had filled her heart til it had near broken it. But, this time, she didn't cry.

Rose was used to her father and other cowboys. She knew how to cuss. She thought to herself, "I'm tired of all this leaving shit."

Rose Strong went home to think.

For weeks Preacher Smoke had been telling different members of the congregation, "I'm worried bout that Rose out there in that big ole house all by herself! I'm gonna start checkin up on her; see is she doin alright!" The congregation was glad because they were mostly too busy trying to work and survive. Except Bertha, she checked every day.

The preacher lived in two small rooms at the back of the church. He had no wife. The congregation fed him every Sunday, but, naturally, being the man he was, he wanted more, needed more. He had, secretly, wooed a few of the women in the church. The ones he knew were alone and lonely. He stood for a god to them, so naturally they gave in to him.

He never brought anything with him, food nor money, and times were hard, so they couldn't always feed him. But giving him some loving, his secret favorite thing, was easy. Besides, they needed some their own selves.

But Preacher Smoke didn't know how to do his secret favorite thing too well. It wasn't his size, because size doesn't make the man. He just wouldn't have known what to do with any size "down there." Soon the ladies began to pull back, and fly from his reach. He had a few who were older, lonely sisters he ate with, but he didn't want them. They smelled of assifidity and cheap soap.

So, the next couple of weeks he did stop by Rose's house in the evenings, to see how she was and if she needed anything. He had nothing to give her, and nothing to do there, except maybe kill a spider if there was one there at the time, but he stopped by the house to check and see anyway.

People with families were moving into town. There were other young men in Wideland now. Some of them called upon her, or just stopped by to see if there was anything they could do for her. She didn't need Preacher Smoke. In fact, away from the church or a funeral, she never thought of him.

But he thought of her. A great deal. As he lay back in his cot, one hand under his head, eyes looking through the dark at the ceiling, other hand on his crotch, he thought of her. "She such a childlike little lady. I know she got confidence in me. I can see it in them soft eyes a'hers. She real gentle, too, got that soft voice. Young, smooth skin. Got a full body; woman's body, plump, but pleasin. She pretty! She do look like a rose, soft and gentle and, Lord . . . she lonely too. She ain't got nobody else! Up there in that big ole house all by hersef! It's my duty, as a man of God, to do my duty and answer her call."

One Sunday, as he preached, he looked down to the front-row seats, and looked directly into the eyes of Rose. When he held her eyes with his own, she blushed, embarrassed, and turned her eyes away. He thought, happily, "That's what girls do when they love you! She really fallin in love wit' me!"

He began to seek her out, always trying to look into her eyes again. She always blushed because she was young, and didn't know why he always seemed to want to look into her eyes. "I know he isn't thinking of courting me!" She thought she was surely mistaken, but then he appeared at her side several times in the next few weeks, reaching for her hand, in a preacherly way, of course. She stopped sitting up close to the pulpit. Instead she sat in the back with Bertha.

Preacher Smoke began to stop by Rose's house during the dinner hours, when he thought she would have cooked, to try to have a meal with her. He thought he could eat *and* talk. But Rose didn't eat much, and hardly cooked anymore since her father was not coming back.

Preacher had to make another plan. He decided he would go to see Rose after he had eaten at another good sister's house, and his stomach would already be full. But in the afternoons and evenings, someone, usually Bertha, was always there.

And so it came about very early one morning, he got up from his lonely, musty bed to make a home-visit to Rose. Preacher Smoke knocked on the big oak front door. Rose had been asleep, so it took her a moment or two to get to the door. She was thinking, "Who in the world is knocking on my door this early?"

When Rose saw Preacher Smoke so early she blinked, thinking, "Something must be wrong with somebody. Somebody has died!" She said, "Good morning, Reverend. What's the matter? Has something happened?"

She let go of the door to pull her thin robe

closer around her neck. Preacher Smoke walked in through the loosened door and turned to wait for her to close it. "I'm jes out on my early duties and said to myself, 'I betta stop and check on lil Rose while I'm out here.' Is your coffee ready?" He smiled.

She knew he had no wife, and that he lived in rooms in back of the church. She decided to make some coffee or, like she usually did, heat up what was already there. These were not times to waste anything.

He followed her into the kitchen, talking. "Mz. Rose, your house always so neat and clean comfort'ble." She stood at the stove to light the fire, and was putting on the coffee pot to reheat. When her back was turned to him, he came up close behind her and, putting one arm around her waist, pulled her to him as he placed his other hand over her breast! She dropped the pot she was holding and tried to turn to face him, and push him away from her.

"Preacher Smoke! What are you doing!? You get your hands off me, and get out of my house!"

He didn't let go, and he didn't leave. He believed she really wanted him and was too shy to be her natural self. He reached down and raised his hand up under her long robe, searching eagerly for that one place he wanted to cup in his hand, saying, "Hush, chile, hush, just let me show you how good you gonna feel. I got somethin here for . . ."

But Rose fought him. She was a virgin, and did not completely understand his actions. She prayed for her dead father . . . or Wings or Bertha to come through the front door. No one came.

She had struggled from the kitchen back into the parlor room toward the front door. But she couldn't get away from the grip he had between her legs. She was in her night-clothes, she had no underwear on. She pleaded with him, "Let me go, please. Stop!"

And he pleaded, "Let me show you, dar-lin, jes give me one minute . . ." He pressed her against the wall so she could not move away from him. His hand and fingers had found the place. No matter how she struggled she could not get that hand to move. She felt his fingers moving to get inside her.

She raised a foot to kick him, but that was a mistake. Swifter than a second, first one, then another finger pushed their way further inside her.

The thrill, the feel was too much for Preacher Smoke. His face and body en-gorged, even strengthened. He took his free arm, lifted Rose off her feet, and threw her solidly on the couch. With some invisible hand he got his own pants open. His body pressed upon hers, and in a few feverish humps the deed was done. He was finished without really entering her body. The rape was accomplished, but the physical harm did not go deep.

Rose was sobbing, her legs askew, nightgown rumpled and torn. She tried to sit up, and pull her gown together. She was sobbing, not at the pain, she didn't feel that so much yet. She wept from rage and her impotence. She looked at him with hatred. She thought, "This dirty, ignorant, old reprobate man! Stupid ignorant bastard!"

Preacher Smoke was saying, "Now, Rose, it didn't have to be like that. If you'd a let me, you could'a enjoyed it more. Now, look what you done done!"

Rose pulled herself together; still crying, she stood up. He reached to hug her, saying, "I'm gonna love you, Rose. We gonna get married!" Her sobs grew louder. She snatched her insulted body from his arms, turning to go toward the kitchen.

Preacher Smoke stopped to adjust his clothes before going to find her. But she found him first, with a butcher knife in one hand and a frying pan in the other. She screamed, "Get out of my house! You dirty son of a bitch preacher!"

Preacher Smoke was startled. "Rose, I'm gonna marry you! Didn't you hear me, girl?" He started moving backwards toward the front door. "What chu gonna do with that there knife? Where you learn to cuss like that? You a lady! Ladies ain't sposed to talk like that!"

Rose reached and flung the front door wide open as she said, "And you a preacher! And a grown man! You're not supposed to do what you have done to me! Get out of my sight! I don't want to see your face!"

His eyes stretched wide, he moved, stumbling, out of the door, still talking. "Rose, I'm your minister. I ain't gonna hurt you none! I wants to marry you! Didn't you like what I did, none?"

She screamed, "Get out of my house!" She hit him with the frying pan on the side of his head, and raised the knife to stab him with the other hand.

Swiftly he finished stumbling out the door and down the steps. The wily preacher kept in mind the neighbors or anyone passing down the road. He turned back to say, "You sho is a liar, Mz. Rose. I didn't know that chu lied like that! I sho can't keep company with a liar, Mz. Rose. Emph, emph, emph!"

Rose followed as far as the porch, breathing hard, tears and snot flying, screaming, "Don't you ever, never, come back to this house as long as you live!!"

Then he was gone. Rose leaned against the closed door, and slid down to the floor, sobbing, and feeling defeated.

CHAPTER 12

Rose bathed herself several times a day for a week. She still didn't feel clean. She had decided to keep her business to herself.

Rose spent the first night crying in her bed, trying to sleep, yet listening to every sound around the house. Every noise sounded strange and frightening.

But after crying herself to sleep several times that week, she told Bertha what had happened. Bertha, aghast, asked her, "Does you need to go to the doctor?"

"I have cleaned myself. I'm not cut nowhere."

Bertha shook her head, slowly. "Must not'a been no big thing enough to hurt you. But maybe you should tell the polices, cause it's some things you can't see."

Rose sighed a sound somewhere between tears and disgust. "The police don't care what happens to a colored girl anyway, Bertha."

Bertha said to herself in her heart, "This chile has done changed. That nasty preacher man destructed her."

Wings came by, checking on her. Rose wondered if he knew. He brought his nephew, Dreaming Cloud, whom he called "Cloud" for short. They were checking all locks on the doors and windows. When Wings was leaving, he said, "This is what we do for now, but I will have someone watching. Cloud will be here to check on you regular. I bring you Brave back, too. You need someone here with you." Later when he brought Brave, the dog wagged his tail, happy to see an old friend.

Dreaming Cloud was a quiet, shy, but intelligent young man. He was even handsome in a way, his body was medium height, and thin. He also had a persistent cough that he couldn't seem to get rid of. He liked Rose because she was Val's daughter, and had become like a member of his family.

When Cloud met Juliet, an instant friendship was struck. Juliet liked him very much. They had something in common and seemed to know it. He always stopped to sit and talk with her a good while.

In the meantime, Bertha kept a steady eye on Rose and her house. She went by often. Once she stopped in to leave one of Juliet's little handwoven baskets, trying to distract Rose's mind. As Juliet grew older her work greatly improved. The baskets were simple, attractive in colors, and in useful sizes. When they could afford it, people were buying them. And Rose was distracted; she decided to help Juliet sell them.

On another day, soon after the rape, Bertha asked after Rose's health, then was silent a moment. She leaned toward Rose and asked in a low secret voice, "When your monthly due?"

Rose sighed that sorrowful, pained sound again. "I never kept up with that. But I'm waiting for it, now, watching for it." She shook her head, sadly, as she said, "It's a sin against God to have a sinner like the preacher sitting in any church teaching people how to live right!"

Bertha put her comforting hand on Rose's shoulder, and patted it. She said, "But that is why we go to church, Rose. To learn. Everybody sittin in church is a sinner. None is good but the Father, God. God put that in the Bible so you know all people are sinners, and it ain't no tellin what one of em will do! You s'posed to r'member that in all your dealin's with men, and women, too. Everybody can, and might, do you wrong. Sometime the least one you expect, chile.

"God teach us that so we will be extra careful cause the devil is everywhere, and tryin to get inside everybody. Some people do not believe that, and I know they has plenty sorrows."

Rose just looked at the soft-spoken Bertha, with more respect. Bertha seldom talked much, but obviously, Rose thought, "It isn't because she is dumb. That's twice I have made a mistake in judging."

A week later, her period came. She breathed much easier. She had positively dreaded the possibility that the preacher might have left a baby inside her private body.

Preacher Smoke never came back to her house. Bertha had let everybody at the next church meeting know what had happened between the preacher and Rose.

The Church Board asked Preacher Smoke to leave. They were all guilty of some sins, but Preacher Smoke had gotten caught. He told the Board, "You know that that there girl is a awesomeful liar. Lyin on a poor man, a good man like me! I done caught her lyin many'a time! But, I will go cause I know the devil always punish the good ones! Ya'all be careful round that girl, cause she will lie on you next! Watch what I tell ya!"

They let him go before they had found a

new minister. That was no problem in those times; many ministers were walking the land looking for a home. That's why they had become ministers. Some borrowed money to buy a Bible to preach from . . . or stole one.

CHAPTER 13

Unfortunately, it was at least a year before Rose let any man come in her house unless she really, really, really knew the man, and she wouldn't let herself be alone with one, anywhere. She prayed often. "I am a ruint woman. What am I gonna do, Lord?"

Rose also thought, "Now, I really do need a husband. But I don't get to meet anyone. I don't know how to act around men, like Tante did. I don't know how to dress cause I don't ever go anywhere except'n church, and I haven't been going there lately.

"And I look like a frump, and I'm so stupid. These young men don't have any way to take care of nobody. And suppose I have a baby? What will I do then? Besides all of that, I don't know anyone I like enough to marry."

Time and circumstance had brought Rose very close to Bertha. She was always giving Bertha some food for her family, or something she could use. They had so little. Wings and Cloud kept Rose supplied with meat they hunted around their woods. "But, no birds, Wings. I hate to see birds killed," she told him.

But she had found out she didn't like to be *asked* for anything important. It would make her feel a little bit used. Bertha very seldom asked for anything that would set that frown on Rose's face.

One day Bertha was about to leave Rose's house, then turned back, with a sigh. She took a deep breath, and said, "Rose, I don't like to ask favors of nobody. Your family always been so good to us." She ran out of nerve, waved her hand in disgust, and said, "Never mind, never mind."

Rose urged her on, "No. Go ahead, Bertha. You are my neighbor, and my friend. Everybody else is gone. What is your favor you want to ask me?"

Bertha shook her head, sadly, saying, "Well, it look like we gonna be gone, too. Joe jes not makin enough money for us to keep rentin that house we got to live in. Don't know what we gonna do. Don't want to be no sharecropper again. And you know, Joe will work hard, but you got to have somethin to work AT. So we probly be movin pretty soon."

Rose immediately felt the blow of her near neighbor leaving the vicinity. "You want to borrow some money? Bertha, I don't have much money. My daddy was my help. I got my class, but, shoot, you know those classes don't put much in my hand. I don't have no husband helping me, none. My blessing is I don't have to pay rent. This house is free and clear. My parents saw to that, thank God.

"I've thought of renting my schoolhouse, that shotgun house? Renting it out, and going back to that storage shed Mama used to use."

Bertha's heart sank. "Oh, that's jes what I was gonna ask you, could we rent it."

Rose had been thinking about renting that house for some time. Some people said the Depression was over, but it surely wasn't over everywhere. Especially not in Wideland. Rose answered, "You can't afford no rent, Bertha. If I rent it to you, then we both will be sittin here worrying about what to do!"

They sat in silence for a few moments, both sets of eyes looking off somewhere in the future.

Finally, after thinking to herself, "I need to keep some friends close," Rose asked, "You know what we can do?"

Bertha looked up.

Rose continued, "This is a good size piece of land, with all these trees. I love them all, but I don't need them all. Why doesn't Joe build you all a little two or three room shotgun house, way over there," she pointed, "on that corner away from this house so we won't be right on top of each other? I'll let you all do that."

Bertha looked up, thinking, "Thank the Lord!"

Rose asked, "How much you pay to rent that house you in?"

"Three dollars a month."

Rose began to say, "I'll lend . . ." She thought of Tante's advice, and changed her mind. "I'll give you two dollars this month so you can make your rent. And he can get started while you live in that house, and work on your . . . the new house. It won't be no fancy shotgun house, so he might be through in a month. He will have to work on it every day, but that's the way life is now. He has to work on it every day! And, surely, he has friends who can help him!"

Tears slid down Bertha's face as she said, "Oh he will, Mz. Rose, he will. I'll help him. I'm gonna go find him now, and tell him, so he can ease his mind. Oh thank you, and thank the Lord!"

Joseph was heartily thankful. A poor man carries such a burden, sometimes hard, sometimes happy, trying to keep his family safe and eating.

Soon Rose heard the sawing of trees, and the hammering of nails. She smiled; they were getting a home, and she was improving her property and income.

CHAPTER 14

Even with old Brave home sleeping on the floor beside her bed every night, and Bertha's family soon to be on her land, Rose was lonely.

Tante called now and then, and even sent small amounts of money to her. But it did not look like she was coming home anytime soon.

There were times Rose felt saddled with the house; she couldn't leave and go off seeking life. Then she would think, "I love my home. I don't care what anybody else is doing. I'm just tired of being here all alone. I know I have Bertha and Juliet to talk to, and I'm glad of that. But I need a man; I need a husband to have my own children!"

Wings was getting older, and did not do much, if any, short distance travel. He was settled in with his children and grandchildren, one of which was named after Val. When the beloved old dog, Brave, died, one of Wings's sons came into town with Cloud to get the dog and bury him near the reservation. Wings tried to keep all the things he loved near him, and the dog had been Val's.

Wings passed away quietly one night while he had been outside sleeping under the stars. His family and his people greatly grieved over him. Wings had been a good, kind man. He was buried close to Val's grave, in his own family plot. He left several grown children, and many handsome grandchildren. Many people of all colors came to his funeral. Rose was right in front. Tante didn't come, of course.

One day, not too long after that, Rose sat in her porch swing thinking about life and death. The sun shone down on her, warming her body. She was thinking of her father, mother, and Wings. Of how long she had been alone, and her own age. "This world and time is just going by too fast!"

Her thoughts turned to marriage again, so she thought of the young man who had helped Joseph build the little house. "He seemed nice; he had manners, nice teeth, and he could read pretty good; he was in one of Mama's classes." She pushed the swing into motion with her feet. "But that isn't enough for me. There just seemed like something was missing! I deserve better."

She leaned back in the swing, eyes closed, thinking, the light breeze blowing gently on her body. She heard the sound of a wagon stopping in front of her house. She opened her eyes and watched as an older lady made her way out of the wagon with the help of an old man. He led-pushed her to the gate, and waited as she made her way to the front steps, not too slowly, but certainly not quickly.

She was a portly, older woman dressed in an almost neat, slipshod way. Rose thought, "She works for a white lady. Secondhand clothes." The woman obviously had a corset on, under a red dress with a black velvet collar, and was wearing thick cotton stockings with only one or two little holes in them.

She reached the steps, looking back for the man to help her; she gave that up, waved him back. She pulled herself up the steps to speak to Rose. Rose got up, going to the edge of the steps, asking, "Good evening, ma'am. How can I help you today?"

The woman reached the top of the steps, breathing heavily. Rose lifted her hand in the direction of the swing. "Would you like to rest a minute?"

The woman took a deep breath, tried to

smile, said, "Sure would . . . and a cup of water, if ya please."

Rose nodded, saying, "You just sit right there. I'll be right back."

While Rose was gone, the woman settled herself on the swing, gingerly. She was a large woman, and any sudden movement would have made the swing unsteady.

Rose returned and, handing the glass of water to her visitor, asked, "What may I do for you, ma'am?"

"Well, you can let me get my breath. It's hot and ya just gave me the water. And them steps was a lil bit hard on me this evenin."

Rose smiled, and moved toward a small stool, saying, "I'll just sit on this stool while you get ready to tell me."

The woman fanned herself with one hand, and drank the water in the other hand. She handed the glass back to Rose, saying, "Ya' a mighty bless'd woman! I hear ya haves a little house . . . sittin out here, empty!" She turned to look at the little house Rose used as a classroom. "And that is jes what I needs to talk to ya about."

Rose opened her mouth to speak when the lady spoke again. "I got a daught'a, a grown daught'a, and she got a husband who works at the hospital (she said this proudly), a good steady job! All they need is to rent a nice lil place like yourn."

She leaned closer to Rose as she said, "I seen you at church . . . sometime, and I knows you are a good, kindly lady. Ever'body say so. My name is Alberta Wilson. I knows you is Rose Strong. Your daddy passed on not too long ago, and your sister done left you here all on your own to take care this here place all by yoursef. I can help ya!"

"I use that house for my classroom."

Alberta Wilson asked, "You got any pupils?"

"Not too many, but enough."

Alberta Wilson smiled. "Well, it's summertime now, and everbody is out of school for a lil while. All we need is a place for a lil while. You can use the rent, can't ya? These hard times is lastin for years, ain't they?"

Rose frowned as she answered, "Everybody can use money. How long would they be here?"

The woman sighed, carefully sitting back on the swing. "Oh, not so long . . . two weeks? A month?"

"Why don't they stay where they are, if that's all the time they need?"

"Cause they stayin with me, and childrens don't pay their mama no rent."

Rose had to smile. "Your daughter got a

lot of furniture? That's a small house."

"She ain't got too much. Her stuff got burnt up in a fire."

"They smoke?"

The woman heard the alarm in Rose's voice. Shaking her head, she said, "No, no. Just a fire was somebody else fault. I don't like them smokers either!" Mrs. Wilson reached her hand out to Rose, saying, "Chile, ma'am, I don't know if you has ever needed somethin in these hard times everybody is havin, but, PLEASE, please, don't say no. God will surely bless ya for helpin his childrens in need."

Wishing she could talk to Bertha, Rose took a deep breath, and looked at her classroom that someone was always trying to take from her use for their use. It was around 1936, the depression was still going on. She had no help since Wings had died but the little money Tante sent, and a little pay from her students. But her students struggled to pay five or ten cents a lesson. And she always prepared something for them to eat because she knew they were hungry, and that's why they came with their little nickels and dimes. Well, she thought now, "if it's only for two weeks or a month." She said, "How much are you planning on paying for two weeks?"

"Oh, ma'am, at least a month, please, ma'am. How some much ya askin for?"

"Nothing, don't want to rent it." But she was beginning to feel sorry for Alberta Wilson.

"How much'll you take?" Alberta sensed the weakness in Rose.

Rose's heart felt sorry for Alberta, but her mind didn't want to. "How about ten or fifteen dollars a month?"

Alberta almost laughed, but this was too serious. "For that there lil house?! We ain't tryin to buy it, jes rent it."

Rose didn't laugh either. "You need it?"

"How about four dollars? An that's a lot!" Alberta hastened to add, "They ain't gonna be here that long."

"When they need to move in?"

"Tonight, sometime. And he'll, her husban will do a lil work round here to help ya. Everbody wit some land always needs a lil help doin somethin."

"They can spend their time working for themselves, and looking for another place to rent. Is that right?"

Alberta nodded her head quickly. "Tha's right!"

"Well I'll rent it for a month. My overseer will help see you all in when you come." She knew people needed to know someone was with her, so she was talking about Joseph.

"Ya'r overseer?"

"Yes, the man who looks after this land. He lives on this land. He sees everything happening on this land."

Mrs. Alberta Wilson looked off in the distance for a moment, then said, "Don't ya worry none, ma'am. We c'n do it. Do it need a key?"

Rose stood up, saying, "I'll open it for you now, but I'll keep the key. You don't have to worry about any lock; it's safe here, and I don't want any new holes put in that door for a new lock . . . for just a month."

Sometimes you just be trying to take a little breather in life and darn if something else don't pop up. It may look alright, but it don't always turn out alright. Somebody always lookin for a place to lean on. My mother knew Mrs. Wilson; said she wasn't too bad, but she wasn't too good either. And her daughter, Ethel, would argue with God if he let her.

Late that night the couple, twenty-five-year-old Ethel Moore and forty-year-old Will Moore, moved in the little house. There wasn't too much noise. But Will was a large man with a large voice that boomed out over the land in the stillness of the night.

They were only there one whole day

101

before Ethel forgot everything Alberta Wilson had admonished them about. The arguments started.

Rose walked over to Bertha's the next day to ask her about the new people. "Do you know this tenant's mother, Alberta Wilson? She says she goes to our church."

Bertha laughed lightly. "I know her, but she too nosy and gossipy too much. I don't talk to her too much. She even have ask me about you; lots of times. She members your mother, but they wasn't close or nothin. I don't know the daughter, Ethel, none at all."

Rose and Bertha, each in their own house, had heard the argument the new people had. Bertha looked scared when she said, "Lawd, I thought for sure that two-hundred-pound man would kill that little one-hundred-pound woman. It sure sounded like it. She didn't even sound scared of that man!"

"Sure didn't," Rose rejoined. "But I'd take more care with him, if I was her!"

Bertha said, "I watched out for um this mornin. The husband left for work like nothin happened, and I seen Ethel empt'in the night slop-jars this morning, too. Everybody is still alive."

Miffed, Rose said, "Well they ought to be ashamed. She was yelling as loud as he was.

102

Louder! Her voice rattles through the air. I'm going to be glad when their month is up and they are moving out!"

Bertha, thinking of the help the big man might be to her husband, said, "Maybe they was just tired, and hungry from movin. Juliet stayed up and listen at um most the night."

Rose noticed Juliet listening, and decided to say less in front of the young lady. Juliet's infirmity, and the fact that she was always sitting still in a chair, made Rose think of her as a child. So she just answered, "Maybe so; I hope so!"

Bertha went to hug her daughter, saying, "You know, she makes a few dimes a day with her baskets now? She make em out of everthin. Peoples comes by and ask her bout them baskets! Even some white folks who still got some money."

"Good! Keep up that good work, girl! You'll be taking care your own self one of these days! And that's the best thing you can learn. You see anything you want on this land for those baskets, you just take it. I'm glad to see you making your own money."

Juliet waved them off, wishing they wouldn't treat her like a child because of her infirmity, saying, "Aww, I'm not gettin rich! A few pennies's ain't nothin but a few pennies's." She changed the subject. "I got those books you loaned me, Aunt Rose. I finished em. Can I get a few more? I like the lying history books, but I like the philosophil books, too. I can't understand all the words, but I'm waitin for that dictionary you said you was gonna get for me."

Bertha butt in, "Hush, chile! She already doin a'plenty for us."

"It's all right, Bertha. I understand. But I have to wait until the new class starts to see what I can harvest. That reminds me, I've got to plant some food so I can eat these next few months. Something beside those canned goods we made last year, Bertha."

Bertha wearily smiled. "Yeah, work is never finish. Always got some more to do. Got to eat, got to eat."

CHAPTER 15

As the days passed, adding up to the month for the temporary tenants, Rose was watchful. The arguing never stopped unless he was at work, or they were asleep. Every evening, deep into the night, sometimes starting again early in the morning before he left for work. Weekends were the worst.

The angry, violent sounds were making everybody sick and tired of the noise. The air, once so peaceful and serene, even if poverty was staring you in the face, was now rent with ugly, angry words. Everyone's peace was gone. Everyone waited for Monday when Will would be gone back to work.

Rose once spoke to Bertha. "I can't hardly stand this much more. I sleep, still listening for him to hit her."

Bertha answered, "I can't sleep my own self. I done passed my limit long time ago. Joseph don't hear nothin when he sleeps. But I ain't sure it's the man's fault. That lil woman makes a lot of noise in a real mean voice."

Three weeks went by the same way. On the last week of the month the Moores were to stay in the little house, Rose went to speak with Ethel. "There is one more week left in our agreement, Mz. Ethel. I hope you all have found another place."

"No, ma'am, we haven't, but we lookin ever day."

Rose frowned. "I hope so, because I can't take all that arguing, fighting, and yelling and cursing anymore. You all are driving everyone round here crazy!"

Ethel tilted her little head, said, "I know, I know. Cause he drives me crazy, too. I poligizes to ya, Mz. Rose. He just workin hard, and scared this pression is goin on for too long."

"Well, for the little time you have left here, tell him to try and keep his voice down, please. And you can work on yours also."

Ethel said in a meek, soft voice, "Yes'm, I sure will."

At the end of the month, they hadn't moved, didn't seem about to. Ethel came to see Rose, saying, "We ain't got no new place yet, Mz. Rose, but I blive we almos do. Let me give ya this money . . ."

Rose said, angrily, "I don't want your

money. I want you all to *move* so I can get some peace. Every evening and every weekend is ruined! Full of nothing but your arguing! How can you live that way?"

Ethel tilted her little head, looked sorrowfully down at her feet and said, "It's mighty hard on me, I can't tell ya how sorrow I am, to have to live this here way. I never like to argur; never like to fuss and cuss. Not used to it. My mama and papa got along jes fine. But since I been wit him, married, I don't get no peace neither. Pleasssse take this here money, Mz. Rose, please. Else I have to worry bout that, too. We gonna find a place. Jes give us one more month . . ."

Rose was aghast. "Another month!? No, Lord! Don't take any more time than you need to find another place. Have you asked the new minister? Your mother knows everybody!"

"I don't know him, yet."

"Your mama does!"

Ethel held her hand with the money out, saying, "Take half."

Rose looked into the sad, darkened eyes of Ethel, and said, "I'll take one dollar, but you better move. I hate to tell you this, because you have enough trouble; but you married him. Take one more week, and then

I'm going to the sheriff. I'm going to have some peace, or someone is going to be sitting in jail, or on the street with no peace. And I mean it!"

Ethel walked away with her head bowed down, thinking, "That ole bitch! Just cause she got a house, and some kinder edukertion, she want to treat peoples like they's dogs!" But it was quiet that night. Everyone rested, even Will Moore.

The next evening, after work, Will Moore had a visitor, and he brought him to meet Rose.

Evenings were Rose's lonesome time. She looked through her window when she heard the two men approaching her porch. She didn't want to answer the door, but it could be that the handsome man with Will might want a reference for their rent application. She sighed and answered the door.

Will smiled at her, while she searched for all that anger and any signs of violence in his face; she did not see it. "I'm a poor judge of men," she thought. Will indicated his friend with his hand, saying, "Mz. Rose, I know I'm gonna be leavin here soon, but I been workin with my friend here. He a good friend, a good person, and I wanted ya to know who was comin by here to help us find a place. His name is Leroy, Leroy

Aimes. Leroy, this here is my landlady, Mz. Rose."

Rose had been looking at Will as he spoke; she was thinking of them moving soon. Now, she looked at Leroy. She remembered him from somewhere. He was a tall, handsome, brown-skinned man. He had a dimpled smile which showed off his shiny white teeth and strong chin to good advantage. Dark attractive eyes with long, sweeping lashes completed his face of promising romance.

On closer inspection a wiser person might have seen that his agreeable smile, his air of sympathy and interest, his carefully worked-out laughter, even his smile, were studied, practiced.

Will said a few more words, "He the mos poplar man at my job. We works together! He the supe'visor of the janitors, under the white boss, of course."

"He is going to help you find another place to rent?" Rose asked, looking at the neatly combed dark hair atop the playful, yet serious dark eyes. She thought, "He is handsome. So many new men are moving to Wideland."

"Well, yes'm, Mz. Rose."

Rose answered, looking into Leroy's eyes, "Good. We need some efficiency around here! How are you doing, Mr. Aimes?" Rose was thinking as she looked at his clean-shaven face, his crisp white shirt, open at the collar.

She looked down at his shoes; her mother had always said you can tell a lot about a man from his shoes; they must be clean and polished. His shoes were highly polished, and not run over. She didn't show her impression on her face. Her mother had also said, "When it comes to a man, keep most of your thoughts to yourself." But she thought, "Why, he's beautiful!" He reached out to shake her hand; she saw his long tapered fingers and clean fingernails.

Leroy spoke in a soft baritone. "I've seen you at church, but you never look at anybody, and you always leaving right after the service."

Rose tried to smile and say "Yes," but she was suddenly very nervous. Tingly, with a tremor of excitement.

Leroy pointed at a section of the fence seen from the porch. "You got somebody to help you patch that fence, Mz. Rose? Is it Mrs. Rose or Miss Rose?"

Rose blushed in spite of herself, and thought of Tante for some reason. "Yes. It's Miss. Rose Strong, and yes, I do have someone, Joseph, but he is so busy he just didn't get to it yet."

"I might be able to get to it for you. I just want to do *something* for you, Mz. Rose, to show my preciation for you helpin my friend. Anything you need. You are such a nice lady, livin here all alone. And I understand you are a very kind person, too."

Rose smiled, but said, "Well, thank you. But I'll see when Joseph plans to get to it. Thank you, anyway."

They said their good-byes then, and Rose watched them walk away toward the little shotgun house. Leroy had a lazy walk, casual. His body was loose and relaxed. Rose thought, "Is that what they call sexy?"

She thought about Leroy all that evening. She didn't run over to tell Bertha about her visitor; she kept her thoughts to herself, and they were warm in her heart. She thought about herself. "I am twenty-five and a half years old. I need a man, a husband. They even have automobiles in the streets here in Wideland, and I still don't have a husband. I need to keep my eyes looking up instead of looking down; maybe I'd see someone sometime. Where'd all these men come from anyway? To work? Here?"

Before that week was over, the tenant, Will Moore, died. Hypertension heart attack.

Rose said, "All that fussing and arguing

killed that man!"

Bertha shook her head sadly. "I'm shur glad I got Joseph; a peaceable man! And that poor lady; all alone in the world now."

Rose tightened her lips. "She got her mother. And I can't put her out before she buries her dead husband."

Bertha agreed. "No, I wouldn't do that."

"She can't pay me and bury him, too."

Bertha looked closely at Rose. "So . . . I reckon this week is gonna be free?"

"Nobody gives me anything free! I have to eat and buy ice for my icebox just like everybody else!"

Bertha placed her hand on her friend's shoulder. "Well, the Lawd will bless ya for your helpin them, now the Lawd done called him away to heaven."

Angry and defeated, Rose stood up, saying, "Nobody called him away! He kept himself upset and angry all the time! It killed him. God does not want anybody like him arguing up in heaven."

"Hush, chile."

Rose, exasperated, said, "Well, it's true! The Bible I read says everybody is not going to heaven!"

Bertha was alarmed. "The preacher say they is."

"Who you believe, Bertha, the preacher or

God? The Bible speaks for God. The preacher can only speak for himself!"

Bertha replied, "Well, I rather know what God say."

"That's smart. I'll give you an A."

That night Ethel's family and friends came to console her; they brought liquor. There were sounds of loud argument almost all night with Ethel trying to get her money together. Ethel's voice was the loudest among them. And Will's voice was dead and quiet.

In a few days the funeral was over. Will Moore had been laid to rest in the Restwell Cemetery. They held a little gathering in the small rented house. Will had quite a few friends who came; many people had liked him. But the new widow didn't have anything to serve them. She screamed at her mother, who was trying to help her, "Who got some money to spend on the dead?"

Leroy Aimes was one of the pallbearers of the big wooden box the friends of Will had built. Rose introduced him to Bertha, and he helped Juliet inside to a seat. He stood so straight and handsome that Juliet blushed when he helped her.

During the service he had cast glances at Rose several times, and saw her looking at him. He would quickly shift his eyes down, smiling. Later Rose told him she was sorry about his friend dying; then she couldn't think of anything else to say. Leroy answered, "I'm really sorry, too. Will was a kind, peaceful man, worked hard. I'm really gonna miss him."

Rose looked at him, thinking, "He must be crazy! Peaceful!? That man was anything but peaceful. But how could he have so many friends if he was such a mean person?"

The sermon was brief; just a few words over the body, then the funeral home presided over getting the box to the hearse. A few people from the hospital went to the cemetery with Ethel and her mother, Alberta. Leroy said he had to get back to work.

But before he left he walked Rose to her porch steps, saying on the way, "I'm sorry I didn't get to finish that patch in your fence, but I'll get to it again in a day or so. I got so many things I got to do."

Surprised, Rose asked, "You are working on my fence?"

"Yeah. Didn't ya see it?"

Thoughtfully, Rose asked, "Well . . . why?"

Leroy smiled down at her. "Cause I . . . like you. And you are all by yourself. I didn't think ya have a man. I done asked, and nobody knows of a man with ya."

"You asked?"

"Sure, I said I liked ya, didn't I?"

Rose smiled up at him. "Why?"

The white teeth glittered between his soft-looking lips. "Cause you pretty, you nice. Ya was kind to my friend."

Rose held on to the gentle words, then grew serious, "What is your friend's wife going to do now about the rent money? I'm not charging her except for the time they already been here. I know, with this funeral and all, she won't have any money. She can stay the week out, but she got to go. I need my classroom back."

Leroy looked like he was thinking. "She could move in with her mother."

"She sure can," Rose thought, "and I better go see her and the minister, and the sheriff, if necessary." She looked at Leroy, who was watching her thoughtfully. "You going to help her move?"

He shook his head a little. "Well . . . I have responsibilities of my own. One thing is to finish your fence!"

When they reached her porch, they stood there a moment. Rose looked up at him again, asking, "You really think I'm pretty?"

"I think ya beautiful! I'll tell ya all about it when I come back to finish the fence. Don't let that other helper of yours mess with it!"

Looking back at him as she went up the steps, Rose said, "And I'll fix you lunch . . . or breakfast, when you do finish."

Leroy turned back toward Ethel's rented house, saying to Rose, "I betta see if she have enough money to last her a few days til she can get to her mama's house." But, he didn't ask Ethel nor give her any money; he was just trying to impress Rose that he was a kind, capable man.

All but a few people were in wagons and cars waiting to go to the cemetery. Leroy pushed the door gently, and went in. The conversation between Leroy and Ethel was like this:

"I just paid your landlady two dollars for you. So ya have at least a week here, then ya go to your mother's. I needed that money for myself, ya know? You gonna have to pay me back."

"Ohhh," Ethel groaned. "How ya gonna ask me that, now, in the middle of all my sorrows?"

Leroy replied in his fine voice, "So I can keep out of sorrows my own self. I was tryin to get her to give ya more time, but I had to give her two dollars. I needed that money. Ya got any money?"

Ethel turned her back to Leroy as she

116

reached into her bosom and turned back to him with two dollars in her hand and a frown on her face. "Here! Taken money off from widows and orphans! God lookin down at ya!"

As he put the money in his pocket, he answered, "Ya don't have any orphans! And you ain't no widow cause ya wasn't married to Will, and I did help ya! We betta get on outta here, cause I'ma have to get back to my job! Where the preacher? If he outside already, let's go!"

CHAPTER 16

Rose had looked for Leroy to come finish the job every day, but she wasn't paying him, so didn't know how to fuss about it. She had prepared lunch a couple of times, expecting him. When he didn't come, she put it in her little icebox and ate it later herself. No one came to the little house she had rented to the Moores.

Leroy didn't come back for a week. When he did show up, he came mid-morning. Rose was a little angry with him, but didn't let it show, and didn't fix breakfast for him either. He finished the fence patching early afternoon, then came in to eat the lunch she prepared after her anger waned.

He looked at her with his pretty eyes, said, "I had to take a few hours off from my job to get over here to do this for ya. Ain't had no time to do nothin for myself. I'm always running, tryin to help somebody, 'til I can't catch up with myself."

118

Rose, with her hand on her hip, said, "I never asked you to do that work. You started that all on your own. I don't worry people to do anything for me! I told you I had a man to do these things."

"Well, don't look like he doin em, so I helped ya. Ain't nothin to get upset about. It's done, and I'm glad I did it. I like ya, a lot."

Rose softened a bit at these words, and was about to sit down and visit like a lady. Then Leroy continued, "I took off from my job; I sure would love to sit here with you all day, if I had time. But I got to get back to work." He stood up, brushing crumbs from his lap and picking up his cap as he continued talking.

"But I sure would like to come back for a real visit with ya. If such a pretty lady as you are will let me." He reached out, touching her cheek lightly. Then, quickly, he was gone through the front door.

Rose daydreamed, night-dreamed, and waited. "He is not my type, he is just handsome, is all." She watched for him every day all day, when she wasn't trying to catch Ethel at her mother's house to get any back rent. Finally, she said, "Hell with it, let them go. Both of em. No sense in wasting my time." She concentrated on cleaning the classroom and putting things back into some order.

Then Ethel came to see her. "I have done moved."

As she poured Ethel a cup of coffee, Rose replied, "I know. I threw away the things I'm sure you did not want."

"Well, we even then. Cause I don't want to leave no bad record behind me. I'm a good church woman."

Rose reached for a tablet near the kitchen table. "No, ma'am. You still owe me from before your husband died. I have kept a calendar so I can show you."

"Well, alrighty. Ya don't have to show me. I trust in the Lord." Ethel took a sip from the cup, and said, "What kind'a coffee you give me? What kind'a coffee do ya use?" She didn't wait for an answer. "Whatsomever it is, they sure cheatin ya! This stuff taste baadddd." She pushed the cup away from her.

Rose was speechless as Ethel put a few dollars on the table and stood up to head to the front door, saying, "This a big ole house. It could be real pretty and nice, but you probly too busy courtin." She looked at Rose. "Or is ya lazy? Ya always tryin to make peoples think ya so nice an clean an busy? Ya so busy, Mz. Rose, I jes don't know what to say bout ya!"

Rose frowned. "You don't have the right to say anything about me. I am clean. I just cleaned up your mess you left behind! You've said enough, thank you."

Ethel smirked. "Tryin to get ya'self a man! Had to find em offa somebody rentin that little ole dumb classroom house." She looked toward the little house. "I betta check that ole house one last time, just to make sure I ain't f'gettin nothin."

Rose followed her to the little house where paper wrappers and cigarette butts still lay outside on the ground around the door. There had been so much work that had to be done inside the house, Rose hadn't gotten to all the outside yet.

Ethel told her, "Ya can't even let me leave here in peace; got to fowler me round. Don't be tryin to find nothin for me to fix, cause this house was a mess when we moved in here."

"I teach in this house. It has never been a 'mess' before."

"I guess it all pends on what ya used to, Mz. Rose."

"You begged to live here, Mz. Moore."

"Mr. Moore put me to do that. I didn't want to. I could'a gone with my mama!"

"You're a liar, Mz. Moore. Look here. This

door is loose from the hinges. How did those cuts and holes get on these walls? And look at that sink. I told you this was just a small kitchen for fixing students lunch."

Ethel cut in, "And don't show me that stupid toilet. The floor is ruined because that barrel ran over! In fak, the floor was already ruined. Yo 'students' peein all over it."

"You're supposed to empty the barrel every morning or evening. I always emptied it every evening!"

"Well, Mz. Rose, cheap things jes does not work!"

"No, YOU don't work, Mz. Moore. Stove full of ashes, lid broken. You can never pay me for what you did to this house. But, you can now get out of it. You don't need to be here ever again."

"Sho don."

Rose started toward the doorway, and stood there holding the door. Rose watched as Ethel went through. Then Rose asked, "And what do you mean I'm trying to get a man?"

"Cause that's what ya doin! I know why ya got Leroy to 'fix' yo fence! Ya jes tryin to fix Leroy." She gave an ugly-sounding laugh, and went through the fence gate. "But ya can't get Mr. Leroy. Mr. Leroy got hisself plenty women better'n you!"

"I don't want Leroy, for your information."

"Now, Mz. Rose, who is a liar!?" Ethel hadn't intended to tell, but she couldn't hold it in. "And another thing, Mz. Rose, I done already got another place for me to live. My mama got that house cross the street your friend, Bertha, use to rent. It's big, but we gonna rent some rooms out. Colored peoples need some place to rest in this town."

Rose started to say something else, then caught herself as she thought, "Why am I talking to this woman?" She turned to go up the steps and into her house. She locked the door, then leaned against it, moaning, "Oh, Mama. Aw, Tante."

CHAPTER 17

Before Rose's classes started again, Joseph had cleared up the problems in the little classroom. His young friend Herman Tenderman had helped him; not for money, just for friendship and a little food. Joseph also had a friend who knew some plumbing. Rose used some of her little savings she had and put plumbing in the classroom. She had a cesspool placed some distance from her house. "I'm tired of having to clean out my outhouse after everybody!"

She didn't put plumbing in the big house. "I'll wait til I get married, then *he* can do it." She didn't quite know who "he" was just yet. She was hoping it was Leroy. "He'll have a job."

When her classes did start there were fewer students coming. There were some small secondary public schools in Wideland now. As time passed a few students, shamed in the larger newer schools by their poor clothes, returned to her classes, somehow embarrassed among all the students and teachers at the larger school. Prejudice was not a great pressure on the colored people, not as horrific as in other Southern places, but it was in Oklahoma just the same.

There were people who helped, and you could relax a bit, if you had the money. But times were still hard, and jobs still hard to find. Rose took on an extra job watching little children for a white family. It wasn't much money, but it came in very handy. She could afford to make lunch or dinner for Leroy, who now came every day except on the weekends. He said, "I work harder on those days. They really need me. I have to be there all day."

Leroy became a mighty regular visitor. Leroy was speaking love to Rose. He realized Rose owed nothing on her house and land, and had no real bills to worry about. She was frugal, and she grew her own food. She even had eggs to sell to the grocery stores. Sometimes she walked a few blocks over to the better part of town and sold her eggs directly, saving some of her own money from the middleman.

Leroy had kissed her, but it had gone no farther than that . . . yet. She was talking marriage. In consequence, he proposed, even as he thought, "I don't have to sure-nuff go through with this here marriage. I can change my own mind any ole time." He chewed on his fingernail a moment, thoughtfully. "But, you know I kind'a like this here woman. She ain't that hard to take no way. Fact is, she is really nice. Cooks and everthin.

"I didn't get none of that poontang yet, but hell, there ain't no bad poon; just better poon." He grinned to himself at his wit.

He even began to give her a few dollars every week, to help with the food he ate, and to make a good impression.

Then everything did go farther. One night, as he was gently kissing her, he slid his hand under her dress. He felt her stiffen, and stilled his hand, whispering, "What'sa matter, baby?"

In a soft, tiny little voice she answered, "I'm scared, Leroy."

"What you scared of? I ain't gonna hurt ya." He felt her body trembling; something in his heart softened him, made him care for the woman who was so kind to him. "You'a virgin or somethin?"

"I don't know."

"How you not gonna know?" He stood up. He had no intention of leaving, he was himself excited and surprised. This was a new experience for him. A woman he knew cared for him, backing away from him. "Mercy me!" Somebody no one else had had?! He thought of Tonya, his usual regular girl. He had thought he loved Tonya!

So, yes, he had a regular girlfriend. They were supposed to get married . . . some day. But, she was a hell-raiser. "She didn't take no shit!" That's where he spent most of his weekends. He was ready to let Rose go in a minute, if Tonya found out.

But, he thought, "Rose is so peaceful, so, well . . . nice! She clean, and she got a school. And this house; it's always clean. Tonya ain't got nothin but a good lovin, a rent shack, and she pretty. And I guess I love her."

He looked down at Rose sitting huddled, quietly, into herself. He felt sorry for her. He kneeled down on the floor beside her, putting his arms around her. She wrapped her arms around his neck, leaning her head on his shoulder. Rose nearly whispered, "You can do it; I won't be scared anymore."

He had almost made up his mind to leave . . . for that evening. But he felt her warm, sweet-smelling body, clinging to him. He laid her back in his arms, on the couch, intending only to kiss her again. He laid her back, but she held on to him. His hand just automatically moved to her knees again.

As they kissed, Rose grew warmer and warmer toward Leroy. She relaxed. His hand slowly moved up her firm, warm thighs. Neither one of them was thinking much. His hand covered that place the minister had abused; Leroy's hand healed it. She became moist, but he still didn't hurry. He soothed, and rubbed, lightly, caressing her private, secret, and sweet part.

Then things just happened. Slowly and naturally, they happened. They were alone. It was quiet. It was a warm night. She smelled good, so did he. It just happened. It hurt a little, but Leroy kept his lips pressed to her lips, his tongue was soothing to her. He just made everything so easy . . . so smooth, and natural. It just happened. And then, it was over, and she was truly a virgin no more.

It was good enough, personal enough, that Leroy forgot Tonya, and whatever their plans might have been. He decided, "I am gonna marry this woman. Rose is my woman. Only mine. I'm the only one!"

It happened several more times, just naturally, but then Rose was deep into planning her wedding. She was so happy. "And sex isn't all that bad neither after that first hurting. That was really bad, but Leroy says

128

it's going to get better!" she thought happily, to herself.

Of course, as everyone heard the news, some people came by to spend a short spell with her, to talk. We have a whole lot of old people round here, and you know they always watch the young'uns. But Ethel wasn't watchin cause she was old, but because she was a trouble makin little woman who would argue with the whole world if she could. She was watchin Rose cause she was jealous. Jealousy is a dangerous thing; you should never take a jealous, envious person lightly.

One morning, a month or so later, Ethel caught Rose out in the yard and came from across the street, saying, "Girl, why don't ya just live wit em? That be nough of Leroy for anybody! Ya gonna have to eat shit a mile long, chile. That man don't love ya. All them pretty womens who want him! Why he gonna pick ya?! All ya got is that ragiddy house over here, and a few scraggly, skinny chickens! I heard he said ya ain't even got no shape on ya; them skinny legs of yourn."

Bertha happened to hear everything because Ethel was standing in the street when she said it. Bertha hollered out, "Rose, don't ya listen to her, she jes jealous. Moore never did really marry her. They jes live together.

She ain't never been married her own self!"

At last, and anyway, the marriage was accomplished. They said, "I do." Leroy was a little slow in saying it, but he said it. He was bruised a bit, from Tonya fighting him. Rose looked at him, waiting for him to say the words, bewildered a moment. But the words came out, and then she said her words. The minister said his words, and the marriage was complete. They were married. Man and Wife.

Leroy moved right into the house Val and Irene had left to their children. Tante didn't come. "My work," she said, but she sent a silver tea set. Real silver plate. Beautiful silver plate.

Ethel and her mother, Alberta, were among a rather good crowd of guests. Ethel looked at the silver set sideways, saying, "That ain't real! That some cheap stuff, or her sister done stole it from somebody she work for. I knows good stuff when I sees it! and that ain't good!"

Ethel didn't have a new man yet, and only one male tenant in her new-to-her house. Her mother, Alberta, moved in with her to help her, and to save money. Then all the voices raised in arguments heard in the neighborhood were Ethel's and her mother's. Long, fierce, ugly arguments that Ethel started and wouldn't let go.

Finally even the badly needed tenant moved out, and soon, Ethel's mother was packing up to go back where she had been before she came to help her daughter. She slammed the front door behind her as she left, saying, "I got high blood, and sugar! Ya ain't gonna kill me like ya did that last man of yo'rn! That's all you do is argue and fuss." Alberta did not move back in with her daughter, but time had healed wounds, and they came to the wedding together.

There weren't many wedding gifts, but they weren't expected. People were still struggling to survive even though the depression was lifting somewhat. Rose was a beautiful bride in her homemade white cotton gown. She loved the bouquet too much to throw it away, but she threw a few flowers at the waiting ladies. Three or four of them, feeling beautiful in homemade handmade bridesmaid gowns, were happy to catch even one or two of the flowers. Juliet, watching, didn't even try.

Rose was surprised, and very happy, to see some of Wings's family there. Especially Dreaming Cloud, one of Wings's favorite nephews, who had come with him several times to check on Rose. Cloud spent most of his time talking to Juliet. They both loved books, and beauty, like most dreamers.

He had begun to come alone, bearing gifts; Juliet was so happy to have someone who came just to see her. Juliet had even begun to spend her little basket money for things like cologne, makeup, bangles, and bows.

Bertha had thought a bit fearfully, "Lord, I ain't ready for no problems with my cripple child." After a few moments looking at her happier daughter, she thought, "Well, ain't she a woman, too?" She didn't want her daughter hurt. She was preparing things in Rose's kitchen, but she watched as Cloud had helped Juliet get to the wedding, seating her in a perfect place to see everything. Bertha shook her head slowly, and breathed a small sigh of hesitant happiness and relief.

Rose's heart was so full of love and appreciation. It felt as though Wings had come to wish her life his blessings, and, she felt, a part of her father was there.

Bertha had baked two lovely, two-layered cakes with jellybeans sprinkled on them (stolen by Bertha, who was not a regular thief, but this was different, this was her friend's wedding!). Everyone was able to get a small piece of cake, and some of the little fingerfoods on the buffet. Too soon for some, people were leaving the gay little wedding party.

Leroy kept on the lookout for Tonya to show up. He was nervous, and was relieved when she didn't. He put his arm around Rose's shoulder as they walked to the front door to say good-bye to their guests. They looked good standing there together, smiling.

The young boy, Herman Tenderman, had followed his aunt to the wedding, but she wouldn't let him come in. "Because," she said, "ya too raggity! Ya makes me look bad! Go on home!" He could hear the sounds of gaiety inside the house, and he knew they usually served food at these things. He wanted, needed, some food. The young man was near starving; not only for food, but for some joy in life.

So the boy, Herman, hung around, leaning on the fence near the front door. This was where he came to school, sometimes; he knew Mz. Rose, he thought proudly, and Mz. Bertha. They helped him with some of his problems. They all liked each other.

Just as he thought, when Rose saw him, she waved to him; he knew he would have a piece of cake, or some of anything she had left. Herman had become one of the important students to Rose. Bertha prepared a plate for him when she had prepared one for Joseph.

The next few months seemed blissful to Rose. Leroy made her happy, and she made him happy. He could mostly do any of the things he liked to do. But, other than perhaps a few brief stops a week at the local juke joint, he went home after his job was done. He gave Rose his paycheck because he could see the evidence of where she spent it. He always kept a few dollars for his own, just to feel them in his pocket.

Time passes quickly when you can fill the hours with happiness. Except for rumors of war, President Roosevelt's New Deal had, for the most part, pulled the nation out of its crushing slump. The whole banking world was involved. Other nations were suffering. Stalin had been robbing Russian peasants of their land and bodies, for big industry. There was a Gulag; people were reduced to slaves. Stalin called it Socialism.

The devil was jumping around with joy; he thought he was conquering the world.

Bootleggers thrived, Prohibition happened; yet, and still, even more liquor flowed over the drinking world. The Keystone Kops and the Marx Brothers ran across the screens. The Ku Klux Klan came back stronger. Ragtime and George Gershwin were part of the background music for souls who just wanted to listen, or dance. Most of the world worshipped speed. Automobiles and planes, whatever.

The world and Life had picked up much speed now. There had always been wars, but now so many more people at a time were killed. Or starved. Or maimed and crippled. Or made homeless. Or childless. Fatherless, motherless. Just like now.

Many would make fast money. Fast money; not all were known, except the underworld *(as they are called)*. Yet the world and Life were not going as fast as they would go. Yet. But Mankind was gaining traction.

But Leroy and Rose did not involve themselves with all that. Their world was small. His job, the garden, the chickens; everyday things filled every day.

I believe it was late 1937 when Rose discovered she was pregnant. I'm not sure; it's all I can handle just remembering my own business from that long ago. She was so bright and happy when she told Leroy, it infected his feelings. He did not really care for children. It was enough for him just to have them coming to the little classroom.

As time passed, and Rose's little belly started poking out, Leroy adjusted. The thought of his own child was now different. "At least I ain't gonna have to worry bout feedin it, or if it's mine. And I ain't gonna have to look for no place to rent! We doin just fine here. So come on, son!"

When Rose's baby was born it was a girl. Because it was not a boy, Rose felt the baby was her own to name. She thought about a special name a long time. She thought of her family; her mother, her father. You can know in your heart that you have someone on earth who is your family, like Tante, but if they are not there for a long time, you feel alone.

She prayed, "Oh, thank You, dear God, for the gift of my little baby girl. I will love her. I will cherish her, and protect her. I will tell her all about You, God, so she will know right from wrong, and have a good life. Because I know you have to know right from wrong to see which way to choose in life. Oh, thank You, dear Father."

Because it was a girl, Leroy didn't mind his wife naming the child. Since her mother's and father's deaths, Rose's soul had longed for something, someone of her own. She named the baby Myine Wee, because her heart told her so; the baby was hers. "I will never be alone again, God. I have Myine" (pronounced as Mine). "And we are a Wee!"

Let us leave the little family attending to their life for a while.

I got to tend to something for a minute.

Now . . . there is a whole lot of things I haven't told you. I can't get everything in all at once. I have to stop and breathe, or go to the bathroom, or eat.

My mama is sitting here looking and listening to me, seeing that I get it all right. She likes hearing this story again.

Now . . . Let us talk about the other side of that "Y" I told you about at the beginning of this story. The Herman Tenderman side.

And love, chile, love.

CHAPTER 18

HERMAN

Now, I need to tell you about Herman Tenderman because I watched him grow up also. He was always so quiet he was almost invisible. The community finally came to know him as a very nice, studious, hardworking young man, even as a child. Always helping his mother. He sure did love her. I didn't know her too well, just from church was all we knew.

Now, I'm starting at the beginning of the time my mama started paying attention to Herman, so we have to back up, go back to the beginning again. His story is happening simultaneously with Rose's, before she even married and had Myine. Keep that in your mind so I don't have to repeat myself in EVERYTHING that was happening at the same time to these people. It's a good story, but you have to pay attention.

We are on the other side of that "Y," getting to the crux where these lives join, and we get into the stem of the "Y," or story.

Herman Tenderman grew up in a father-less family. There was just he and his mother, Odessa. His father had been long gone from the time he was a baby. They were very, very poor. In those times, like in these times, poverty was spread all over the world, except for the fortunate few who were rich and had survived the wars, and the Wall Street crash in America that had affected the central banking centers almost everywhere in the world.

His mother, Odessa, died when he was about eight years old. She had tried to raise him right, but could hardly keep food on the clean, bare table, or clothes on his back. I'll tell you.

Odessa had worked like a man for years as a field hand, picking whatever was in season. Every season. ALL long days. And she begged the overseers for more work. She worked too hard for a woman. Always tired, always hungry, always needing everything. And having babies three times, and losing one.

She had been able to keep a small shotgun shack for Herman and her daughter, Pearl. But they lost that shack when Pearl got sick, and Odessa had to use the little money she had for medicine. Her sister, Peach, called

Aunt Peachy, let them use her closed-in back porch. "Only for a lit'l while, Odessa, cause it too crowded up in here!"

Pearl died at four years of age, and Odessa cried tears that seemed like her blood, because they came from such a deep place in her heart. She blamed herself because she was unable to afford a doctor or any medical care for Pearl. She had taken bone-thin Pearl, with her rasping breath and mucous-filled nose and eyes, to a white female doctor. She had thought, "I knows a woman won't let no chile die."

But the doctor had said, "There is nothing I can do for this child if you have no money. I have to keep up with my own patients!" The doctor handed her a pill. "Here, give it this aspirin. That is about all I can do for you." Then she had spoken to her nurse, "Who's next?" and turned away from Odessa, and the congested child you could hear struggling to breathe.

Odessa had wrapped the ragged, but clean, blanket closer around her baby, and turned to walk, slowly, out of the doctor's door. Disheartened, broken-spirited, Odessa took her Pearl home, and cried for two days as she watched her small beloved child die. She blamed herself. Her young son, Herman, did everything a child could do to comfort his mother.

He tried to bring his mother tea or even just hot water in a cup. His Aunt Peachy would look up, see him in the mildly dirty kitchen, and run him out. "Ain't nothin in here for ya! You let yo mama git her own! We all got to face dyin, this ain't nothin new, chile. Now ya get on outta here mongst my things!"

Stay close with God, dear chile, and try never to get too poor around anyone. Work; work hard, save; go to school, learn something, lest you be caught poor one hard day, without a God perhaps, and counting on human beings on this earth, and you will mostly, and surely, suffer for it.

Odessa couldn't grieve long; she had to get out to find some work, make some money. She had to get another place of her own, away from the hard, selfish hands of her sister, Peachy, so Herman and she could have some little peace in their dreary, bare life.

"Peachy don't owe me nothin, but this here chile ain't have no fault in me bein broke. I got to take care my son!"

She found work at the garbage dump, earning barely a few nickels a day. With her sister, Peachy, pushing her, Odessa finally found a really broken-down, dilapidated two-room shack for herself and her son. She paid, and also did work in exchange for that condemnable shack.

She also walked and walked until she found a butcher shop to clean up, and a few toilets in cheap diners. She was dying on her feet. She didn't cry anymore, just lived on deep sighs. No more tears left. She would get on her knees and pray til the dawn came glimmering through her hazy windows. Sometimes she fell asleep as she prayed, her head resting on the foot of the worn mattress they used for a bed.

Her eyes were always seeking some new job to do. She forgot how to sleep; when she did get to lie down her eyes stared into the darkness, looking for an answer to how to keep Herman alive. And, above all, keep him well. "Don't get sick, son! Heah, pull that sweater tight round yo neck! That there rain is sho cold rain. Don' want it runnin down ya back."

Herman tried to help. He went around to the garages that had sprung up in town since automobiles were on the newly paved roads. But he was so young, so small. Sometimes a thoughtful man would let him sweep the floors, or wipe the oil off of whatever was soaking in it. When his mother, Odessa, found out, she fussed with him.

She wanted him to get over to the school. "You get on ovah to that there school Mz. Rose is teachin. I done spoke to her, she gonna let ya. We find a way to pay. I wants ya to get you a edercation. Don' be no fool like I is! Learn you somethin! I means that, Herman. Let me do the worryin round heah! You do the schoolin!"

Odessa did outdoor jobs; chopping wood, cleaning yards. She even patched a roof once. Cheap labor, paying almost nothing, sometimes a few eggs. Even that was all right with Odessa. Her son would eat breakfast.

Usually they had one good meal a day; Odessa worked hard for that. That meal had to hold them until the next day. She kept a pot of beans simmering slowly, and ready. Herman didn't like to eat alone, without his mother. He wanted to be sure she had something hot to eat whenever she came back to the shack. Coming and going to school, he was always picking up stray kindling to keep the fire in the stove going, so his mother wouldn't have to worry about it.

As Herman grew, he learned. He watched everything his mother did, and learned to do it. He went to Rose's school as Odessa wanted. Sometimes, she would come home from some field with a few vegetables and a few pieces of fruit for "my boy," with a smile on her weary face. "God gave us these, son."

For his part, her dinner would be ready and waiting. Not usually anything special, but hot rice and beans. If he had done some work at the butcher's, he got a few chunks of chicken to put in the beans, or a chunk of a ham hock; that made it special.

Everyone knew Herman was a good worker, even as small as he was, and that he didn't steal. His not stealing helped him a great deal. When people trust you, you go farther in life. He helped his mother in every way his little body could. He was learning love all the time. He dearly loved his mother.

His mother was painfully grateful, and thanked God all the time because her son was so kind and good. She loved her son.

Herman was a brown-skinned boy. He looked out from large, round, clear, black eyes with surprisingly long beautiful lashes. A long, narrow nose, flaring at its end, was set in a narrow face. His lips were firm and medium sized, but not thin. He looked a bit unattractive until you really looked at him; then he was handsome. His was a man's face. He had long arms with large hands, and long thin legs with large feet. He moved neither fast nor slow, but rather, steadily.

Odessa could not afford even the small school fees. Rose hadn't asked for any money; she knew there was none. But Odessa had gone to talk to her. "I'll scrape by best as I can, and send ya somethin ever time I has a nickel over. I mean that, Mz. Rose. Jest, please, let my son come here for some learnin."

Rose had taken only a few moments to decide after looking into the dark, intelligent, sad eyes of Herman. She didn't believe in people getting something for nothing. To Rose, that was part of learning to live also.

So as she pressed his shoulder, she said, "All right. In exchange you can help me clean up after we help the students get their lunch. I'll throw in your lunch, too. Maybe even breakfast, depending on how good you can work. But I am afraid you will have to get most of your own supplies: paper, pencils." She smiled, and Herman thought she was the most beautiful lady he had ever seen.

Herman replied, "Tell me where the supply store at, and I c'n go do some work for em, and get what all I needs."

Rose looked into the earnest eyes, saying,

"There must be some other way. Let me talk to the store lady, Ms. Day, and see if she might have something for you to do on a regular basis. But, first, we have to wash your clothes, clean you up so you will be comfortable, and presentable."

"I'm alredy comf'table, ma'am."

In time, Rose clipped his hair as best she could, having practiced on many little heads. Bertha washed his clothes, and made him underwear from some material in Rose's sewing room. His clothes weren't always ironed, but they were always clean. He was so proud. His mother cried as she prayed, and thanked God at the kindness of these few people toward her son.

Bertha thanked God that young Herman was the helpful kind of young boy he was. Joseph liked him. He steered little clean-up jobs to Herman, suitable to his size. It was like having a son. Joseph was working pretty steady. Bertha's heart was just happy Joseph and Juliet had some company besides her. So Herman was a busy young man.

He was doing clean-up work at the lumberyard, also. Joseph helped him get that job. When there was not too much to do at the lumberyard, Herman worked at the automobile garage on Saturdays, and some evenings. He was learning a great deal about cars; how to rebuild small things, clean parts, and stock them. He gave all the money he earned to his mother. Now they had, not a good shack, but a cleaner, better shack that did not leak very much at all.

In the colder seasons he wore secondhand shoes from the barter store. He had so many places to go to do his piecemeal jobs that it was never long before the soles were flapping at the bottom of his feet. When Odessa had no work in the winters, they made do with newspapers in worn shoes. When it stormed or snowed, and there was no newspaper, sometimes he went barefoot because he was embarrassed to be seen by others at school or work. One day, after it had rained, Mz. Rose saw him come sneaking into the classroom with mud squishing between his toes.

Rose exclaimed, "Oh, Lord!" and went immediately into her house to get an old pair of her father's boots. As she was leaving the room she said to her small class, "First one laughs will have to clean boards and erasers for a whole week. No laughing at being poor in my class. We are all poor!"

Herman studied the books Rose gave him at school. *Thoroughly. Remembering* his mother's words, how she always talked of wanting him to go to school. "It gonna be ya only way to somethin! Ya only way." At first that is why he went. But he had a bright, quick mind, and soon he went for the pleasure he found in learning.

By nature he was reserved and serious. He listened hard, then studied intently, and learned quickly. After learning how to read, and understand well, he found all books interesting. He worked two months at the bookshop for a newly published book on auto mechanics. In a year or two he was even loaned some of Tante's thick books of learning.

As time passed, Rose began to speak to him about college. He put that out of his mind as an impossibility. In the meantime, Rose was excited about being in love and planning her marriage, at that time, to Leroy.

(I have already told you about those times, but we are at the beginning of Herman's story, and I have to tell it this way so you understand what was happening to them at the same time. It's my way of telling; I'm not trying to confuse you, just trying to tell you something.)

Time was moving along; President Roosevelt's New Deal was working for many people.

(I loved President Roosevelt. Ain't hardly been another one like him.)

148

Still, a few people slipped through the cracks, as is always the case. Do not think Herman was making much money; he made little money, but he learned. Sometimes he did grown-man-size jobs; his employers chose to think he was "still a child," and pay him that way. But he worked, and he learned.

Herman would think, "I have so little to help my mama, besides a little food, and a piece'a roof." He heard her every night, on her knees praying, and crying when she thought he was asleep. He didn't know if she was crying for his father, or crying because she was hungry. It gave him a pain in his heart that never left him.

She didn't eat much, in order for Herman to have more. She was working less, because she was ill, and had been for a long time. She never complained out loud. But it is a terrible, hard thing to hear your mother cry. Tears would slide from his own eyes down his cheeks to the rough mattress, softly, quietly. He didn't know he was crying for the same reason Odessa was crying; about life. Just life.

Odessa was happy about one thing; Herman was in some school. "It ain't the big white school that lets coloreds come to it. But if you learn the ABC, it don't matter where at you learned em!"

She would go by to offer Rose some small offering, but Rose looked at the tired, overworked woman, old before her time, and burdened with the weight she had carried, alone, for so long. Rose tried to think of something to give Odessa without it appearing to be charity.

She would make a mental note to pick up a decent coat, and some sweaters, at the secondhand store. She thought, "I can pretend they are old things of my mother's I have been planning to give away for a long time."

Odessa was beginning to feel mighty low lately. Worse than ever before, and she had suffered many pains doing men's jobs. She didn't know why, or what was causing her loss of energy. She didn't even have any appetite. "I neva did think I wouldn't be ready to eat anythin. Hungry as I been!"

She had so many ailments acquired over the last, long years doing all kinds of hard work. Of course, she had no money for a doctor. So she just lived, and worked with the pain in her stomach, sides, and back. No good nutrition, no medical attention, and unnecessary worry about her son finally helped the thing growing in her body to take it over, and kill her.

She died when Herman was about eight or ten years old. By that time Herman was working pretty steadily at the several odd jobs he had acquired with Rose and Joseph's help.

CHAPTER 19

Something ran through Herman's mind daily now. "I want something that is mine; nobody else's, just mine. Like my mama was mine. I've got'a have something that is mine!"

He wanted to die and lie beside her in the homemade box that was her coffin. Herman had built the coffin of plywood he was allowed on credit at the lumberyard. Odessa was almost tiny by the time of her death. Rose and Bertha had lined the box, quickly, with quilting and a lovely piece of shiny material.

When she was buried, Herman made a simple cross to place at the head of her grave in a potter's field for the poor. Rose was going to take her out to Wings's family and have her buried in the beauty of the reservation. But Herman cried it would be too far for him to go see her often enough.

After she was buried Herman went to the

graveyard two or three times a week to sit by his mother's grave until it got too dark and cold. He was quiet and thoughtful during this time of mourning, always staring off into the distance. "I don't got nobody now. I want something of my own; something belongs to me."

There was an old, shaggy brown dog that hung around the general area of Herman's house. He had often given the dog the slim scraps from his own meals, because he liked the friendliness of the dog's eyes. He called the dog "Buddy," and took him home with him. The dog, usually wary of young boys, answered his calling, followed him, and slept on the shaggy mattress beside Herman, under his arm. They trusted each other. Both needy hearts had a friend.

Finally Herman had to turn to the only person he thought he could turn to in town, Aunt Peachy. Herman did not want to go to her when his rent was up and due. His mother had suffered the arrows and wounds of hurtful words from Aunt Peachy. But he thought he had no one else. Actually, he had other friends.

Peachy had come to Odessa's funeral because she said, "I don't want no talkin goin round this town bout me and kinfolks!" After the brief funeral she had told Herman, "Well, boy, I know you ain't got no place to go, so if you jes has to, we'll find some place for you at the house. Ya can work and feed yourself cause I ain't got much to feed my own family. But come on if you has to. You need to quit that school-goin, and get ya a real job! Ya old enough for somethin!" Herman didn't want to go to her house then.

Herman held out for a long time. He continued to work, and he saved his money, little as it was. But when winter came he couldn't keep sleeping out under a tree or in anything he could find to crawl into. Brokenhearted, feeling like he'd rather die, he went to his Aunt Peachy's house.

She was sitting at her kitchen table gossiping with a friend as she chewed and sucked on a chicken bone. She looked at Herman, laughed, and said, "Well, boy, I thought ya had done married, and done moved in with somebody or somethin!"

(She was taunting that boy!)

Herman said nothing, just shifted from one foot to another, quietly.

"Well, open ya mouth, boy! Tell me somethin. What ya plannin on doin here? I can't have no lazybones hangin on me. You workin?"

"Yes'm, a little."

"We don have no money here, so." She paused, silent a moment. "Ya see this here room on the back porch? The one your ma used before?" Herman nodded in silence. "Well we gon try to round ya up some bedclothes, and you can make a pallet out there . . . for awhile. Ya think ya gonna be here long? Cause this house too small for too many peoples. We's already full, ya can see." She turned to look at her guest, saying, "Lawd, where is my brother when I needs him."

(She lied, for nothing. Never had a brother.)

She looked back at Herman. "Go on, boy, go on an look that porch over, see is it alright. And ya ain't gonna keep no dog here in my house. This a clean house!"

Herman's heart plummeted to the bottom of his soul, and fell into the pit of tears always waiting there. He took a deep breath, and said, "It'll be just fine, Aunt Peachy, it'll be just fine. I'll move first chance I get." As he made up his mind at the same time to try to find some way to keep his dog, Buddy. He thought, "That's my buddy. How am I gonna let him go away?"

His aunt kept talking. "Quicker than that, son, cause ya got to quit that school ya be goin to, and get ya a real job, like a man!"

"Yes'm." He went onto the back porch,

and sat down on the floor to think. He looked through the torn screen covering the back porch. He sat for a long time, tears filling his eyes, thinking, "I want somethin of my own. Just mine."

The dog hung around the different neighborhood in spite of the kicks and rocks thrown at him. Buddy learned when, and where, to hide, to stay close to his friend who continued to bring him food scraps he was stealing from his self, and Aunt Peachy.

Chapter 20

In a very short time Herman arranged to be
night watchman at the lumberyard, so his
dog could rest warm and safe there. Pay was
extremely low, but he didn't care. He had
his dog, and his regular jobs that kept him
afloat. He just wanted a place to be safe in
with Buddy off the streets, and not at Aunt
Peachy's.

And he didn't quit school like Aunt Peachy
wanted. Instead, he paid more attention to
his studies than ever. He went to Rose's
school. Now and again he brought Rose and
Juliet wildflowers when his eyes were caught
by their bright colors against the green foliage. He liked them because they liked, and
fed, Buddy.

He watched Leroy and Rose living together in their home. He marveled, yet, at
the beauty a family could be. When he
learned about Tonya being Leroy's girlfriend
again, he saw something bad coming out of

all of it; but he did not know how much he did not know. He stayed out of everyone's business. *(That boy had some sense!)*

He did everything Rose told him to do; read everything she thought he should. He still did some work at the bookstore, so he was able to get books at reduced prices. Rose and Bertha both fed him when he let them. He liked them to wrap up whatever food they were giving him so he could share it with his Buddy.

Time passed quickly, as it always seems to in hindsight, and Herman became very accomplished in all his studies. Rose, having fewer students now that she was married and a mother, helped him all she could. She wrote many letters seeking help. Finally, she helped him get a scholarship to a newly established African American junior college in Oklahoma to help him round off what he needed to get registered in a three-year college for a degree.

Herman had saved his money. He had gone without almost everything but the bare essentials, as usual. But he persevered; on his way . . . somewhere.

His Buddy, though well fed, was old, and had many injuries from kicks and the blows from stones thrown at him through his life. He was now crippled. Who knows what all people do to a defenseless animal. He was in pain most of the time. Buddy looked at his friend with so much love in his eyes it seemed to flow out of them and cover Herman.

Joseph told Herman he must take Buddy into the woods and shoot him. "That dog'll shorly live a painful life full of suff'rin an such, less'n ya put em to sleep fore ya go. Take my gun and go on back up in the woods, and put Buddy out his mis'ry."

Herman cried, Rose and Juliet cried. Finally Joseph did it, Herman couldn't. Herman was about seventeen, I reckon it to be. I ain't positive, but I reckon.

After two years, he had a B.A. degree, and his money ran out. He enlisted in the navy (See the World!), seeking a way to complete his education. After three years he came home. Twenty-something years old. He wasn't sure where "Home" was, but he had saved his money, as usual. He got his own place; a small shotgun house in good repair, in a decent neighborhood where Blacks were allowed. He had been gone about five or six years.

To get his new home ready, he shopped for a few things he wanted in his own place, and filled the tiny refrigerator and shelves with food. Fresh new sheets were on the bed he had bought for himself.

He stood at the window looking out at the street, and the sky filled with fluffy, happy clouds. Herman smiled. He felt good. He had a degree. He was also a certified mechanic. He was home. The only home he knew.

Now he decided to go out to see Rose, Bertha, Juliet, and Joseph; his friends. And he decided to look in on his old jobs; his living. Thinking, "I'll think about getting back to college, after I rest a bit. Let's see what is going on since I left this place. Wideland. How wide did it get?" He laughed to himself. "I am home."

He was welcomed back with opened arms by everyone. Rose looked tired, but smiled with pride at all Herman's accomplishments. Mostly she was just glad he was home safe. He looked with a little surprise at Myine. He smiled, saying, "You were so small when I left. You are a very beautiful little lady. I'm gonna have to wait for you to grow up and marry me."

Myine folded her hands behind her back, and answered with a smile. Everyone laughed.

He went to talk with Bertha and Juliet, who just grinned all over herself. Juliet was happy to see him. "Oh, Herman! You have gotten even more handsome!" Rose and the young Myine had followed him to Bertha's house.

Rose chimed in, "He sure is. You thinking about getting married, Herman? These girls around here will go crazy about you! And you're going to have a job forever, being a mechanic. Every car in town needs some work done on it."

They stayed there talking about an hour. Then Joseph came in for his lunch. Herman could see Joseph was really tired. He had worked hard all his life. He showed all the years he carried, and the scuffling he had done for his family to survive. Life hadn't improved that much for Joseph. His lack of education kept him at a sorry low level. They didn't even pay him fairly for the work he could, and did, do. Naturally the men talked a little man-talk about war, and making a living now in Wideland.

Joseph told Herman about how Wideland had grown and changed, especially the night life. "They got some real nightclubs here now. A few of em even have live music! Oh, they got some new kinder ways to get ya money now. Womens just be hangin out in them places all the time. You got to be careful, Herman, cause ya just the thing they be lookin for!"

Everyone laughed, but Joseph. Joseph nodded his head, saying, "I mean it! Ya gon have to be careful out here now! All kinds'a people is makin more babies than they is money! They needs help! They's on the look-out!"

The child Myine, maybe seven or eight years old, laughed lightly at the words because the grown-ups did. Then as Herman and the others said their good-byes, Juliet just looked at Herman all the way to the gate and beyond. She was wishing she could go down to all those places where everybody was out there looking for a mate.

Soon, Herman checked on his old job at the automobile repair shop. It was still small, but he said his hellos to everyone, and went by the new garage Joseph had mentioned to him. Larger, brightly lighted, and busy, it was named Pink's Automobile Shop. He spoke with the manager, who had frowned when Herman first mentioned employment; well, Herman was a Black man, and everyone knew they were just manual laborers.

Herman explained most of the things he could do, and where he had learned. At the end of his speech the manager was nodding. "Yes, we can sure use somebody like ya. And ya can fix boats, too, huh? Well sure, ya got a place here then." Herman left, saying, "I'll let you know for sure, after I get a few days of rest." The manager's eyes followed Herman as he left the building. He was a little stunned that the Black man had those skills, but they really did need someone with Herman's skills.

He proceeded to find the nightclub Joseph had spoken of. The Lark's Club. His eyes had to get used to the darkness inside. The club was really crowded, and it was early afternoon! And it was full of the ladies Joseph had spoken of. Some of them were attractive, most were not. Herman smiled to himself, thinking, "I'm not looking for a wife anyway. That's a looong way off from now."

He took a stool at the bar, and while sipping on a beer he just looked around, gauging the place, listening to the jukebox; it was too early for the musicians to play. He listened to, and laughed with, the women who came up to talk to him. Finally, he bought a drink for one of them, named Wanda.

He refused the gambler who proposed a "little game." He had smiled at him, saying, "Don't know how, partner. Don't know how. Never do anything if I don't know how." The gambler had walked away with his crooked dice, but he couldn't argue with that smile.

Herman was just passing time, looking at Wideland. When he left a few hours later, he had decided he would return one day. It was something to do, some place to go to talk to people.

The days passed slow and relaxed. Comfortable. No rushing done by anyone Herman met. He went back to see Rose a few times. He could tell she was not happy, but she didn't seem to want to talk about it. He left her a couple hundred dollars. "That's not much, I know. But it's just for now. So you can help some kid like you helped me."

He took a few gifts to Juliet. Pretty gifts. Girl gifts. Makeup, hair curlers, flowers, bangles, and beads. Even perfume. Bertha said, "You spoilin her, Herman!" Herman replied, "She will never be spoiled. She has too much sense for that. And she is pretty, and deserves little things like these."

Juliet repeated those words to herself over and over, for many weeks; even months. She remembered the words when Dreaming Cloud, now called simply "Cloud," came to bring her tree bark, wildflowers, and various things of beauty for her baskets from the reservation.

Cloud was a strong-looking Indian brave,

but he was not strong. He coughed, lightly, but often. He didn't seem sick; his eyes were bright, his cheeks rosy and smooth. But the cough was always with him.

Cloud was a very gentle man. He was usually shy, and embarrassed around strangers, even after he knew them awhile. But he had liked Juliet a long time by now. Juliet was still sharing with him reading, drawing, and dreaming. She even read fairy tales with him sometimes. Even though they both knew there were no things like these, they both liked the idea of golden apples and beautiful horses that could fly.

Bertha always smiled big when someone was paying her lonely daughter some attention. She still worried about her daughter, and a man. It frightened her. Still, she always served them a nice lunch she called "tea-time lunch." Theirs was a nice, comfortable relationship. They enjoyed each other. Bertha had to remember Juliet was old enough to be someone's wife. She didn't trust anyone. *(She needn't have worried. Juliet might be crippled in her body, but I think her mind was pretty smart.)*

After a few weeks Herman became bored with doing nothing. So he registered for a class in political science at a junior college in a nearby town, two evenings a week. He also started working regularly at Pink's Automobile Shop.

Herman had also been going by the Lark's Club once or twice a week. At first it was out of boredom, now it was for company. Soon school would relieve the boredom and he thought, "I will not have time to go to the Lark's Club."

He had seen the woman, Wanda, at the club a couple of times. He had bought her drinks and talked for long times. Wanda was an attractive woman, lots of makeup, but well built. She had a full head of jet-black hair, and almost all her teeth. She had two children at home. A home that was often full of neighbors and kids.

About the third time she met him at the bar, she asked, "How much home cookin you had since you been home?"

"Not too much; not enough at any rate."

She tilted her head to the side, saying, "You always so nice to me; why don't ya let me fix ya a nice dinner one night? I'll clean the house out so we can eat in peace, and I'll fix somethin ya will really, really like."

"What?"

"Well, Herman, I won't know til ya tell me! But I'm a good cook and I can fix it no matter what it is! Or I will do like ya told me you do; I'll get a book and learn how to

166

fix it! On your day off. When is your off-day? How ya like that?"

"I like that, but you decide. Fix me what you really like to eat. That way I know it should be good. I work all week and some Saturdays, if I feel like it."

Wanda was impressed. "Welllll, a man who can choose his own days off!"

"I didn't say that," he laughed, "but I don't have to work every Saturday."

"Okay, Herman, let's make it next Saturday." Then she moaned, "Oh, no, the house be all full of kids on Saturdays! That's ya only day off? Ya sure ya ain't got some woman out there lookin for ya to be at her house, or ya'll's house?"

"It would have to be dinner, then, because I work all other days. And no, there is no woman looking for me to be at her house."

Wanda smiled a great huge smile, said, "Well, alright then. This Saturday. I'll figure somethin out so we will have us some peace. Just be two of us, alone together."

CHAPTER 21

The next Saturday Herman met Wanda's two young boys, Gary and James. Gary was a round-headed, talk-a-lot boy that grinned all the time, and James, the quiet one, was long faced, and barely spoke. He just looked at Herman steadily. Their mother finally rushed them out with show fare. "Come home af'ta the show; don't stay but maybe two pictures!" The boys left nodding their heads in agreement, but not really paying attention to their mother.

The kitchen smelled good. Short ribs smothered in thick onion gravy, rice, collard greens, cornbread, and a sliced tomato salad. Herman ate his full plate with all the proper appreciative sounds, and then she led him to her bedroom. His smiling questioning face made her say, "We gonna sit and talk in here. Too many people come by and we won't have a chance to be alone none. If they don't know nobody's here, they won't try to come in."

Wanda really liked Herman; he was different from the men she knew. She thought, "He don't lay around the bar all the time. He must don't gamble, but that don't really matter long as he don't spend all his money out there that I needs round here."

She played the few records she had: Sam Cooke, Arthur Prysock, B.B. King, and others that spoke of love and lovin. The Blues. They each drank beer. She smoked a little pot, and he did, too. The evening turned out to be very interesting. Before he left they had made love twice. "It was not bad, in fact," he thought, "it was pretty good!"

Good enough to come back for more; and he did, just as she wanted, had planned. Herman was a good man, quiet, hardworking, kind, and trustful. He gauged most women by his mother, Odessa, Rose, and Bertha. He had experience, but it wasn't the rough kind, the cold-blooded people kind.

Within two months Wanda told Herman she was pregnant . . . with his child. He did not love her, but she was alright. After much worrying, and a lot of thought, Herman did the "right" thing and married her.

His place was larger than her little shack, but his landlord did not want children, especially young boys. He found a large house that would even have enough room for the coming baby. He was making good money, and now he would have a family. "No child of mine is going to suffer like I did."

Herman dropped the class he had registered for, and took an extra part-time job because something, it was never quite clear what, had happened to Wanda's income; it had just disappeared.

The house was always full of the kids, their friends, and a few adults that obviously didn't have jobs. Music was always playing. They were always drinking beer, and liquor Herman didn't know he was paying for. It reached a point where he couldn't sleep the few hours he had to sleep. Wanda finally put a cot in the laundry room, and told him to lie down on that. She was never downright mean; she always smiled as she used him up.

The baby was a boy. Herman was a proud father, he filled the nursery with baby toys, and all the things a little boy would like. There were even some things for when he grew up. Herman talked about the school, and even the college the baby might attend. He did not forget Wanda's sons. He bought socks, shirts, shoes for them; they really needed everything.

Herman wanted to name the baby Herman, Jr., but Wanda said that it was bad luck to name the baby after the father. She wanted the name to be Jerome. So the baby was named Jerome. Herman didn't really believe what she said about bad luck, but rather than argue, he agreed. It didn't matter anyway, she was going to do what she wanted in the end.

The laundry room became dirty, and smelly with unwashed diapers. She always ran down and bought some new diapers, thinking, "My husband makin good money! I done washed enough dirty clothes in my life already!"

The next year brought another baby; a girl. Herman almost lost his mind he was so happy. "A girl! My baby girl! I'm going to name this one. Her name is Rose."

Wanda asked, "Rose?"

Herman replied, "Yes, Rose Bertha." And the name remained Rose Bertha Tenderman.

After Rose was born, Herman felt a little better going to work every day. He had been getting tired and weary lately. Couldn't see why he was working all the time, and everybody else at his house was playing.

He was having trouble with his stepsons.

They were becoming willful young men. Herman tried to talk to them about school, and maybe college. They both listened to "the ole man," but Gary couldn't care less about his words of advice. In fact he didn't understand the words. He brushed them off, saying, "Only fools be sittin up in some dark room stud'in books!

"He too old to unda'stand life today. Ain't like in his day. We smarter now-a-days. We men!"

James usually copied his older brother, but, as time passed, and he saw the things Herman did for his mother and Jerome, he became more thoughtful about listening to Herman. He had seen how other men had treated his mother; he had thought it was normal, until now.

He began to absent-mindedly pick up one of Herman's books, and leaf through it. Herman had seen him and was encouraged, and encouraging. "What do you ever think about that you would love to do, James?" James didn't answer, just smiled in his quiet way, and went outside. The truth was, he had never been asked to think about anything serious before. He didn't know how, or what, to answer.

Gary was the leader because he was the oldest. The brothers used their mother's marijuana, and drank any liquor they could steal from the house. This was difficult; their mother watched it closely, until she got drunk, which was often now. They encouraged her to drink. Then they stole some of her money. Didn't dare take it all. "Cause Mama is tough when she come to herself!"

Lately, Herman would come in from work, and find Wanda drunk, stretched out on the couch he had bought her. Dress or robe hiked up showing her thighs; mouth hanging open, hair a mess. He would think, "This my wife. Lord, I'm glad my children are too young to understand this, and my friends don't come here. I am not happy, Lord. What have I done to myself? I had a future, Lord!" He held the tears back. "But I'll take care of my children You gave me, Lord. I'll sure do that!"

Now he went out to the laundry room to sleep on the cot without any fussing or encouragement from Wanda. He thought, "I would rather be out there alone." Sometimes he took the baby, Rose, out there. Just to hold her while they both slept.

And he was too tired to fuss about all the partying going on at his house. Things didn't get better over the years. They seemed to get worse every day. Always some new faces he didn't recognize. The only thing he could count on from Wanda was waking him up to go to work. She would wake herself up to do that no matter how hung over she was.

Then Gary and James started staying out all night. Once Wanda had to go down to the police station to talk to them about Gary. She would moan to Herman, "Herman, what we gonna do? I needs money for a lawyer."

He replied, "I don't know, Wanda. Gary should have had a job. I'm not going broke for someone who does not care about his future or himself. And he certainly does not care about anything I say."

When Gary was not around, James began to talk more to Herman about life. He was interested in the navy. Herman was glad because he thought that would be the best thing for James, to be separated from Gary. James was also interested in the mechanics of automobiles, and admired Herman for what he knew. "When I gets a lit'le older, I'm goin in the navy, like you did, Herman."

Herman replied, "You could do with a few days in school, James. Even the navy wants their men to know how to read. You're smart, you can do it. Let your brother make his plans; you make some of your own. Now, let me get some sleep; I got to get ready to go to work later."

His last thought before falling asleep was "I have to go see Mz. Rose and Mz. Bertha. It's been a long time. I heard Rose was sick. But these are modern times with modern medicine. I know she'll be alright. But I got to get over there." Then his mind floated away in unrestful, mind-numbing sleep. But, with the new day, old thoughts faded away; he did not go check on the friends he truly loved. Life was heavy on his back. Time just seemed to evaporate.

Herman began to save all the money from his second job. He continued, every payday, to give Wanda the money from his regular job. "I'm married to her; I got to take care of her. But this second job money is going into a savings account for a house for my own children; and I am going to see that they go to college."

For two years James went to school, sporadically, and finally found his way into the navy. Gary laughed at him, "Ya ain't nothin but a square, man, a fuckin fool." But still, he looked forlorn and lost when James left. Wanda had sense enough to be proud of James. Herman breathed a sigh of relief, and kept working for his own children.

Herman's life went on in this way for

years. Years that took a toll; he got older, more weary, tired, and disgusted. The money not being so abundant as it once was, Wanda found ways to steal from her husband. With Wanda's encouragement even Herman began to drink to escape his weariness. What stopped him from going too far was he had to be sober to see what happened to his children. They were his life. Rose more than Jerome, because she was a defenseless girl.

But, lately, he had been hearing about things people did even to young boys. "This world is really changing. It wasn't like this, or as much as this, when I was growing up. I slept outside at night; hobos and all kinds of men were out at night. But these kinds of things didn't happen to me. I didn't hear of them happening much to anybody.

"The Bible is right, and Satan must be running this world. This sure looks and feels like Satan's system, and it is killing people or making them kill themselves. No one is safe anymore. Everything is moving so fast, too many people can't see what's happening. I've got to watch out for my children." Then sometimes he would say to himself, "I've got to go see my friends, Mz. Rose and Bertha. And Juliet. Those are the kind of people I want my children to know."

(He was beginning to feel as grown as Bertha and Juliet, so he had dropped saying "Mz." He respected his teacher, Rose, too much for that.)

But in the rush of life, the steady run of problems, jobs, and trying to rest and get some sleep, he didn't go see his friends. It was always "In a few days, next week or tomorrow."

There were many, many more people in Wideland then, with more coming every day. And it seemed as though they all needed their cars worked on. Wanda was fighting all the time for more money. Gary was in and out of the jail, and Jerome was admiring Gary for being a "man." Herman had to worry about his daughter because he knew Wanda had company when he was at work, and she was drunk.

It all crowded in on him, and he was already tired. So, much more time passed, like time does pass: slowly, but fast, at the same time. And much had happened to his dear friends.

CHAPTER 22

ROSE AND MYINE

As Wideland was making its history, and Herman was living his plans, the Leroy Aimes household, with Rose and Myine, had been living their history.

The birth of Myine had completed the happy family. For the next few years no other child seemed to be on its way. The first years of Myine's life were filled with joy and laughter. Her stomach was always full, and whatever was good for a little girl, Rose made sure to get it for her.

Rose was very happy with her family, grateful not to be alone anymore. She loved Leroy more and more every day. Sometimes she could not believe her life; it was so good, so full. She awoke each morning eager and ready for the day and her daughter. If Leroy was slipping away she did not, at first, notice.

Over time, while living a life he had never

come close to before, Leroy became used to
the sameness of his home, even bored with
it; the cleanliness, the good meals, and
peace. Some human beings are that way.

In the beginning of his marriage he had
stopped in at the juke joints two or three
times a week. He was popular. People liked
him, and he liked them. He liked to laugh
and talk with all kinds of friends.

A year or so more passed quickly, and he
began to drop in some of the new clubs and
joints to socialize almost every night. But
not Sunday. That was his family day, he told
his friends. And he was proud of his family,
his house. Then the Lark's Club had opened
with its live music and the club became part
of his daily routine. Finally he began to go
out, after he had gone to church with his
family, Sunday nights.

He never ran into Herman or Joseph,
because Joseph was home when he wasn't
working. Herman was too tired to go out.

There was no way to avoid a meeting with
Tonya; they had seen each other several
times, smiled and waved at each other.
Finally, one night she placed her hand on
her hip and stopped at his side; she stared
at him, and waited. He smiled as he asked
about her two daughters. She replied, "They
jes fine!" He wanted to ask, "Who the

daddy?" but didn't. Instead he said, "Well, I'm glad you doin so well." He called the bartender and ordered a drink for her.

Tonya took a sip of the drink, smiling as she did so, making her dimples show as she had practiced. She looked at him with those eyes that were meant to look as though they had a secret. "Ya been busy ya'self! I hear ya got a little baby. What was it, a boy? a girl?"

"I have a daughter, Myine."

"What kind'a name is that? Ain't neva heard it befo."

"It's jes some name that Rose picked out. It's okay. What you doin out here if you got a new daughter? You still runnin the streets!"

"If I wasn't I would'n'a met up with ya." She smiled again, looking at him through lowered lashes.

"Yea, well." Tonya was still looking good to Leroy (which is different from good looking). She still looked sweet to Leroy. He remembered their old days; how good she was in bed making love to him. He thought of love-making a lot. He thought, "I got plenty at home, but, well, a strange piece is . . . Tonya wouldn't be a real strange piece, but strange enough. It's been a long time now."

When she turned to speak with someone,

he looked at her behind, and smiled. When she turned back to him, he asked, "Who your man now, Tonya?"

"What ya wan'a know for?"

"Just askin."

"Ya see somethin ya want?"

"I just might."

It didn't happen that night, but he had a warm spot in his heart for her anyway. In a short time, it didn't take long, she had wheedled herself back into his arms, and deep into his life.

They became an invisible couple. Every night he was out, he wasn't at the Lark's Club, or a juke joint anymore. He was holed up at Tonya's rented shack. That made Tonya more than happy. In an ugly mean streak of her mind, she thought, "Mz. Lady got all that house ova there, but I got her man deep in my pretty yeayea ova heah!" She gave him as much good loving as she could. Because of her hatred of Rose; because Rose had her own house. Rose, who did not even know Tonya existed.

Rose was always waiting in some way for her husband. As she was cleaning house for her family, washing, ironing, shopping for food, cooking for her family. Or playing with Myine as though she was a child, herself. She thought of Leroy, her husband. "We are a family!"

This was a long time ago, so Myine was only going on seven or eight years old. She was reading well, and could write. She loved words and pictures. Tante's old books were almost worn out, though still well cared for. Aunt Tante sent new books, including large art and sculpture books. Even school books for teaching calculus, and Latin.

Aunt Tante wanted Myine to go to college. "I'll pay for it!" she wrote. She lived in Europe now, but asked for pictures of her sister and niece all the time.

She sent many things, beautiful fabrics, buttons that had struck her fancy. Ribbons, hair clasps, scarves, everything that a big girl and a little girl might want from Paris. But she did not come home . . . herself.

Leroy and Tonya were growing closer. Well, all they had to do was make love and laugh together. Rose cooked his food, washed and cleaned his clothes. She took care of him when he was not well, and worried mightily when she would see him looking sick. Or even too tired. All Tonya had to do was concentrate on moving her hips, and she loved doing that.

Leroy made love at home when he grew ashamed of neglecting his wife, and Rose looked at him with confusion and hurt on her face. In those intimate moments with Rose, Leroy felt his love for his wife. He could not understand why he kept Tonya. He would promise himself he would let Tonya go, be faithful to his wife. Somehow in Tonya's company he forgot his family, and his promise.

Rose knew something was wrong, but she was not used to the different ways a man can change. She would think, "I haven't changed, I still love him just like the day I married him."

Tonya had always been poor, every day of her life. Struggling to survive, one day, one week, sometimes even for one hour at a time. She had always wanted, dreamed of, the kind of life Rose had, just in general. Now, Tonya's dreams and desires became stronger. Satan was really working on her. In fact, he had plans for her; plans for everybody, including Rose, Leroy, and My-ine. Satan thinks large.

Tonya looked at the life Leroy lived, and wanted it for herself. "That house! Now he got a car, even if it is used. He got nice clothes, an he don't buy me none! He done even got bigger on his job at that hospital."

She counted, in her head, the money she thought he took home. "He give me a lil money, now an then. My cleanin jobs don't pay me much." (She hadn't had time for school so she couldn't read except for a few words, nor write very well at all. She had hated school.)

Tonya hated, and envied, Rose. Coveted her life. "Of cou'se she got it easy! Cause she got that house. And that's why her life so easy. She prac'ly rich!"

It took over a year, but Tonya convinced Leroy that Rose was in their way to true happiness. She tried a few magic spells on him; she gave that up because magic didn't work fast enough.

Then she began to withhold her loving from him; not too long, because she knew there were many yea-yeas out there who would love to catch him between their legs.

She always gave in to him, at the right time. Gave in, in a dramatic loving way. They would hold tight to each other; she for one reason, he for another. She kept whispering into his ear, and into his dumb, blind heart. He listened, actually without intending to, until even Leroy did not know how the thing went so far. Some mojo must have worked. They were planning to get rid of Rose. Forever. He, halfheartedly, but Tonya was persistent.

Rose was naive, and her daughter was much like her. She did not tell Myine the truth, as she knew it, about life. The ugly things that lay beneath the surface of people. About the choices that came in so many ways, in so many things on earth. Nor the ugly things that lay beneath the surface of even very nice people.

Myine was doing well in all her studies. She had always been around books. She was now mentally beyond all her mother's classes. As her Aunt Tante wanted, she was dreaming of college. She was dreaming of becoming a scientist; she wanted to study the ocean, the land, even the heavens. She loved all the mysterious life on earth.

Her mother had taken her to see the ocean a few years ago. They went on a bus ride, supposedly to the Pacific Ocean, but arrived and sat by the Gulf of Mexico, really, all day. They were immensely pleased with the expanse and depth of magnificence. Then they ate a hot meal, boarded another bus, and went straight back home.

Myine browsed through her two new books, thinking, "Just to see a piece of that huge, beautiful body of water that God created, and all the magnificent, unusual, wondrous life in it." Of course, they also saw some of America. Juliet loved to hear about the trip, and see the pictures as often as possible. She borrowed them to show to

Cloud, to dream about going one day.

Rose mailed all Myine's letters to Tante. Myine kept the ones she received from Tante, and read them over and over again. They were fertilizer for her dreams. They were about college, and going one day to meet her aunt. And so Rose and Myine dreamed.

Bertha, meanwhile, did not know what to do. She did not want to hurt her friend, Rose, by telling her about Tonya. She knew because even ailing Joseph knew from his friends. Juliet had told Bertha, "Mama, if you really are her friend, you have to tell her that Leroy is not doing her right. He got another woman, He ain't livin his married life right!"

But Bertha would reply, "You ain't sposed to meddle in nobody's business, Juliet. They grown." Juliet would not let her off the hook, "Mama, what is a friend for if they not sposed to tell you when somebody is lying to you? And hurting your life?"

"Hush, girl! That's jes the way life is!"

"I don't believe that, Mama. They sposed to have some Christians in this world, and that's sposed to mean something more than what you're saying. And a friend is sposed to help a friend."

"You don't know what you sayin, Juliet."

"But I know what I'm talkin bout, Mama."

And so it went, but Bertha did not tell her friend Rose. She didn't want to hurt her.

No one told Rose.

Slowly, day by day, Rose became sicker. Didn't go to the doctor until a few weeks had passed. Leroy kept saying, "I work at the hospital, head of my own department, and it's lots of people have come down with the flu or a virus. The doctor say you just have to wait it out. Drink a lot of juices, and soups. Wait it out is all you can do, Rose."

Rose heard him calling her "Rose," instead of "Baby," as he used to. She missed him. She still loved him so much, and blamed herself for not being well enough to make him a better home.

Then, one day, he told her, "I'm gonna get one of the ladies from the hospital to come over here and help us out with things, so you don't have to worry none."

In a very weak voice, Rose said, "I guess we could stand a little help cleaning the house. But that would only be once a week or so."

Leroy patted her shoulder as he planned his lie. "Let the help-lady do that, and fix your lunch so you don't have to eat no cold sandmich."

"Who is it, Leroy? Have I met her? How are you going to pay her now that I'm not making any money to help the house?"

"Rose, I don't want you to worry none. Jes let me take care it . . . for a little while, til ya get well. It's gonna be that little ole lady what goes to the church. Mz. Willis. She need a little help. She ain't gonna do much; just keep the house from gettin too messy is all.

"I'm gonna send you food from the hospital so don't nobody have to worry bout no cookin. That way I know ya gonna get the very best food to get well. Cause ya know hospital food got to be good to make everybody well. Myine will pro'bly eat with Bertha cause she over there all the time now. I told her not to be round ya too much, til we know what virus ya got."

Rose raised her head, weakly. "But my students, I've got to get back to work."

Leroy turned his head, dismissively. "I told all them kids to tell their mama that you was sick, and school was out . . . until you get well."

Rose dropped her head back down on the pillow, and tears filled her eyes. "Ohhhhh, my kids. My kids, who depend on me, will suffer." After Leroy left, she cried into her pillow. "Oh, God, I feel like I'm dying. I don't want to die. I want to live to help my baby grow up. Oh, God, I don't want to die. Help me get well, please." And so her prayers went. Leroy began to sleep in another room. She cried throughout the nights.

Bertha knew Leroy hadn't really cared for Rose, lately. He didn't know what Bertha or Joseph knew about him and Tonya. But Bertha offered to bring her own good food to Rose, her friend. "I know jes what she like, Leroy. Shoot, I'll be glad to do something, anything, for Rose. Ain't no sense in paying nobody to do what I want to do, be my joy to do."

"Well, thank ya, Bertha, but we better leave things like we got em, cause nobody don't know how long Rose gonna be sick. I'll be gettin somebody to come in already, if I need em. They say, what she got last a long time. But I sure do thank ya, and Rose thank ya, too."

Bertha started to speak. "Won't matter how long . . ."

"I say 'thank ya' Mz. Bertha, but we gonna be jes fine! And I hope Mr. Joseph is feeling much better. I been seein em at the hospital sometime when he come in to see his doctor."

Bertha stood at their front door, and it was open and shut before she could plead her case.

Rose was upstairs, a little thrilled because her husband was really taking care of her. "Oh, God, I thank You for my good husband. I know I'm going to be alright as soon as I find out what is wrong with me."

No one told Rose anything about her sickness; and no doctor came to visit.

Then Leroy told Rose he had a cousin. "She need a job. I was helpin her get one, but I was wonderin if maybe ya could let her help ya, til the one I get for her come through? She a good worker. Her name is Tonya. Ain't that a crazy name for a' old woman? But, she a good worker! We need a little cleanin up round here. I try to do it, but I got a full-time job."

Rose was continually getting weaker. She said, "Leroy, you are so good to me. God bless you, my husband. But we could ask Bertha. She can use the money, and I know her ways. I haven't seen her lately. I miss her. I want to see her any . . ." Rose started choking on something that had come up in her throat, and couldn't talk anymore.

"Rose, Joseph ain't doin so good; he ailin. She got her hands full. So I'll tell my cousin to come on, an get started. She be in here today to fix your lunch so ya don't have to eat no cold sandmich."

Rose put the rag she had coughed into down and reached out, expectantly, for her husband to hold her a little bit, and kiss her check. "What I would really like is you staying at home these nights and make me a married woman again." She smiled pitifully up at him.

He stepped back from her, patted her hand, saying, "Rose, I'm workin at the hospital; don't want to give ya nothin I pick up out from there. Jes hold on, we gonna be together real soon. I cain't wait myself. Been a long time. Now ya just need to concentrate ya mind on that! Cause I'm gonna be here, waitin."

A tiny shiver of a thrill went through Leroy's heart; he had loved her, he remembered their first love. "I'll stay home tonight, baby. I didn't think you missed . . . my lovin. But, Rose, ya too weak for me to fool around with ya. It takes all my stren't to stay away from ya, but I got to do it cause I want ya to be well again."

She fell back into her pillows. "I miss everything about you; me and Myine miss you."

Leroy looked at Rose, hard, for a few moments. Then he said, softly, "Ya know, once ya had you a baby . . . ya forgot all about me."

Rose's voice was weaker from her exertion. "I didn't forget about you; Myine added to us; all three of us were one together. I still sleep with you every night you come home." Her eyes widened. "Where are you when you don't come home, Leroy? Juke joints don't stay open all night. Where do you go? Who are you with?"

"Rose, I stay out cause I don't blive ya miss me. An we jes be sittin round talkin bout shit . . . nothin. Okay, I'm gonna stay home tonight." He turned to leave the room, then said, "Don't forget ya said ya'ed let my cousin work here, part-time, for us . . . you. We got money in the bank. I'm gonna be home more, watchin to see if she works good. That way I c'n get to see bout my daughter, too."

And so it came to pass that Tonya came to cook, and care for Rose every day. Leroy even paid her. Said, "Don't ya do nothin to my daughter. Nothin! Don't ya make no mistakes."

Tonya began to hate Myine then.

(She didn't want that man to love his own daughter!)

Tonya was thrilled to be in that house. She looked around every room with delight.

Hardly able to keep from shouting the words out loud, "This gonna be mine! Mine! One day soon now." Her own daughters stayed at her old shack; she left them alone many nights.

She often stayed with Leroy, sleeping downstairs behind the kitchen on the porch. Far enough from Myine's and Rose's rooms not to be heard. They made love stealthily. And the loving was good! It got better, because it was stolen, and she thought they were making a fool of Rose.

By this time Rose had much poison in her system; Tonya was doing it slowly. They did not want the doctor to be suspicious. Leroy had called the doctor, at last, because too many people knew Rose was sick.

Remember, in those times small police departments did not think of poison. They were used to guns, knives, fights, and beatings. Usually no one suspected poison among Blacks; and there were so many strange diseases everywhere. With all the drugs Leroy brought from the hospital, Rose was almost already dead as she slept.

She heard nothing, not even the loud moans that Tonya made, on purpose, on the nights she slept there with Leroy. Leroy tried to keep his hand over her mouth, but sometimes he lost his concentration on his hand, replaced by his concentration on the business in his hand.

In the next few weeks Rose tried to eat the nice-looking lunches Tonya prepared: chicken and dumplings; meat loaf; lima beans with pork neck-bones. Things not really good for the ailing; things easily mixed with poison. As little as Rose was able to eat, Tonya spoon-fed her; she ingested more than enough of the poison.

Rose grew weaker and weaker. She often vomited up her meals, slimy glucose, green and yellow, streaked with blood. She cried often, from bewilderment, and frustration, and the lack of her husband and love. Finally Tonya had to move to the house full-time, stay every night, to take care of her.

Bertha had tried again, and again, to see Rose. She cringed, and ached inside her heart when Tonya moved in her friend Rose's house. She knew what was going on in there. Juliet had given her mother a dirty, accusing look when Tonya had moved in, and Bertha did not do anything to stop it from happening.

Bertha's second mistake was to try to hide some truths from Myine that would be very important to Myine's life.

Being older, Juliet was able to take care of herself much better. Bertha now had a steady job. After keeping Joseph supplied with his medicine each month, she was able, with credit, to buy a good wheelchair for Juliet.

That wheelchair made the poor little family very happy. Especially Juliet! Juliet was in her early thirties, and could, at last, go outside on her own whenever she wanted. She loved to sit in the chair, in the wind, and listen to the sounds of trees, birds, and just life. Just life. Cloud visited and began to dream deeper dreams with her.

Juliet was almost independent. And, too, Cloud visited regularly, almost every day. Myine was usually there, also, because Tonya would run her out of the house. "Stop all that cryin and fussin round yur Mama! Ya gonna worry her to death! Get on out. Go play or somethin! Ya got all this big ole yard! Get!"

Myine, a young child, was confused, bewildered. She had never known such attitude and treatment in all her days on earth. "Who is this woman who can do anything she wants to do in this house?" Myine began to do something she had never done before: talk back to Tonya. She had the feeling Tonya would not hit her.

Rose tried to control some things. But her strength was gone; she sometimes blacked out, and one day turned into another day without her understanding how or when. She was helpless; her end was very near. She began to understand that, when she was too weak to do anything about it. Leroy seldom came into her room. It was now her room. Alone.

Juliet was nearly going crazy; she was frustrated and angry. "I can't knock that woman down, nor go up them stairs either. The doctor never comes so I can't tell him, and I don't even know his name to look him up. Oh God, Oh, God!"

She wished for Herman to come by, but he was busy with problems that took up his whole mind, keeping him away. Juliet found out he had recently moved, and had been married. But she had no way to find him. He didn't come to her church anymore, and she seldom went to the church herself.

She wanted to tell Rose, "Don't eat what that woman gives you no more!"

Juliet asked her mother to try to find Herman, and Bertha tried, to no avail. Joseph was sick also. Well, he was old. He had worked very hard all his life, eating poor food, and getting little rest. He was dying, also. Bertha counted on Juliet to take care the house and Joseph. Bertha had to go to work because there was nothing or no one else to count on. "What will I do when my man is gone, God, and my friend is gone, too?"

Then, one evening, Myine came downstairs bringing the tray with two soup bowls she and her mother had used. She had fed her mother, dripping most of the soup onto Rose's nightgown. She came into the kitchen as Tonya was cooking steaks for Leroy and herself. Leroy had his hand possessively on Tonya's behind.

Her mind was shocked; this was her father! Then it became clear in Myine's mind, but she couldn't have explained how or what was clear. She just knew! She watched as her father leaned over to kiss a smiling Tonya, who was pressing her hip into Leroy's crotch.

Myine set the tray on the table, hard. Her father turned at the sound, as he let Tonya's behind go. "Baby! Ya want some'a this steak?" Myine broke into tears, shook her head "no," and ran from the kitchen.

He started after her, but Tonya stopped him, saying, "I been thinkin, we betta get her to go stay some'eres else for a lil bit. Rose bout to die, and I don't need to go through all what's goin to be goin on in this house!"

Leroy looked alarmed. "This is my chile.

197

Where ya gonna send her off to?"

Tonya replied, "A very nice place I know. Been thinkin on it for a long time now. She'll be jes fine, Leroy. Let me," she placed her hip back on his crotch, "jes let me handle yo'r sweet baby, Baby. I ain't gon let no chile get hurt no where round me!" She looked down at his crotch as she said, "Ya jes handle this juicy thing! And this juicy steak I done cooked for ya. Let me worry bout the baby. I done learnt to love her jes like ya do."

Soon thereafter, one night lying in bed, Tonya kept filling Leroy's glass with liquor, pretending to drink right along with him. He was drunk and sleeping when she jumped out of bed, quietly, of course. She hurriedly dressed Myine, pushing and dragging her to the old raggedy car Leroy still had. She drove her about fifty miles away to a little cafe named Mom's Cafe. The child was half asleep. "She ain't never gonna know where she at, do she take a mind to find her way home."

Inside the cafe two older white people, the Whipets, were a little surprised when Tonya came in carrying a child. Pa Whipet said, "Well, ya done finally made it. We bout done gave ya up!"

Tonya looked at Ma Whipet, asking,

"Where her bed?"

"Over hind the kitchen. C'mon, I'll show ya!" Mz. Whipet said. "My, she a big little girl." Tonya motioned with her finger on her lips. "Shhhhh. She sleep."

When Myine was placed in the makeshift bed, they returned to the dining room. Mr. Whipit gave Tonya one hundred dollars for Myine. "We sure been needin help! Ma is gettin old, and I ain't none too well."

Tonya placed the money in her purse, and said, "Don pay no tention to nothin she say; she tell lies to get some tention. She a good worker. Good-bye, ya'll." It was 1947, and Myine was about eight years old.

Tonya was gone back to the house. In the morning, Leroy woke up, mind hazy, and late, rushing to work. He looked through the door, checking on Rose, but didn't notice Myine was gone.

Juliet and Bertha always looked for Myine to stop for breakfast on her way to school. When they missed her, they couldn't get any answers except from Tonya. She said, over her shoulder, "That baby don't need to be over here at yo house with her mama dying."

Rose did die soon after that. She kept asking for her child; Tonya kept saying, "She be here soon. Now ya jes rest."

When Rose died she was thinking of her husband, and her child. She raised up a little from the bed, holding her arms out. She cried out, "Leroy? Myine? Myine." Rose's head fell back onto the pillow, she exhaled a long breath, and then she was gone.

The funeral was small; it wasn't held at the church. They held it quickly, in the parlor of the house: Leroy, Bertha, Juliet, Joseph, Cloud, and a few others who just happened to find out Rose had died.

After Rose's death, the thrill of making love dulled for Leroy. It wasn't as good, or desirable. The heavy, horrible truth of what Tonya had done frightened him. Sometimes the sight of Tonya, even her big behind, made Leroy frown with annoyance. He would think, "Ya know, God? This wasn't none of my idea to hurt Rose. I miss Rose; she was clean, and sweet. Her lovin was never bad. She was clean all over. Don't put this on me, Lord."

Tonya noticed Leroy had slacked off making love, no matter how she flashed her behind, or rubbed up against him. She rolled her eyes, thinking, "This negra better wake up. He ain gonna get no other woman! Not now! This house is . . . ours!"

In every moment, every day, there was

something unexpected for Bertha; the death, the funeral, the disappearance of Myine. Everything always seemed so sudden. "Just life and all these things," sighed Bertha through her tears, "goin too fast for me."

But not for Juliet. She cast many dark looks at her mother. "I told you, you should have told Rose. Told somebody, even Myine, what was going on in that house. Now look. Our best friends. The one is dead, the other is gone. And we don't know nothing!"

Life and death seemed to keep Bertha and Juliet too busy to try to find out more about anything. Juliet, in her new wheelchair, would roll herself over to the house to throw rocks at the doors, front and back, until Tonya answered.

"What ya want?"

"Where is Myine?"

"Her daddy sent her off so she don't have to go through all the pain of her mama's dyin."

"Where did he send her?"

"Well, now, missy Juliet, I think ya is gettin in somebody else bizness! What ya need to be thinkin bout is the rent ya gonna have to pay, now Rose is gone!" Then Tonya slammed the door shut. That happened several times. Then Tonya stopped answering the door.

Bertha did not want any problems. She could not afford to pay any rent. Joseph was sick unto death, and hadn't been able to keep up any work. Bertha was working a domestic job that kept them all going. They worked together to keep the front yard weeded and clean. Cloud mowed the small front lawn.

In her grief, Juliet called Rose "Aunt" to feel closer to her. She frowned, saying, "But Aunt Rose would not have charged us, Mama. We can still do things round here. We watch this place, and keep it pretty clean."

Joseph was quietly crying at the circumstances he was leaving his family in. His heart stopped pumping the feeble blood, and he died with the tears rolling down his face. They held a memorial in the little shack they called home. The house Joseph had built. It was a sad, sad, terrible day. They didn't know what was going to happen to them. A disabled young woman, and a tired, ill, old woman. The family.

But they had Cloud. Cloud loved Juliet, and thought a great deal of Bertha. He still coughed his low constant cough, even with the syrups and herbs they prepared for him. He wanted to marry Juliet, but Bertha told Juliet, "No. Just no." But, he brought them money he earned at whatever he could find to do. He hunted and brought food. But, it wasn't much.

Bertha kept working, Juliet kept weaving baskets, Cloud sold the baskets. Life went on, even as dreary as it was. Rose's death and Myine's absence stayed on Juliet's mind. Stayed on all their minds, but Juliet's in particular.

As expected, Tonya came over to their little house ready to argue about the rent. "Ya jes gonna have to come up with some money! Things is tough, and I . . . we all need it."

Bertha said, "We don't have any money, Tonya. My husban jes died. It took all our money to bury him."

"Well ya jes gonna have to get some, or move on way from here and let somebody else have it that can pay."

Juliet spoke up in a regular tone. "Aunt Rose would not charge us for this house. My daddy built this house. We still take care of this land, and watch it for her."

"Then don't do it no mo! She ain't here no mo. Cause I will call the sher'ff and ya c'n get put out! I didn't want to make no trouble for nobody, but we done done all we can do!"

As Juliet patted her sniffling mother's

back, she turned her face to Tonya. She said, almost gently, with a faint, but distinct threat in her voice, "Yes, you can call the sheriff. We would love to go to court about everything. So many strange things been happening round here . . . since you came, that I would really want to find out what the sheriff would think about them. Healthy people dying; and young, strong children disappearing. Yes, the sheriff would probably be interested his own self."

Tonya narrowed her eyes at Juliet and Bertha. Bertha was a little frightened, but dare not show it. But Tonya was the most frightened. Juliet was not frightened at all. Tonya did not know how much these people knew, or what they had seen.

She said, weakly, "Ain nothin goin on round here. What ya talkin bout?" But she began to back away from their door, speaking in a different tone. "If ya ain't got the rent, ya ain't got it. But I'm tellin ya this can't keep up. I'll let ya stay for now, but ya betta think bout gettin some rent money."

When they were alone, Juliet told her mother, "I told you something was going on that didn't seem quite right to me. I believe they killed poor Rose. Poor Aunt Rose. Lord, please have mercy on her little child."

Every time Leroy brought Myine up,

Tonya said, "We gonna go get her soon. We jes want to be sure everthin okay round here." Or she would try to put her arms around him, asking, "We can get married now, da'ling. You ain't got a wife no mo, cept me. We don't need no big wedding or nothin.

"We just sneak off one morning on ya day off, and get some preach'a to make us man and wife. Oh! Leroy! All the things ya wanted for us is here now." Leroy looked at her as though she was crazy, and walked away, laughing, as he went out to get into his car.

Tonya began to encourage Leroy to have a drink before he went to work. She would say, "to get ya ready for the day." When he came home from work, she had a drink waiting for him, "for to relax ya afta a hard day. I know them people wor'y ya to death." She had a glass of ice, and a bottle of liquor on the bedside table when he went to bed. "Hep ya sleep betta."

He knew, somewhere in his mind, what she was doing. He thought he was the strongest, but he wasn't really too sure in his mind. His mind was always a little fuzzy with liquor lately. "After all," he would think, "Tonya loves me; look what she done done to get me."

It didn't take long, because he already had things he wanted to forget. He began to rely on liquor after the death of Rose. Tonya didn't really know why she kept him full of liquor; it just seemed like a wise thing to do. And it was something she could do. Her house was more peaceful when she didn't have to listen to him asking about Myine.

So much fear at the thing they had done pressed on his mind and hers. But the police never did come with questions. So Tonya began to concentrate on Leroy's death. He was becoming a job; she always had to be careful, even with what she might say about Rose!

Tonya did not want him to die in that house. "Be better all round if he pass on away at the hospital."

She wanted to move her daughters in the house with her; then she could stop paying rent on that shack. Her youngest, the baby, had already died. TeeTee, who was fourteen, already had two abortions. Dolly, who was sixteen, had one baby, Lola. Tonya finally felt they needed her help, and concern. "They might as well be here with me. I got this house now. We need to stop payin rent somewhere else."

Leroy was mostly drunk now, and he was about to lose his job. So Tonya told him she moved her daughters in to save money. He grunted, raised his hand, and waved it in a way he thought meant, "No, no." She paid him no mind. If Leroy lost his job before he died, she would need her daughters to each get some kind of job.

First, they fought over Tante's room upstairs. Dolly won because she had a baby. And the room was larger than the last empty room.

Her daughters liked living in the large house. They talked excitedly. "It gonna be perfect for parties!" Rose and Leroy had had plumbing and electricity put in. TeeTee liked not going outside to the outhouse. "This house perfect for me, too!"

Soon, even Leroy, half high all the time now, began to notice how the house was changing. Always dirty and greasy looking. Dirty clothes scattered everywhere. Dishes piled high in the sink. Pots and pans, greasy and burnt, sat on the stove until he washed them or got on Tonya about them. The young girls didn't know how to take care of a house.

He did miss the neat house and appetizing table Rose had kept. His clothes even began to disappear, given to boyfriends, or the girls wore them themselves. Once the clothes were dirty, they were cast aside, it didn't matter where they fell, even in the middle of the hallway.

One sober night he told Tonya, "Ya'll got to do better'n this! I ain't used to livin like this! I'm'a have to put ya'll out, if this keep up! My house was clean!"

He shouldn't have done it, but he shook his finger in Tonya's face, saying, "I ain't gonna live like all this no mo. Ya'll got to do better'n this, or ya'll can go on back to ya own house! Them are cows ya got, they sho ain't no ladies! Ya'll are destroyin my house! This bout ain a house no more, not like Rose had it. It's a dump now!"

Tonya's thoughts were a little confused. "He wou'n't put us out. He jes talkin." Tonya loved that house. She felt like a Lady in that house. She had envied Rose for years. That house meant Tonya's world to her.

She repeatedly thought to herself, "Never was nothin said bout Rose dyin. Didn't nobody ev'a say nothin bout polices. Nobody thought about why she die. Evabody knew she was always sick."

She poured herself a drink, and sat down to enjoy it as she continued thinking. "If he was mar'ied to Rose, then this his house now. He herited it from her cause he was married to her. Don't nobody know if he married to me now, or not. So if he die, I herit it from him. This be my house! My house!" She smiled to herself. "An I c'n leave that chile out there where she is at, cause ain't nobody ev'a gonna find her, an Ma and Pa Whipet ain't gonna tell nobody cause they needs somebody to do all that work for em."

Leroy's days became numbered. She didn't have all the poisons they used on Rose, but she thought she had enough for Leroy. "If I don't, they got rat poison, but I ain gonna use that; they looks for things like that. I seen it on TV."

Then she thought about the people on "her" land. Juliet and Bertha. "I ain't gonna bother em jes now, til this here house is all mine. Won't be long. I c'n wait. Then . . . they got to pay or go!"

She did holler at her daughters about the mess in the house, but she didn't do much better than they did. Often they stole enough from her purse to get a six-pack for her so she would go to sleep, just like Tonya did for Leroy when he didn't have to work.

The girls didn't care about the house, really. Not like their mother. And they hadn't been taught to think. So they only thought, "It jes a good ole place to get a party on, and slip all my boyfriends in."

Time passed, slowly, as Tonya began giving Leroy small doses of poison in his food. Slowly. Just to sicken him a little. Stop him from asking about Myine.

Friends had warned Leroy about losing his job. He began to cut down on his drinking. He also began to look at Tonya through suspicious, narrowed eyes, suspecting her of having something to do with his constant illnesses. He didn't want her to sleep in the same bed with him any longer.

She didn't want him to die too soon; she needed his money. She was saving the big dose to serve him one morning as he was leaving for work. "Let him die at work! So them people, not nobody, can't blame me."

She wanted to go get Myine to bring her home, but not for a good reason. She was thinking, "This house needs more work en I can do. And TeeTee and Dolly ain gonna never do no betta. I'm gonna have to put em out jes to keep my house clean." As an afterthought, "Or I c'n make Bertha a maid in exchange for the rent."

In this way, a few years had passed.

Myine's life was painfully sad. All work, starting at about 5:00 a.m. They had given her an alarm clock, so no one would have to wake up to wake her up. She started the fires in the kitchen, and pumped the water in. They could have had more modern conveniences, but they weren't looking to live much longer, so why waste the money?

Myine had been at Mom's Cafe almost five years. She often looked out over the trees, trying to read the stars, wondering which way was home. When Tonya had brought her, she had driven many extra miles in different directions until the child had fallen into a deep sleep.

She was only about fifty miles from Wideland. Myine wanted to run away, her life was so sad and desperate, but she did not know which way to run. The north star didn't mean anything to her sense of direction.

She had no social, mental, or physical life. She was not allowed to go to school. School had been stopped, never thought of. "What ya need to go to school for? Ya already got a job!" They were not mean to her. Ma Whipet was even some ways kind. Pa Whipet, for his own reasons, did all the whipping that needed to be done.

As Myine grew older, her little body blossomed, and you could see she was going to be a good-looking young woman. Pa Whipet liked to spank her by bending her body over his knees. He would spank her behind, then rub her behind. Spank and rub, spank and

211

rub. He didn't hit her to really hurt her. He hit her for the chance to rub her buttocks; his shaking hand slipped lower each time he rubbed. In time he let his fingers rub over the exposed private parts, but not too often, because Ma Whipet was there.

Sometimes Myine heard creaking noises in the kitchen, behind which she slept. She grew used to that; she knew it was Pa Whipet sneaking in to steal the covers off her, and feel around her private parts, quickly. Thank God he was frightened of staying too long.

She wanted to tell Ma Whipet, but Pa Whipet had whispered to her, "We bought ya, ya know. We can sell ya to some real mean men who would love to work ya to death, and do plenny more things to ya. If ya tell . . . Well, ya know what c'n happen to ya. Ya have a easy life here with us. Think bout that! Fore ya opens ya mouth bout anything!"

Her little cot was in the supply room surrounded by boxes. She used one wooden box for little personal things she wanted to keep. Pretty rocks, lovely, colorful birds' feathers, a beautiful leaf, or a dead flower sat atop the box. Her clothes, the few she had, were kept inside the box.

She looked longingly down the roads leading away from the cafe. She wanted to run away so deeply in her heart; she did not know which way to run. The Whipets kept her frightened as to what was out there in the world . . . waiting for her.

So she worked each day the sun came up, and prayed each day to the God she had grown up knowing. "Please, God, oh, please, God. I want to go home, I want to see if my mother is still alive, and my father. And I'm tired, Lord. Lord, I am so tired. Help me, please, help me."

She cried, "Lord, Lord," as she washed dishes, cleaned tables, learned to cook simple things. She cried, "Lord, Lord," as she fell, exhausted, to sleep, jerking awake from deep tired sleep only when she heard unusual sounds from inside the supply room. She began to sleep with a knife under her pillow.

In Wideland Leroy finally died, an angry frown twisted on his face, forever. He had known it was coming if Tonya continued staying at his house. But there was nothing he could do to get her to leave. When he died, he whispered in his brain, "Lord, what have I done? I had a good woman. Look what I got . . . now. Where my little child? What have I done?" But he knew what he had done. That hurt the most. It was all his own doing.

People had always held funerals at home in their parlors. Now funerals were a business. The funerals were held in funeral parlors, and you paid; sometimes dearly. But still, Tonya did not take him to a funeral parlor. The few words said over his cheap casket were said quickly. Tonya rushed the preacher, as she moaned, groaned and screamed out, "Take me wit ya! Leroy! Lord, I loves my husband. Don take im from me! Jesus!" She cried, but there were no tears.

CHAPTER 23

When the funeral business was all over, and the few visitors were through dropping by, and a few days had passed, Tonya went to bring Myine home.

She just walked into the little dingy cafe, and said, "I come to get Myine." She told Myine, "Get ya things, we goin." Naturally the Whipets fussed, and tried to get her to change her mind.

Pa Whipet spoke first. "It's been five years, Tonya! She like our own child now! Ya can't take her away!"

"Yea, I can. Let's us go, girl."

Ma Whipet tried to make the best of the situation. "Well, ya should give us some of our money back! We done fed her, and raised her all these years."

"And I bet ya got ya money's worth, too." Tonya waved their outraged spittle away. "No, I know ya did! Com'on child. Get!"

And they were gone.

Tonya held Myine's hand as they went into the house. She told her, "Ya mama been dead, and now ya daddy is dead. So it's jes us now; we the family." It was as though another stone wall had come crashing down on that child's head. She must'a been just, as they say, out of it. Lord, Lord!

All that was happening to Myine was startling and amazing to her; unbelievable. She cast her eyes toward Bertha's and Juliet's house. Tonya pulled her, and directed her inside the main house, where Myine began to grieve deep in her tender soul. She felt it yet more deeply, because she was home, here where they had all lived. But they were not; they were gone . . . forever.

Dolly fussed and fumed about Myine, this intruder to her room, but she had to give in, and share her room (Tante's old room) with Myine. The baby Lola was sitting on the floor crying.

Myine looked around the room she knew so well, and was amazed still further. Dirty dishes and clothes were strewn over the bed. Soiled diapers were atop the dresser, bed and tables in the room. It smelled to high heaven with Lola's urine-soaked diapers

216

cast everywhere. Even inside drawers, and on the closet floor.

Myine didn't know where to sit, so didn't sit. She just stood looking in wonder. She had her wooden box with her; her five years' worth of possessions. Tonya said to Dolly, "Ya'll get this here mess cleaned up! All a'it! We got a washin machine, use it! Show Myine where it at! How c'n ya stan it in here?"

Dolly moaned in disgust, "Ya messin up my day, Mama."

Myine moved some things aside with her foot, and sat her box down. She opened the window first, then turned to Dolly. "Let's get started so we can get through." Dolly slowly began picking up things and throwing them in a corner. Myine thought, "At least they'll all be in the same corner."

Dolly said, "I'll pick up all Lola's things, diapers and stuff, and I'll go downstairs an wash em. Ya c'n take the rest a' this mess, an do whateva ya want to wit it."

When all the diapers and dirty dishes were removed from the room, it made the job look much clearer; you could see all the real dirt. Myine pulled the sheets off the bed she was supposed to sleep on, and rushed them to Dolly. "Here take these. They need washing for tonight."

"Ain nobody told me to do all that!"

"It has to be done sometime, so let's do it, and get it out of the way." Myine smiled at her.

Dolly waited a moment, standing with her arms full of smelly diapers, staring at Myine. Finally, she huffed a big sigh and said, "Put em on top. I'll put em in, but ya gon have to take em out the washer, and put em in the dryer. Or hang em up if that ole dryer ain't workin. I got this here baby to look afta."

Myine agreed, because she was thinking of Mz. Bertha and Juliet. She was dying to run over the yard to their house. She wiped and washed the furniture, lingering lovingly on the bedroom set that had belonged to her Aunt Tante, probably made by her grandfather. By the time she was finished, Dolly was back.

Dolly closed the window, saying, "It too cold in here for the baby." Myine said nothing, but reached out to smooth Lola's hair. Right away, Dolly jumped up saying, "Watch the baby for me, sister, I be right back!" In a second, she was gone. (She didn't return for three days.)

Myine stood amazed, it had all happened so fast. She went downstairs to give Lola to Tonya. Tonya told her, "Ya let 'er go, so ya got to watch that baby til she come back!"

"Well, I'm going outside, Mz. Tonya."

"Take the baby wit ya."

Myine lifted the child, and went out the door, running to Juliet's house.

There were such screams and cries of joy when Bertha opened her front door and saw Myine. "Oh, Lawd, oh, Lawd. Look here, Juliet! Jes look here! Here is my little Myine. Oh, child, where did you come from? Where you been?"

Juliet was just as happy to see Myine. "What has been happening to you? You have grown, girl! We have sure missed you." Neither Bertha nor Juliet could control their tears. "I think of your mother all the time, and I think of you all the time. I wondered where you were. What had happened to you? I was so scared of what that woman had done to you!" Bertha signaled to Juliet; Juliet lowered her voice.

"Are you staying here? Are you going to leave again?"

"No, I'm home now. My mama and daddy gone . . . she told me."

Juliet replied, "Well, I'm sorry to say that ain't the worst of it." Bertha gave little Lola some cookies, sitting her in a wooden chair. "I'll give ya a glass of milk when ya finish eating that cookie."

219

So they talked, and talked; and they hugged, and hugged. When they had brought Myine up to date on all they knew, they made plans.

Bertha sighed. "We been tryin to find Tante's address, but nobody who we know knows it, and Tonya ain't never gonna let us in that house to look for it."

Juliet took Myine's hand, saying, "But you live in there now. You can look for your aunt's address."

"I was looking for my mama's things, but they are not upstairs in Tante's old room. I went into Daddy's and Mama's old room for a quick minute, chasing the baby. But Tonya is always up there laying on the bed, eating or drinking something, so I couldn't look for anything in there. I didn't know what to look for anyway."

She hugged Bertha, and squeezed Juliet's arm. "But now, I know. I want to find my aunt. Suppose she's dead, you all?"

Juliet placed her hand over Myine's. "Tonya goes out, plenty. Nights. Then you can look in that room. But I don't blive anything important to Rose is still in that room. Girl, they are too lazy to put things anywhere neatly; if Rose's papers and letters are anywhere, they are stuck away down in that basement. Cast off in some corner."

Myine asked, "Is that where the clothes dryer is?"

"Yes! When you go down there to wash clothes, that's your chance to look around, dig around. I remember those letters. Some were yours, Myine, from your aunty!"

Tears filled Myine's eyes. "I remember them; I remember so many things when I was growing up."

"You still growing up. You ain't but round fifteen . . . or so. And you look beautiful! Beautiful! I'm so glad to see you, Myine." Tears filled Juliet's and Bertha's eyes again. "Did you suffer, Myine? I just hate that woman! Hate her!" Juliet wiped her face with the back of her hand. "She just ruined everybody's life! And I still blive she killed your mother! Poisoned her!"

Myine reached for her friend. "I remember believing that, but I had no way to prove it; I was so young, so small. And she was so grown, so big." Myine broke down crying then. "It was horrible, just horrible. I worked so hard, all the time. Work, work, work. Clean, wash, polish, cook, oh, everything you can think of.

"I have not been in school one day since I was taken away. Yes! Yes! I want to find my aunt. She never seemed to care about us, but I'm gonna make her care when I find her. If I find her."

Juliet tried to console her friend, but it was awkward from a wheelchair. "We'll find her. We'll pray and look. We have to make arrangements to talk, every day. Tonya gonna try to keep us from doing that. But she can't stop you if you don't want her to. Just find some way to say 'police.' "

Bertha gasped, "Juliet! You tryin to get this girl killed?"

Juliet narrowed her eyes. "Don't eat nothing over there unless you see everybody eatin from the same plate you are. Better, come eat over here."

"Alright," agreed Myine. "Then we can talk."

Bertha, excited, said, "Herman been coming by. He worried bout you, too. He ride around lookin for ya sometime, but he got so many troubles with his family, he can't hardly do nothing. He ain't been by lately, the last day or two, but I know he still lookin!"

Myine sighed. "It's good to know somebody was looking for me. I still don't know exactly where I was, but it was a long way from here."

She awakened the baby, Lola, who had slumped over in the chair, her stomach full of cookies and milk. Myine took her home to work on the wash . . . in the basement where the papers with Tante's address might be.

So the search began at every possible moment when she could search without waking Tonya's anger. She knew Tonya would be even more severe and mean if she knew.

Herman came by to check on her often as he could; he seemed especially glad to see Myine back at her home. He helped her with money.

Myine volunteered for all the basement washing work. That was hard enough, but now Tee and Dolly left the children with her all the time. They could be gone an hour or even a month.

She cooked, cleaned, and washed dishes, and clothes. She refused to wash Tee and Dolly's clothing. Most of the time the dryer did not work, so she had to hang all the clothes outside. They asked, or would try to sneak their clothes in with the children's clothes. But Tonya backed Myine up, saying, "Ya'll betta get yo'r own clothes washed."

Dolly was twenty-one years old, and Tee was nineteen; combined they had three children, and several illegal abortions. Drugs and liquor were what they had built their life on.

Dolly fussed and made so much noise, coming in so late when she finally came home, Myine asked to sleep in the basement. Tonya thought she understood, and was just happy to have the girl there to do all that work; she agreed. Myine furnished a neat little corner with things no one else wanted. She kept her things there. That way she could also search through the boxes without interruption.

Myine had thought she was tired before; now she was exhausted every day. She almost wished she was back at the cafe; but no, she did not want that. "Here, I have a future." Bertha, Juliet, and she had agreed this was her home. "I'm going to get my house my mama wanted me to have." She continued her search among the boxes of "trash."

Then the unexpected happened. A letter came . . . from Aunt Tante. Everyone in the house was sleeping when the mail came. Myine was up fixing the children's breakfast; she heard the mailman, whom she was always friendly with. She took the letters, knowing there was none for her. She was about to set them down on the table when she noticed a foreign stamp. She looked closer, and it had her mother's name on it.

She kept herself from sobbing . . . in

gratitude. When the children were settled at the table, she told them, "I have to run over to Mz. Bertha's right quick. Eat, I'll be right back." The children knew they could believe Myine so they stayed in their chairs and ate.

She ran to Bertha's, keeping her small screams low. They watched her read the letter, happily.

Dear Rose,

Why haven't you answered my letters? I know you blame me for not coming home, and not writing for a long time, but I was married, as I have explained to you. My husband has been sick for a long, long time. I am the only one he trusts. Finally I found someone I can trust, a round-the-clock nurse.

I want to know what is happening to you there — How is the baby, Myine? Of course she is no baby now. My own daughter, Monee, is about her age, perhaps a little older. I don't let her tell her age.

Lord, Sister, we are getting to be old women now. But I have had a very good life. My husband has prepared all our property so I will not have to worry about small things. His Will is intact. But I worry about you! We are almost old now, Rose!

Answer me, or I am coming there, and you know I have always hated Wideland. I love living in France. It is my home. I have already told you everything. Write me. I don't know why, but, lately, I need to hear from you! Please, sister, PLEASE!

They read the letter over again, and again. Myine's heart leaped with joy. Bertha tried to jump, but her old body, tired and weary, wouldn't let her. She wept a whole lot, though. Juliet laughed and cried all at the same time. They were happy; at last the light was shining at the end of the road. Not only for Myine, but for all of them, because they loved her.

Bertha hated to say sad things amidst such joy, but she had heard something she thought Myine should know. "I have friends at my church with grown children, and they have told me Dolly is using drugs. Heavy drugs, they say. And she is whoring on them dan'geous streets near the clubs. And they say she a heavy drinker too! There's many a liquor store in that neighborhood now. The police's don't even come in there, less'n they jes have to!"

Myine looked at Bertha, thinking about

all the times Dolly and Tee had acted so strangely. What were they thinking about? What were they going to do about their children? Aloud, she asked, "Tee is not doing those things, is she, Bertha?"

"Not like her sister is, but she do it sometimes too."

Juliet said, "Listen, life is life. They are making their own choices. And I don't think Tonya is going to be able to do anything about them."

They all sighed, then Juliet spoke again. "You got that letter, Myine. You are going to have to make some choices yourself. Let's write that letter to Aunt Tante! I see what they mean when they say people make their own beds!"

Myine, upset, spoke. "But I . . . love Lola, and I like all the children. I hate to see their life destroyed."

Juliet, always the realist, said, "You don't have anything they can steal right now, but you better plan on sleeping over here pretty soon."

Bertha agreed. "They have wrecked that house, an Tonya tryin to get a loan on it. But she don't have no marriage papers. She jes got his death papers. The bank say that don't mean the house is hers!"

"She needs a marriage certificate," said

Juliet. "But it wasn't his house anyway."

Myine finally spoke up; she hadn't been hiding it, just never thought it was important. "She tried to get me to fill out some papers, applications, I think. But I wouldn't. What would I be applying for? She screamed at me, threatened me, and stuff. But, I just didn't see what I had to do with any part of their business."

She sat down, with her hand over her heart. "Now. The letter from Aunt Tante! Oh! Thank You, God!"

Myine answered the letter at Bertha's house. She went to the post office the next morning, while everyone slept. She mailed that letter filled with gratitude, love, and dreams. Even though she had Bertha and Juliet, she was love starved. Family starved.

The next few weeks crept by. All three women, Myine, Bertha, and Juliet, watched for the mailman every day. They did not tell him what they were so eager for. He was a white man, and some white people still did not like Black people. They didn't know what he would do with a letter from France. So they just watched for him . . . and waited.

CHAPTER 24

MEANWHILE HERMAN TENDERMAN

Time was going by swiftly. The world was moving so fast millions of people did not know from day to day what would happen to them the next day. You might even say the world was raging as it spun around. So many people were angry, and they didn't always know why. Society was slowly sliding back to the old dream of the rich; the poor would work for almost anything, and the rich were getting richer.

Of course, the middle class were struggling to maintain the new system that gave them a chance at the trough; they hadn't had that chance often, some never. And there were the poor, the very poor, who were exploited by almost everyone, even each other.

Many races, all over the world, were fighting for their rights. In the United States of America, African Americans stepped up their fighting in the fifties.

Herman had traveled extensively in the navy, and he read voraciously, so he knew what was happening on the earth most of the time. It was why he had tried to make his children and stepchildren study, and become aware of the choices they *MUST* make. It was also when he came to realize there really was a God. "If there is no God, we are all doomed. This is not just a nation of liars, this is a world of liars. God must have some plan for mankind, or else why did He create us?

"Wars are always going on . . . somewhere. Why does mankind like killing? World War II is just recently over. I saw the cruelty of that one. Then there was Korea.

"Well, the world is in turmoil. And my life is in turmoil."

He didn't have to go to war anymore. He had a family, such as it was. In his own mind, he didn't have a family because his mother was gone. He smiled to himself when he thought of Jerome and Rose Bertha. He prayed that they would turn out better than it seemed they would.

Herman had finally gotten his stepson, James, to go to school enough, to learn enough, to get into the navy, as he had. He also worked on his son, Jerome, to study when Jerome really wanted to go play basketball, or baseball, or anything but school. He had even paid him, sometimes, to go to school.

College was out of the question, but, finally, Jerome went into the navy also. It had been a long, hard, seemingly neverending battle, done with a smile sometimes, and sometimes with a threat. But, Herman thought, Jerome was gone from the influence Gary had been, and Wanda was.

He held little hope for his daughter; Rose Bertha thought her mother, Wanda, was the smartest person in the world. But Herman didn't give up, even though he could tell it was not going to be much use. She was barely staying in school already. Cutting classes all the time. Going where? he asked himself. He had found out her mother let her stay home and sleep.

There was grey in his hair now. His eyes were puffy from staying up late into the nights, watching his kids. Wanda could sleep through anything, never even know they were not in the house. She wasn't worried, she let Herman do that for her.

Herman shook his head in amazement as he thought, "That was why Gary died. A drug overdose, after the woman he was living with stabbed him about some heroin.

He hadn't even known he was dying; he was still reaching for his drugs."

In Herman's mind, he did not have a family. He had worked and pleaded with them, for years, to do the right thing for their own self. He loved them, but they didn't seem to know what love was. They hadn't even had sense enough to love their own self. Well, their mother didn't seem to do that either.

He knew, now, some people are born with love already in their hearts. Many, many people have to learn how to love, and they never get to see it, to learn. They think it is sex. Wanda was good in bed, but wasn't worth a damn at anything else; especially love, even for her children.

He reminisced about his mother. "Oh, God, I'm glad I had my mama. She loved me, and I sure loved her. I knew all about love. Learned it from my mama. Don't know where she learned it, cause her sister never did have love in her heart."

He had said many times to hisself, "These are Wanda's kids. All of them. They don't want my help, so I won't worry about them. I'll just tend to my own business; take care my own."

Then, one day soon after that, he was disciplining Rose Bertha, when she snapped her little fifteen-year-old behind around, getting away from Herman. She got extra smart with him, probably been smoking some of her mother's pot. She said, "I don't haf'ta do nothin you say cause you not my daddy no way!"

Taken aback, Herman asked, "What'd you say? What do you mean?"

She just stuck her breasts out, chin and shoulders up. "That you not my daddy. I know my daddy! My mama told me when I was bout thirteen years old. My daddy's name is Jerome; same daddy as Jerome. That's why he named 'Jerome'! Jerome, Jr. So you can't tell me what to do! I'm tired'a you always tellin me what I ought'a do! Drivin me crazy bout school!"

Suddenly, Herman's tiredness became too heavy, sitting on his back like a mountain. "The life I have worked all these years for! Oh, God! I knew Wanda slept with other men. I know she is an alcoholic. I knew we didn't have a life, but I didn't know my life was a garbage dump! I have been fooling myself! I'm telling everyone else how to live, and now, I don't even have a life!"

He looked around the once nice house he had bought for his family; Gary's two children were running around in dirty, baggy diapers. Their mother was in prison for killing Gary, but she had a heroin habit she might never quit anyway. "They should have been trained," he repeated in his brain. Wearying despair was falling over him. "They should be trained, but there is no one who cares enough to train them.

"My children don't love me. And it seems I just thought they were my children. They are not my children! My wife does not love me. I haven't loved my wife for years and years, since that first year we married. And now I learn that my children are not even mine. I have just thrown away my life. If I married Wanda because she was going to have my baby, now that they are not my babies, why should I stay?"

It grieved his heart because he wanted to love his family, he wanted it to be his family. He had wanted a family, his own family, ever since his mother had died. "But . . . it is not my family; never has been." He sighed from somewhere deep in his body and tears rose to the top of his head and heart as he decided his life.

"Well, I don't have any reason to stay here anymore, sleeping on a cot in a laundry room. I can sure afford better than that; I take care of myself. Why should I stay? I'm not a happy man. I'm not even content. I'm leaving."

He called out to his wife, "Wanda . . . I'm

leaving." She was sleeping off a drinking binge, and didn't hear him. He grabbed a few pieces of underwear from his dresser-box, and went out the door. He took a deep breath, turned to the right at the end of the path, and walked to his truck.

He had been saving for his children to go to college. He had spent some of it on James's college costs a few years ago. Now James was saving money for himself.

Rose Bertha would probably never make it to college. She was already having sex, calling it love. She dabbled in drugs, thinking it made her grown up and glamorous. If she didn't change, she would grow up to be an even bigger fool than her mother.

So Herman left the house he had bought, worked, and paid for, for his family. His heart was broken. "But," he thought, "I have jobs! I am not dead." He did not look back through the windows of his truck at where his life had been for all the wasted years. Wasted, because he still didn't have a family.

His last thought as he turned off that street was "Jerome might not make it, but if he does, I will help him, even if he isn't my son, just like I helped James. But, from now on, I want something that is mine! Don't care what it is, I want it to be mine! All mine!"

Herman went to his night job, and quit it. "This money is not making me happy. I won't need to work so hard now, and they have never given me my due. I've been working there years, and they still don't like me because of my color." But they hated to see him leave. He was one of their smartest employees.

He kept his day job at Pink's garage as a master mechanic. He had a White boss who knew less than he did, and was paid more. But he was Black, and in Wideland that made him worth less. The difference was this White boss knew his value and even liked him.

He found a temporary room to rent. He didn't have anything but a suitcase and two toolboxes. He was tired, but a new light feeling was giving him impetus. He went to buy sheets, pillowcases, towels, two feather pillows, and a brand-new mattress. "Nobody ever slept on this one but me! It's all mine!"

When he did bathe and go to bed, he slept for two days, waking only to eat. He looked into a mirror, accidentally, one morning and discovered that the quiet rest had restored him. The grey hair remained, but his skin was clearer and looked healthier. The hard work he had done for so many years had kept his body with solid muscles, and strong. "I am getting old," he thought, "but the old man doesn't look so bad."

After a few weeks he found an apartment, and moved in with a few new furnishings. All his.

Sometimes he drove by his old house, just to see where his life had been; he never wanted to forget any part of it. He missed his old family. "I thought I had some sense. I loved those kids, all of them. And I thought two of them were mine, really mine. Nothing was mine; nothing is mine. I want my own. Mine."

He sent James and Jerome his address. Neither one his son, but he loved them; they were friends. In the note he added, "Keep this for when you need me. Give my address to no one."

Once, he had gone to see Bertha too early in the morning; the house was asleep. He knocked on the old classroom door; it was empty. He walked to Bertha's house. There was no answer.

It didn't happen often, but as fate would have it, Bertha was gone off to some little job. Juliet and Cloud were in bed locked in an embrace. They had made love, and now they were sleeping. Juliet heard the knock, and wakened a little, but she could not, and did not want to, move from under Cloud. His body still nestled inside her. She did not wake Cloud to answer the door.

There were so few times they were able to make love. He was so sweet, so gentle with her. He wouldn't make love to her just anywhere in the woods, as she would have let him. He loved Juliet. He wanted to make her his wife; but she did not want to leave her mother and go to live on the reservation. She thought she might not be able to be crippled anywhere but at her home.

If Juliet had known it was Herman, she might have wakened Cloud. But she didn't know who it was, so she just settled down in the bed under Cloud, and continued her dreaming.

Herman didn't know what to do, but he was lonely and wanted to be around people he knew cared about him. He wanted Bertha and Myine to know he was single and alone out in the world; he needed a family, again. They were the only family he knew he could count on. The family he wanted, felt safe with, until he met, somehow, someone to give him a real family.

He had always loved music, jazz, classic,

and the blues. He needed some music in his life. So he went to register in a community college, and to look over the classes offered. "Maybe I'll study some instrument." After registering, he went to a music shop to buy some of the blues and jazz music he had heard lately and liked. He had to buy a record player, also. "I am going to start a whole new life! Even if I am getting old."

Sometimes life curves on you. Sometimes we follow the curve. Sometimes we don't.

CHAPTER 25

Now we are at the stem of the "Y" I told you about. Everybody seems to be at the crux of their life, someway, at the same time. Herman, Myine, Bertha, Juliet, and Cloud. Oh they ain't through having problems; life ain't like that. But there comes an end to some old problems while the new problems move into place.

You don't have to believe me, just keep living.

Herman did return to Bertha's house to see the people he loved and considered like family. He had become, again, the person, the man Bertha and Myine counted on for protection and help. Even Juliet, although she had Cloud to count on.

Herman hadn't told them everything, but enough for friends. They all knew Herman's new phone number. He knew all about Tonya and wanted to go to the police, but

Tante had told them to wait until she came, and she was on her way.

When the day of her arrival finally came, Herman was unable to take off work to take them to the airport, but Bertha knew someone else that would take Myine to pick up Aunt Tante.

At last, Myine was to meet her Aunt Tante. Tante flew in from the south of France two weeks after receiving Myine's letter. She recognized Myine immediately; she looked like Rose, only prettier. Myine flew to embrace her aunt. The tears were ready as they both cried, and held each other.

They were driven back to Wideland, which Tante was surprised to see had grown so much: some tall buildings, and many new stores and offices. She even found an automobile rental business; she decided to rent a new car. They let Bertha's driver friend go. Tante insisted on giving him a few dollars.

As she drove through the area that was now Black, she saw pool halls, barbershops, beauty shops, medical offices, and more. Even a bank. She asked, "They still have prejudice here? As bad as it used to be?" She didn't wait for an answer, but continued, "I used to hate this place. It's one of the reasons I have never come back."

She turned her head, briefly, to look at Myine. "Now, tell me again, everything that has happened. My sister is dead. Ahhhh, that truly hurts me; I never came to help her. How did such a man, her husband, get into our family, our house? What was Rose thinking? And what is that woman, Tonya, thinking of? You, you own that property!"

Myine shook her head slowly. "She thinks she inherited it. That it is hers. I'm the housemaid, cook, laundress, the everything. But there is nothing I can do."

"Well," Tante said in a hard tone, "there is plenty I can do. I need the name of a really good lawyer, fair to Black people. I'll never find a French lawyer here. I don't need a lawyer for much, just a little." Her voice was confident. "I want to see him first. Now. We need to go to the courthouse for the county records."

Myine's heart smiled, gratefully, and she laid her hand on her aunt's shoulder. She said, softly, "I don't know where you will sleep; I sleep in the basement."

Tante almost jumped in her amazement, saying, "The basement! Of your grand-mother and grandfather's house? We will talk about that later. Now . . . show me the way to the police station. I know where it used to be, but . . ."

Myine's eyes widened with fear, and wonder. "You're going to the police?"

Tante smiled, patting her niece's knee. "Yes, I need to understand the law, and get a lawyer, if I need one. But, right now I want some records, and the District Attorney."

At the county records office Tante learned the taxes were seven years delinquent; many letters had been sent regarding the foreclosure. Tante paid the taxes. While she was at the courthouse she got copies of the original deeds, birth certificates, and a receipt for everything.

When she reached the District Attorney's office, he looked up to see the tired-looking, but elegant woman dressed in the classic suit and shoes you could tell were not made in America. He looked into the bright, pretty, but sharp eyes. He asked, "What can I do for you, Miss?"

"Mrs. Deraineau. I was born here in Wideland, now I live in France with my husband. I need some information." From the tone and accent of her voice, you could see and hear her superior education. She did not exhibit a superior attitude; she was simply forthright, and correct in her actions and speech. He gave her his full attention and all the information she would need.

"You won't need an attorney, Mrs. Deraineau. Just let me know if there are any problems. If everything is in your parents' name, and I see it is, there will be no problems."

Tante persisted, "But I need something that will look legal to her . . . so she will understand I mean what I say."

The D.A. had his surprised secretary type a letter with the words, "If I can be of any assistance to you in your family matters, we are at your service. You just have to give me a call and let us know. The Court is at your service."

Satisfied, Tante and Myine drove to the house to rid it of the trespasser. Tante brought the basement up again. "Why do you sleep in the basement, child? You are over sixteen years old; my room should be your room, at least."

"I'd rather be separated from them, and besides, I had to be able to look for your letters to get your address. All my mother's things were stored down there. I had nowhere to turn, except to Bertha and Juliet. And I liked it down there. I have a nice corner I fixed up for myself, and it is the quietest place in the house."

"Bertha and Juliet. Bertha was always a

help to my mother. I never really paid much attention to Juliet, though she was born a few years before me, or a few years after me; it didn't seem important. But Bertha is getting old, and still helping even mama's grandchildren!" Tante reached over to take Myine's hand. "Well, I'm here now."

Tante was in her late forties. She had matured beautifully. Everything about her was completely well groomed. She was impeccable, even after the long flight from France to America.

She had decided, after a good look at Wideland, it was not yet a city, but it had spread out wide, and had become a little more modern. There was a real district attorney instead of a sheriff.

When they arrived at the house, Tante got out of the car, and just stood still a moment, looking at the house. She did not look as though she had ever lived there.

When she spoke, she asked, "What have they done to my daddy's house? Even the trees look sad. It should never have deteriorated like this." She took a deep breath, and started up the path to the hanging half-unhinged gate. She looked at everything with great distaste.

"This would never have happened when my daddy was alive. I used to sit on those steps with my dog, Brave." And a moment later, "I rode my horse all over this land. What is all this trash about!? Why does everything look so raggedy, and forlorn?"

Walking behind her, Myine rushed to say, "I do the best I can, Aunt Tante. Bertha does too. But she is old. Juliet can't do too much in a wheelchair, but she does all she can. Dreaming Cloud helps all of us. They are the only ones who have kept this house up. I eat at their house . . . and sleep there sometimes when it's too cold in the basement . . . or too much is going on in the house."

Finally they reached the steps of the house, when Myine spoke. "Aunty, we better go to Bertha's first, to leave your suitcases until we get things settled. There are thieves in this house. They will steal everything you have if they can reach it."

"My God in heaven! I'm glad my husband wasn't able to come. This is dreadful! Lead me to Bertha. Slow now, child, slow. Aunty is not a spring-chicken, and this terrain can be dangerous." She laughed lightly.

Bertha and Juliet were waiting in the open door. They opened their arms, and held them out to Tante as Bertha stepped forward to meet her. Bertha had tears in her eyes and a shining smile on her face. "Look at ya, Tante! You look mighty good! My eyes are so happy to see you here! This child has been done mighty wrong, and is suffering. I prayed for ya to come!"

They embraced as Tante entered the small house. "I don't remember this house, but I'm glad you are here, Bertha."

Juliet just smiled happily, tears rolling down her face. "Oh! Hello Tante! I am so glad you came home! What took you so many years to come back and see about things?"

Tante smiled down at the woman she remembered as a young girl, and had felt so sorry for. "That's too much to explain, Juliet. Just try to think that I did the best I could do for myself. Now, let's see what we can do about this Mz. Tonya."

After they had talked, and Bertha had settled more things in Tante's mind, Myine and Tante got ready to leave. Bertha said, "Ya can stay in my room here. It's clean as a pin. I can sleep with Juliet."

"Thank you, Bertha. After I look around and decide what I am going to do about things, I'll know. I'm fatigued; that was a long, long trip. I want to see my house now. I'll leave my things here for the time being, but I want to sleep in my own old room."

When they reached the front door of the

house, Tante didn't knock or ring the bell; she opened the door and walked in. Tee and Dolly were in the kitchen arguing about who had bought the last box of cornflakes. Two or three of the children were fighting over bowls. Tonya was just coming down the clothing-cluttered stairs. Clothes even hung over the banister.

Tonya looked as if she had just awakened, as she scratched her back. She looked at Tante, saying, "Whoa, there! Who's bustin in my house witout even knockin? Where ya goin?"

Tante, faintly, smiled. "It is I, Madame."

Tonya looked at the beautifully dressed, immaculate, mature Black woman walking through the hall toward the kitchen. Tee and Dolly, mouths hanging open, stood staring. Even the children hesitated in their struggling with each other.

Tonya turned her eyes on Myine, who was coming in behind the lady, following her into the kitchen. Her face hardened, and looked fearful at the same time. "Who is this here woman, Myine? It's too early in the mornin for comp'ny and shit."

Myine started to speak, but Tante interrupted her, at the same time Tonya saw Tante's resemblance to Rose and Myine.

Tante continued, speaking clearly and

crisply with a slight French accent. "I am Tante Deraineau. I own this house. Myine owns this house. Who are you, and how did you get here? In our house?"

Tonya was speechless, as were Tee and Dolly. Even the small children felt the atmosphere change; they stood still, staring at the lady in black who had hushed even almighty Gramma. When Tonya found her voice she answered, "I married into this here house."

Tante tilted her head slightly, and asked, "To whom were you married? My father is deceased, and I have no brothers."

Tonya's need, and desire, for the house would not let her give up. "Ya sister married, was married to my husban."

Tante looked straight at Tonya. "Isn't he deceased, also?" Then Tante turned, and started up the stairs Tonya had just come down. "I want to see my bedroom, and my parents' old bedroom."

Tonya, knowing her family was watching her, believing in her, tried to find some answer, some lie, for this now hated woman who had come to steal what was rightfully hers. "They ain't ya'll's bedrooms no more. They blongs to us."

Tante, already going upstairs, replied, "They still belong to us, dear."

Tonya sputtered, "Look! Ya can't come in this here house! This here house is taken a'ready!"

At the top of the stairs, Tante turned around to say, "I stopped by the District Attorney's office before I came . . . home. Anticipating that any woman who has done what you have done is an ignorant woman." She opened her purse and withdrew the envelope, holding it up for Tonya to see. "I have proof of our ownership, and proof that you have one night to move. One night! Now, get out of our house! That does not mean move tomorrow. It means move tonight, and be gone tomorrow." Tante turned, and proceeded toward the bedrooms as she swiftly put her hand over her nose.

"Mon Dieu! This house stinks to high heaven!"

Tonya was thinking about what was in the envelope. How much Tante knew or had been told. Her terror came, not just from the tone of Tante's voice, but from her own knowledge of what had happened in the house. What she, herself, had done. Everyone was so quiet, Tonya could hear Tante's voice from upstairs, from where she stood, at the bottom of the stairs.

Tante had gone into the room Tonya used, Irene and Val's old room, Rose's room

250

where she had died. "Does anyone actually live in this room? Get all this mess out of here! I will have this house sanitized!"

Then Tante went into another room. "More of the same! Get all this mess out of my sister's room! I don't need to look any farther. Just get out!"

Tante began coming down the stairs; her voice was harder, her eyes were black ice. "At eight o'clock in the morning, I am going back to the District Attorney and have him help you out."

Myine spoke up. "And have him look into my mother's death. And my daddy's death."

Tante was almost in Tonya's face, her black eyes glittering, threatening, as she said, "You have sold my niece for money. You'd better thank God she is safe, and home where she belongs. You tried to make my niece your slave in this house with all these funky, nasty, dirty people, children included, who live like animals! Raggedy, unclean, uneducated, ignorant woman; who the fuck do you think you are! Mz. murdering peasant!"

Tonya stood silently in front of her children and grandchildren. She wanted to answer, but she kept seeing prison bars, and she was trying to think of some sure way she could blame everything on Leroy. She was overwhelmed by the Black, intelligent, sophisticated woman. So Tonya didn't holler as usual, she just quietly said, "We don have no wheres else to go." Her voice rose, only a little, yet her mind remained the same conniving mind. "We needs money. Ya can't put kids out in the streets. They got laws now. We needs money."

Tante had an answer. "Let me help you understand. You are not here by invitation. You are trespassing on private property, dear. After I count what you owe us for all the time all of you have been here, every dime you ever get will have to come by me, or whomever I appoint; and I will surely appoint my friend, the District Attorney."

Tante turned to go through the front door to the outside, saying, "I can't take that stench any longer." She turned back to say to all of them, "If you take anything that does not belong to you, that you did not bring here with you, I'll have you arrested for that . . . too!"

Chile, everyone around here was so glad to see that problem cleared up and out! We all had wanted to help, but no one knew just what to do! So, as usual, we didn't do nothing. We didn't know everything that had happened to Myine at that time; but it was a damn shame!

But Tante sure took care of it. Tante didn't have to be afraid because she didn't live here. Chile, there are some crazy, wicked people in this here world! You know some of them!

CHAPTER 26

Tante and Myine stayed at Bertha's little house the first night. Bertha took joy in putting fresh, clean white sheets and pillowcases on her bed for them to sleep on. The pillows were feather pillows from their own chickens; not as soft as duck, but the fact that they belonged to their own chickens made up for that little matter.

Tante slept like the proverbial log. She awakened in the early morning listening to the chickens clucking, stirring to begin their day, her mind running quickly over her early years with her parents in her home. After a moment she turned to look at her sister's child, her niece. She discovered Myine had been laying there looking at her aunt sleep. Myine had been thinking of all her aunt had accomplished in one day.

She could hear people already helping Tonya move. They seemed to be scrambling, rushing to get away. Myine thought, "Tonya is afraid of the police."

Tonya kept trying to keep the noise down so Tante would not waken and come out to see what they were doing, or how they were doing it. She did not allow anyone to take anything from the house that didn't belong to them. "Jes get ya'sef together and lets get on outt'a here!" To get a little of her self-respect back, she added, "I don't wanna have to whip that woman's ass! So hurry up!" Her children and grandchildren respected violence, so they hurried.

Hearing them, Tante smiled a tired smile, but her eyes were shining brightly on her niece. "Well, it's started. Now we have to make plans for what we are going to do next. Do you know a cleaning company that can come in here to clean and sanitize that whole house?"

"Bertha will know, or I'll find out."

Tante nodded her head as she answered, "We don't have much time. I have to leave here, and get back home this week."

Myine frowned. "Ahhhhh."

Tante patted her niece's arm. "We don't have time for that either. We need to talk. Talk about your future. What are you going to do? Go finish college?"

"I never started college. I never went to high school. I studied with my mother. I don't want to go back to school. I was about nine or ten when Tonya took me to that cafe; I was gone five years. I'd be embarrassed sitting in some classroom old as I was. I read everything. I know how to study by myself."

"Child, never be embarrassed about improving your condition. Only fools laugh at anybody in school." Tante sat up in the bed, asking, "Now, how do you feel about staying in that big house all alone?"

Myine hesitated. "Well, that is something I wanted to talk to you about. See, Dolly, Tonya's daughter, has a daughter named Lola, and I know Dolly is not going to raise her right. She is not going to send her to school, or even feed her right. Lola will be alone a lot, and hungry."

Tante interrupted her. "Myine, you can't take care of the world. You have got to worry about your self. You were sold when you were younger. You lost many years of your youth; and Tonya's the one who sold you."

"Oh, Aunt Tante, Lola wouldn't take up much time. I have grown to love her; she is helpless. She's smart."

Tante frowned as she said, "I wonder who, in her family, Lola took after." But, she thought, "Myine is weak like Rose. I'll never let my daughter, Monee, be a weak fool."

After a moment, she said aloud, "Well, do as you want. But it is entirely your responsibility. I will not be coming back here like this again. In my world, you pay for your own mistakes. And I think Lola will be a mistake."

After a moment spent staring through the window, she said, "I am going to clean this house out, and I am going to leave you ten thousand dollars in a bank account, this one time. That will be your responsibility also. I will not be able to send more at any time, unless you have a medical emergency. Try to save for it. I am hoping you will be married by then. Anyone can find a husband if they have a house in this town. I don't know when I'm coming back here again. France is my home, where my family is. The family I made."

Myine reached out, placing her hand on her aunt's arm. "I'm your family, too."

"I know that. That is the only reason I am here. My mother, Irene, and my father, Val, would never forgive me if you lost this house because of someone tricking you out of their dream."

"But you didn't know what was happening here."

"My life is very full, so many things to do. But I was trying to reach my sister, Rose,

257

when I heard from you, her child. There was nothing else I could do. This is important to me, also. But let us not waste time talking about the past.

"Now this house is in your name, and my daughter's name. I will tell you about her later, when we have all the things we have to do done. But, when you get married, that's all up to you. What you have can become your husband's. But a piece of it will always belong to my side of the family."

Myine smiled, and said, "Good!"

Tante continued, "I don't like Wideland; never have, except for the Native Americans. So don't think of me when you make your decisions. I may never return here again; and I don't think my daughter will ever come. I have told her the truth about the America I know. Anyway, I have such plans for her; she may live in a castle one day, if I get my way. So this is yours; any added name is really for your protection."

"Yes, ma'am."

"Remember this, someone has taken your mind and life every time there was an opportunity. You can't let that happen again. You could have gotten directions to the District Attorney, yourself. Everything was on record."

Myine looked into the distance of her

mind as she said, "Tonya will get away with killing my mother and father."

Tante put her arm around Myine's shoulders, as she said, "You have to let God take care of things you cannot help. I feel deeply about those things. But, she won't get away with it. And as for your daddy, it was your daddy's fault she was in this house. It was not all Tonya's fault."

Myine laid her head on Tante's shoulder as Tante continued, "Remember, that was a long time ago. We have no witnesses except Bertha, who is old and sick, and we have Juliet and Cloud. My sister is dead; no trial will bring her back. I believe in God, and He said 'Vengeance' is His. Everyone gets what is coming to them.

"You have a great deal to do right here, Myine; getting this place straight, getting yourself straight. Use our time and thoughts for that." After a moment she said, "I believe Rose, your mother, named you 'Myine' because she was saying you were hers. That is so like her; full of love. And look what it got her."

She looked seriously at Myine and said, "You're old to still be single. Have you ever been in love, Myine?"

Myine shook her head, "No. Not with a man. I love Lola."

259

Tante smiled. "Well, start with loving yourself, first. Get your teaching certificate. Get some new clothes, and get a good hairdresser. Do something for yourself so YOU will feel better. Rose, bless her soul, is gone; you are here, alive. I'll send you some things I think would look beautiful on you. I'll send you some real perfume, also. American perfume is not to my taste.

"You think I'm talking about how to look to get a husband; well, I'm not. You don't want a husband who is looking for looks, although you are beautiful to me. I'm talking about you enjoying the things God gave you. I'm talking about the things God put on this earth to be enjoyed: silks, satin, good linens and cottons. Good foods, beautiful, real scenery with beautiful sunrises and sunset. Mountains, deserts, glaciers, and all the animals that live among them. And remember, you are for yourself to enjoy, as well as others. Live, child, live. Lift those worries off your mouth, and smile. You are getting rid of your worst problems!"

"Oh, Aunt Tante. You make life sound wonderful."

"That is what you have to do; make life. And we need to get up and get started making this day a good one. Now."

As they were dressing they heard Bertha

moving around in the little kitchen.

As an afterthought, Tante said, "And travel, Myine. Come visit us. You would love France . . . or Italy, or Spain. Or any place God created, and men have left in peace, so far. That does not leave much, but enough for you right now. Maybe take a year off from college after you get your teaching certificate. Juliet can take care of this house while you are gone. That reminds me, I have to go to this college around here and see what you have to do to get a certificate."

Myine was speechless, laughing happily. Thrilled at having her aunt with her in Wideland. Her Aunt Tante, who loved her.

As Tante went into the little kitchen, she said, "We are going out to dinner tonight, so I'm going to take Myine shopping today. Just get her a few things I would like to see her in. We have to go by the bank anyway. I want to get some money to pay you for all your help."

"Oh, Tante, you don't owe us nothing! I'm just glad you come, and I'm glad everthin turned out so good. They really leavin! But ya don't owe us nothing! I'm so glad they gone from here. Now Myine will be al-right!"

Juliet just sat in her chair looking and listening, a tentative smile on her face.

"Bertha, time is money." Then Tante asked, "Bertha, do you know a piano tuner around here? I want to get that old piano tuned up, and looking good like it did when I was a child taking lessons. I want it fixed, polished and shining! Now, let's look over your list of people coming to help us with this house!"

Bertha smiled as she reached for the list. Juliet said, "We are getting some of Cloud's people to help clean. The women can use the money. And Cloud can do some of the handiwork."

It was Tante's turn to smile. "Fine with me."

CHAPTER 27

Tante made a reservation at the very best hotel dining room in Wideland, after she checked to see if African Americans were welcome there. Her accent negated any but the most absurd prejudice. She wanted a peaceful dinner with her niece.

Myine was a little surprised that Bertha and Juliet were not joining them, but decided not to mention it. Myine and Tante talked about the business they must attend to.

Then Tante asked, "What do you know about men, Myine? Are you a virgin?"

Myine blushed, embarrassed.

Tante exclaimed, quietly, "You are! An old virgin. Any virgin over the age of eleven is an old virgin these days."

Myine stammered, thinking of Pa Whipet, "I've done . . . a little."

Tante smiled, saying, "Listen, I'm glad you haven't been messed over, and some male hasn't left you with a house full of kids."

"I'm only going in my twenties, Aunty."

"Listen, Myine, it happens earlier than that with some people. Fools, I call them. That's why I wanted to say a few things to you. Number one. Never love anyone more than you love yourself. God and children don't count, but watch the children. You can only trust God.

"Number two. Never ask a man if he loves you, unless you know he wants to tell you at that moment in time. If you have to ask, he does not love you. If you have to ask, he will know it is more important to you than it is to him.

"Never do any 'favors' with your body. Your body is too special, too private for that. It is a gift from God.

"Be clean at all times. There should never be an odor coming from you, from any place on your body. Any place. One of the things I like about France is the bidet. It helps to keep you clean and odorless . . . your private parts.

"You can be a bit sloppy in your dress, sometimes, but always in the best clothes. Old or new.

"Always love your lover, never do sex for fun and games. It always works against you.

"Never stop learning. Watch everything that happens to you, and try to understand why it happened.

"Don't confide all your business to anyone.

"Don't trust anyone, completely. Perhaps dogs and cats. But remember, Jesus said, 'None is good, but the Father.' It does not mean everyone is bad, it just means you never know.

"Above many other things, don't be a *liar* or a *thief.* You have no idea how much love and respect will have to do with the most important things in your life. Your whole life. Not being a liar or a thief is a most important thing to respect, to love. It is not true that it is easier to be bad than it is to be good. It is quicker to be bad; you have to think to be good, but the thinking is so much more beneficial in the long term.

"Without respect, there is no love . . . for long, for anyone, but a fool.

"Keep God in your heart. Be friends with God. You will have to call on Him, perhaps many times, someday. You want Him to know you. I must be honest, I am not as close to . . . God as I should be." Tante's face was grim for a moment, then she said, "But I mean to be as soon as my life . . . adjusts.

"That will do for now. Enjoy your dinner. And you can love me all you want to."

Soon, time was growing very short for Tante to return to Europe. By now, Myine loved her aunt so much. She would stare at her and think, "My mother was from the same womb as this fantastic woman who is my aunt. Oh! Why did that hateful murderer come into our life, and take my family from me?"

She would hug her aunt at surprising moments throughout the day. She held her arm around her waist on nights they slept together. Tante didn't mind; she knew her niece was thinking of her sister, Rose.

Myine had gotten her driver's permit to learn to drive. Tante had said, "The important thing is to know how to drive. You can practice after I am gone."

Speaking as she rushed, looked, hurried, Tante prepared to leave Wideland. When Tante finally flew away in the huge silver airplane, so much had changed, much for the better, in Myine's life.

The house now had her name on the title. There was a new bedroom set in her own room; no more basements, or boxes for her dresser. There was even a new bedroom set in Tante's old bedroom. The house was clean throughout, and the steps and banister were repaired and shone with cleanliness and polish.

The kitchen was still being worked on; cabinets were being taken down, and the good, solid wood was being cleaned and polished. Everything looked so much better, cleaner. Best of all, Myine thought, there was a full-size, secondhand refrigerator.

The ten thousand dollars was being whittled down, but she had something to show for every dollar. The entire house had been transformed. It was, again, a wonderful place to come home to.

Aunt Tante had not bothered about the land, saying, "Never mind all this land right now. You can clean, clear, and work all that out to suit yourself. There is plenty of help around. Bertha and Cloud can help you get the right people." She had looked worried then. "Bertha is not doing so well. She works too hard. She had better let Juliet marry that boy, Cloud. I think they are doing everything already anyway, and she needs someone to put her mind at rest about Juliet. He seems a good sort, if he is anything like Wings. And as far as Herman and the other men around here, you watch yourself around men. Herman is at least ten years older than you; that is too old for you.

And he has marriage debris in his life. You just get on with your college exam work, like we have arranged for your teaching certificate, then you will be taking care of your own business.

"Perhaps you will come to France to find your future husband; there is no one in Wideland for you to make the kind of marriage you should have." Tante was thinking of her own daughter, Monee, whom she knew was fooling around with someone other than the wealthy old man Tante wanted Monee to marry. Tante loved money, and would even sacrifice her daughter's love on that altar.

Myine didn't answer then, because she didn't quite know enough, and she was nowhere near close to thinking about a marriage. But she looked thoughtful. She knew she liked Cloud, and she loved Juliet, but that was their business.

She began to watch Bertha closer though; she did look tired, and ill. "The only thing I can really do is not charge them rent, but I wasn't going to do that anyway; they are my only family, here in Oklahoma."

CHAPTER 28

Now, we are getting to the part I love: Love. The stem of this "Y" is not too long, but it's long enough for love to happen where, by the way, I think it should happen. Heavens, chile! I think love is the only thing that makes life worth living! That is why so many fools fall for that imitation love, and end up suffering for not knowing what love is. Look in your Bible; there is the true description of it in there. 1 Cor. 13:4. God created us, so He must know what we really need.

Now, I have told you, so far, this tale from two or three perspectives. After I tell you this last part from my perspective, you can decide for yourself, but I think it's the most interesting part about these people. It is exciting to me that if you live, and think right, you can find love no matter how old you are. And no matter how old you are, it's always good.

Time was catching up to Herman Tenderman. For a long time he had not known Rose was dead, but when he knew he was heartbroken. He had loved Rose. "She put my whole life in the right direction. She helped me. Or I would have been just like Gary, and so many other young men."

He had worried about little Myine, Bertha, and all of them. "Defenseless women" was how he thought of them. He had helped to look for Myine. When she came home, he went to see them. Myine was not so "little" even if she was young.

But his life at that time was so jumbled and chaotic, sometimes he didn't know which way to turn. So he hadn't been there regularly, as even he thought he should have been. He had met Tante during her return to help Myine. "Quite a woman, but not like our sweet Rose."

His life, at that time, was so full of changes, surprises, things he had to do for himself. "I didn't do all I could have for them; I should have done more."

Being alone was very lonely when he first left Wanda; too quiet sometime. He didn't like eating alone, and usually some youngster would be at Wanda's. But he had been sleeping alone a long time. He knew he liked the new peace and quiet. Herman's new life began to steady and develop a new pattern. He began to enjoy his aloneness.

If he put something down, it was there when he reached for it the next time he wanted it. He had to cook all his food, if he didn't eat out, but he could cook and eat the things he wanted, and not plan for the whole family and their friends. Things he had wanted more of were still there when he came home from his job.

He began to think of his family as "my used to be family." He had to keep reminding himself, when he missed them, they were not his biological children. "I still love them, but I can't worry about that. I love my 'almost daughter,' Rose Bertha, but she is her mother's child. She is going to be just like Wanda, no matter what I do. She already thinks I'm a fool. I can't live that way."

Since he had left their old house, money matters had forced changes on Wanda. She had cooled down her drinking. She got drunk less and less. When she had a few drinks she would cry about her life. "Ya'll ran my good man away."

Then again, "That man is such a fool! He had a good home here. Well, at lees I got to keep the house; for all my years in this here world, I got a house! But," she sobbed, "I ain't got no money, and no man. He took all my good years, and left me now when I

271

am gettin old."

Wanda would look at her daughter with anger. "You! And yo big mouth! I jes tol ya so you'd know! Ya wasn't sposed to tell him. Fool! Ya ruined my life!" She sniffled, blew her nose, and glared at Rose Bertha, "Ya ruined my life and yours too, ya dummy! Fool! Fool! Fool!"

Rose Bertha would give her mother a dirty look, which happened pretty often these days. She always had an answer for her mother. "You need to get up and get a job, Mama! I ain't got no clothes to go get one, and I'm too young anyway. And I'm sick and tired of eatin beans and bread."

"Chile, you needs to go to school, like ya father tol ya!"

"You the one said he wa'nt my father! And I'm too old for school."

"Well, ya sure ain't too smart for it!"

"I get along, Mama."

"That's jes what I been wantin to ask ya. What ya doin stayin out ALLLL night? Who you be with all night long?"

Wanda never got an answer, just a pouting frown.

Wanda continued, "Ya need to marry one them mens ya got comin by here!"

All Rose Bertha would answer was "Ugggh!"

Wanda would mock her. "Don't 'Ugggh!' me! Ya needs to bring a man in here to take the place of the one I had that ya loss for me!"

"Get another one, Mama."

Crying again, Wanda would say, "I want the same one back."

Getting up from her seat to look in the kitchen for something to eat, Rose Bertha would holler back to her mother, "Go get em then. He always was a fool for ya."

Wanda was quiet a few minutes, too long for Rose Bertha. She peeked through the kitchen, and saw her mother deep in thought, and decided to press her mother. "You can get anybody back. You still beautiful to em!"

But Wanda said, very thoughtful and serious, "Ya know? Herman was right; ya all are fools. Don't know nothin. If I let ya stay here with me I ain't never gonna have nobody. My best son is James; he writes me sometimes, and send me a few dollars. You don never give me nothing. And ya spreadin ya legs open all over town . . . for nothing. Herman was right, ya are a fool."

Rose Bertha slammed the refrigerator door, which was already broken, saying, "I ain't got time to stand round here and argue with you! I got things on my mind." And indeed she did. She was pregnant. And she didn't know who the father was. She thought, as she looked at her mother, "If I have a baby, she gonna help me take care of it."

She said aloud, "I got to be here cause I'm gonna have this baby. Ya think Herman will help me take care his first granchile?"

Wanda smiled slightly. "Since ya open yo mouth so smart, Herman know that ain't his first nothing. Ya done tole him you ain't none of his, so that baby ain't gonna be nothin to him. And I want ya to get this straight; ya not gonna lay on me either, no ma'am, and drop them babies. Cause ya jes beginnin ya life, and I done already lived mine, and I got me a house. You ain't got nothing but a belly full of baby, and a head and a behind full of men. Don't count on me, fool."

Rose Bertha had moved to the doorway to stare at her loving mother as Wanda continued talking. "I might could have me a future . . . if I didn't have you, so I sho don't want two of ya!"

Rose Bertha looked at her mother with the beginning of hatred; but she thought, "I can't hate my mama, cause I maybe haft'a leave this baby with her." She moved to hug her mother as she said aloud, "I love you,

Mama, we a family. You always tol me that!"

Wanda tilted her head at her daughter, a thoughtful look on her face, as she answered, "I didn't lie to ya, baby, I jes didn't know ya yet. I blive ya growin your own family for yourself now."

CHAPTER 29

After Herman left Wanda he filled his life with his work, and there was peace of a sort. He was reading and getting good sleep again, and he did not really miss his old family, except to feel sorry for them. But he wrote Jerome and James, sent them records, tapes, and love.

He thought of Juliet, Bertha, and Myine often. He would go by there, and they were always glad to see him. But he didn't want to go too often; he liked them to call, or send for him.

He liked being at home. He cooked, and he thought he ate well, but after a physical checkup the doctor told him he was not up to par. "You have high blood pressure, and still, you are anemic. Take a little glass of port wine in the evenings to build up your blood. Other than that, you're alright." He gave him a prescription, and a bill.

Herman didn't like drinking alcohol too

much as he got older. But he got into the habit of having that little glass of wine and developed a taste for it. He started having two or three glasses of wine every evening.

(Well, he was alone, and wine will sneak up on you.)

Soon he began to fall into a deep, heavy sleep in the evenings. Waking a little groggy in the mornings, he had to take a cold shower to wake himself up. It was becoming a habit. Habits are so easy to develop in human beings; you can become addicted to water. Or anything.

Many days went by like that in his life. Days that turned into weeks, and then, months.

Eventually, being the type of man he was, he stopped himself. "I have too much to do. My life is not in a wine bottle."

So he went out just to see some people, or to do something beside work or sit in his apartment and read. Sometimes he looked at television, but so many people on television were dying all over the world in greedy, selfish wars, some of them unnecessary wars, for greedy people; it made his head and heart hurt. He would then go out to one of the clubs and have a little glass of wine. There were so many deaths, and so many new clubs.

If he happened to see Wanda in a club she shouldn't be in, or even Rose Bertha, his ex-daughter, he would leave. He would go home, where he would read, or listen to the lying heads in the news again, or look at the sex and death on his television until he snapped it off and read himself to sleep.

When Herman did go by to see Bertha, Myine was usually at work or studying. He held Bertha and Juliet, saying, "Call me. Call me when you need someone to do something around here. I know Cloud is here, but call me anyway." They didn't call him because Cloud was indeed there, and he could do many things.

At times, he looked closely at Myine, thinking of her as a young woman, not as a child, saying, "Your mother and Mz. Bertha, here, made all the difference in my life. They helped to give me a life; led my education and all. My self-respect, even my hygiene. Your mother cleaned me up, and Bertha kept me clean." He laughed a little as he looked back over those years.

Myine was a darker bronze color than her mother had been. Leroy mixed in her blood, he thought. Her eyes were wide and clear with thick, short lashes. And there was an honesty in her face and eyes; there were no shadows she was hiding behind.

Her smile was quick, and fresh, and glowing. Nothing of secrecy lurking there. Her teeth needed some care, but on the whole, she still had all of them. She had a lovely body, as her mother's had been; slender, medium tall, about five foot four, but rounded and soft looking. She was quiet, only smiling at most everyone; so happy to be doing the studies she loved.

They told him about all Tante had helped them accomplish on her trip. He asked Myine, "So you are now back in school? College?"

Myine smiled, almost apologetically as she said, "I'm not going for a degree, right now. I just want a teaching certificate to teach small children. I need to start working to get some money coming in. Later, I'll go for a B.A. degree, since Aunt Tante tried to invest in me, but I'm trying to hold on to as much of that money as possible. It's expensive just to live."

Herman nodded his head, saying, "You need to go for all you can; an education will never let you down. People may, but the education won't. There will always be some way to use your education."

Myine's face became more serious. "I have a child I take care of, Lola."

Bertha sat in an old rocking chair, listening. She was in her late sixties, perhaps sixty-nine, and still working when she could. She was ailing from the many effects of a hard, struggling life, and no real medical care. She had often gone without food so Juliet could have medicine.

Bertha spoke, saying, "And everybody else in that Tonya family that can sponge off Myine when they can! They been tryin to move back in that house. Tonya and them grown girls of hers, Tee and Dolly. But they are fools with that dope! That's why Myine have that Lola child for a long time now, long time!"

Herman was alarmed, and admonished her, "Don't get mixed up with people who like dope, Myine. You will be the one who will suffer the most. You have no idea what a dope-head will do to take advantage of you. You have much more in life waiting for you. You already have your own house."

Advice-tired, Myine said, "I'm not going to let that little child down just because of something her mother does. I'm not crazy. I don't use dope. I just take care of a young girl who needs help.

"I think I'm too old to be in school. But they let me go to junior college, and study hard just so I can get a teaching credential. Then I can take care of my own self, and my own business."

Herman smiled, thinking, "She still has spunk. That is good, as long as no one wears it down."

Then Juliet said, "She too good-hearted. People take advantage of her."

Herman looked at Juliet; he knew they still didn't pay rent, but he was glad they were there. They were family by now anyway.

When Herman left there he was thinking about his own "business." He wasn't sorry about quitting his old job. They were always trying to give him apprentices to teach them the trade. Young men too ignorant to remember what he taught them, most hadn't stayed to finish regular school. Their minds were always filled with sex, and parties. He wasn't going to teach them all he knew anyway. "Next thing you know, they'd be my boss."

When he reached the place he rented, he thought as he went into his apartment, "I wonder if I should buy myself a home of my own." He had saved a good amount of money, even though he helped James, and sent money to Jerome occasionally.

In the kitchen he prepared water for his instant coffee, thinking, "Instant coffee. Instant love. This world is full of instant everything now-a-days. None of it good.

Instant unhappiness is more like it. If I buy a house, I'll be tempted to move someone in it with me. These lonely days are sad and tiresome.

"I wonder if I should dress and go out to dinner? I should have asked Bertha or My-ine, but I'd only bore them in my dark mood."

He looked in his closet; he had three or four nice suits, several dress shirts and pairs of shoes. He liked hats, had quite a few really good ones. He sighed and closed the closet door.

"Nothing on TV, as usual. Tired of going to the movies alone, and don't feel like see-ing the news on TV; all the wars, killings, and blood everywhere. Somebody always killing somebody. I could go out and buy a new book, or get a little piece of lovin from somebody; buy a piece anyway. I could go to church in the morning, maybe; but I'm tired of them lying too.

"I could go sit by the river's edge, watch people and think, but I did that last Sunday. Do I want to get married again? But you need to be in love to get married. You need love to make it work.

"Maybe I should move to another town. Travel. But I don't feel like it." He went to a window, and looked skyward. "You know

282

what, God? I want to be in love. Life does not count for much when there is no love in it. Help me out here, Lord. Please. I'm serious, God, dear Father. But, I know; love in Wideland, now-a-days, is pretty hard to find. Love anywhere, I guess."

He turned back to his kitchen, opened his refrigerator, and began to prepare himself a drink. "There is plenty free nooky out there, I could go get some of that; that would relax me, make me sleep better, but only You know, God, what would be hidden inside of it.

"Is there another woman, a good woman out there in life for me, Lord? I'm tired of being alone. See, Lord? I'm in the prime of my life. Yet I spend all these lonely nights and hours knowing what it could be like; what I'm missing. I don't have anyone to love. And You are a God of love, so I know You understand."

Feeling a little hopeful, Herman bathed and dressed in one of his best suits, and took himself out to dinner. He didn't go to a joint. He went to a lovely dining establishment that went with his suit. He ordered a sumptuous dinner.

People smiled at him. The waiter smiled for the tip; the owner smiled for the patronage, the bartender for his tip, and a few fine ladies of various colors smiled when their dates weren't looking.

Herman's thoughts were "But she isn't here. She isn't here." He left thinking, "How lonely will this night be?

"How lonely must I be?"

When he turned the motor on in his fancy new truck, he thought he might go to one of the new chi-chi clubs, but he thought of Wanda. He didn't want to see her and remind himself of the twenty-something years he had lost with her. So he went home to his books and the television. "Well, at least I am safe. Can't catch nothing sleeping by yourself."

But, on the way to his home, his car, somehow, turned a few corners and stopped in front of a woman's house. A woman he knew to be clean, fresh, almost honest, and mature; but she begged too much. He relaxed his body anyway, for a little while. He drove home thinking, "God, I know you see me, but I'm still not in love. That wasn't love, God."

He prayed and talked to God through the years.

CHAPTER 30

Cloud had worked on Bertha's house when the laborers had worked on Myine's house. He had plenty of material left over to work with, so the house was looking better as time went by, and it was more comfortable. A few more shelves were added to the kitchen, more needed cabinets throughout the little house. Bertha and Juliet made curtains, tablecloths, face and hand towels for their own use.

Bertha was not working except on really good paying, little jobs. Her body was worn, and many ailments held her back from doing what she knew had to be done. She didn't see a doctor often; there just was no money for that. She didn't complain; she kept her pains to herself.

Myine was steady in her college work; she had to be, because she had lost so many years. She had passed all the necessary tests, and now she was keeping up with the class for the past few years.

Money was stretched, and in short supply, but everyone managed on the garden they all worked in and nurtured. The fruit trees gave abundantly with Cloud's care. He knew about all those things, and since he wanted to be around Juliet, he was always working at something.

Bertha liked Cloud, but didn't want Juliet to think of being with him or anyone. "You ain't strong like other girls, Juliet. First thing ya do is have a baby, and that would kill both a' us." *Juliet had been having her menstrual period ever since she was nine or ten years old. We tributed it to her broken body: it has never stopped! Even now.*

Juliet loved Cloud. She didn't fuss with her mother, she just let time go by, telling herself, "We always together anyway." But she did want to marry her man. She thought Cloud was handsome. "Somebody else could get him from me."

TeeTee and Dolly, Tonya's daughters, came by to eat, now and then, and to try to borrow a little money from Myine. Bertha told her, "First time you give them something, they ain't never gonna stop beggin ya, they be here everday!" But Myine knew that; she spent any extra money on Lola. Usually she spent it on books for her classes.

Once, Dolly thought if she told Myine she was not going to let Lola stay with Myine any longer without Dolly being there, that Myine would let Dolly come back, too. "I can't keep leavin my chile. I miss her too much. I need to be round her. Lets us both raise her up." But the answer was a steady "No. You're late. She is raised."

Then Dolly pretended to be taking Lola away. Actually, Dolly liked to died at the thought of all her time, and little money, having to be spent on her Lola. One day after Dolly took Lola away, Dolly came right back to leave Lola with whoever was there at the time. Bertha was there. Dolly said, as she rushed in, "Mz. Bertha, I got a little bizness to take care of is all. I'll be right back; honest!" She didn't come back for several weeks, and then just to eat a meal. Finally all the play ended and in the end Myine had Lola to finish raising alone.

That was alright with Bertha and Juliet; they had always helped with Lola, so Myine could go to school with a free mind. When Lola was with Juliet, she was well behaved, even doing her homework for school, and helped in little jobs in the house.

Around that time Myine got her certificate and started her little classes for children. She did pretty good, too. Then . . . they heard from Tante again. Tante was sending her daughter, Monee, to Wideland to have a baby that was not by the rich man Tante wanted her daughter to marry. The father was someone Monee loved, but that was not what Tante wanted for her daughter. She wanted that money.

When Monee's daughter was born, Tante called Monee to come home right away, back to France without the baby. And, Tante said, she would send some money from time to time. But Tante reminded them, "Remember, I left a large sum of money, when I visited you, to save for our family estate. My daughter is part of the estate." Monee had named the darling new little baby Poem.

Myine, with Bertha helping what little she could, and Juliet, just carried right on; didn't miss but one or two steps. They would go on that way for several years. Everybody maybe didn't prosper, but they weathered the storms.

Then without notice Monee came to get her baby, little Poem. She had married the man Tante wanted her to marry, and she was taking Poem back pretending it was Myine's child and they would be helping the poor side of Tante's family.

You see, so much was happening to all

these people that you can't tell it out straight!
So I'm doin the best I know how. Ain't people
something, chile? Now, let me get back to
Herman, Myine, Juliet, and Cloud.

CHAPTER 31

Herman usually stopped by Juliet's and Bertha's house every few days to sit and talk. He liked Cloud; Cloud always seemed to be busy. But he knew Cloud did not make very much money from the odd jobs he found to do. From his own experience, he knew Cloud needed a steady income.

He began to bring carborators and other automotive parts from his job to teach Cloud how to clean them. Soon there was a steady supply. "These parts sit around for ages waiting for someone in the shop to work on them. I can get you a little money if you decide to do the work."

Cloud did good work, quick and steady. Herman supplied the cleaning solvents and gas to do the cleaning. He paid Cloud well, from his own pocket until the owner of the shop noted the difference in the "junk," with the old parts looking clean and ready for use; he agreed to pay for the jobs, by the piece. Herman agreed, and made arrangements with Cloud.

Cloud built a nine-by-nine concrete platform behind Bertha's house to keep the parts on, so he wouldn't "mess up the yard!" as Bertha said. He even built a small storeroom to keep the solvents in for safety. It wasn't long before he was buying his own supplies. He grew to love Herman like a blood brother.

Cloud was able to save a good amount of money over time. Bertha welcomed the money Juliet was extremely happy to give her. Juliet was proud of her Cloud. "My man," she called him.

But every day, Bertha was becoming more obviously ill. She seemed to be shrinking, more wrinkled, dry, and weak. They had to physically stop her from trying to drag herself to the few jobs she had that she wanted to keep. "Mama, that money is not as important as you are. We going to send you to a doctor! At last!"

Juliet had the money from Cloud for the doctor. They called on Herman to drive Bertha. Juliet now had an electric wheelchair, and she went with Bertha after Herman and Cloud helped her get in the truck.

Herman was glad Juliet was coming with them; he knew the prognosis would not be a good one, and he did not want to be the bearer of bad news. He also knew that Cloud wanted to marry Juliet, and Juliet was getting old her own self. She would not marry Cloud while Bertha was alive. "It is stupid," Herman thought, "but what are you going to do with some people? That woman has a life she is not living because of her mother." He also knew Cloud and Juliet were already lovers.

A few days later, when everyone knew Bertha's time was any time at all, Herman talked to Bertha. "Why don't you sit out here by your garden, and tell that young man Cloud to help you, to do your planting? He can dig, and you can talk as you sit out here in the sun amongst your trees. All this fresh air will give you a good night's sleep!"

Bertha answered, "I got to work!"

Herman answered back, "You don't pay any rent; you plant what you eat. Anything else you need, I'll give it to you."

"I got to take care this here child!" Bertha seemed stubborn, but she was trying to find some way to still be useful.

Now, Herman was stubborn. "Juliet is no child. She is about as old as Tante is. I bet she is almost fifty years old, if not more. She needs to be married while she can, and you let her husband take care of her."

"Who gonna marry her? You, Mr. Herman?"

"You know Cloud loves her, Bertha."

"Cloud is a Indian. He ain't gonna be able to take care Juliet."

"He already does, Bertha."

Bertha waved him away. "I want her to marry a good Negro man. A colored man. A Black man; whatsomever they calls em these days."

"It isn't about what you want, Bertha. What does she want?"

Bertha sighed, saying, "She don't know what she want. She too young, and foolish."

"Juliet hasn't been foolish since she was born. You are the foolish one, Bertha. You know you like Cloud, and you know you and Myine are getting older. Who is going to take care of Juliet when you die?"

But Bertha ambled away on her old arthritic legs, saying, "You betta get on way from me, talking all that foolishment."

Juliet would not marry Cloud until her mother gave her permission and blessings. *(She was already blessed, she had that man!)*

Herman went on about his own business, or he would work on the little rooms Rose and Irene had used as a classroom. He liked to be there; he felt at home there. Myine was there, but he dared not say anything to her.

CHAPTER 32

During these times, Herman had a lady-friend he visited every once in a while. He knew he was not the only one she was close to, so he prayed each time, before he lay down with her.

He was very careful; he seldom had sex with anyone. "I'm not putting anything of mine in any hole that turns up to me; too many pretty women are sitting on a disease, or two." But Herman loved making love. Not just for the sexual finale; he loved love.

He loved the softness of the female skin, the smoothness of the arms and legs, her body. He loved the texture of her hair, fluffy, curled, straight, or curled tight; all these things made his five senses come alive. He loved the smell, the touch, even the very sight of some women. He loved the taste of a woman's kisses, the feel of her lips, soft and yielding. The sound of a female voice, the right voice, could send little thrills through the canals of his ears.

Then, as happens in life, he met a nice lady about his age, Willamena. She stayed at his house so often, they almost lived together. She had a daughter who lived with her, and she respected her daughter enough not to bring a man home to sleep in her bed. Herman liked and respected that.

Willamena dressed very nice, was always looking like she lived in a clothing store. Her hair was always in place; she went to church, she cooked very well, her house was clean. Everything about her seemed to be good. And, she made "good lovin," as they say.

Herman was more than pleased with her. And though he did not want to be married again, did not trust life to be fair with him, he was tired of being so alone. This time he was really thinking about getting married to his Willamena. True, his heart was not leaping with joy, but he thought, "I'm too old to be looking for love, but at least I care a lot for her, and I won't grow old alone." He decided to marry Willamena.

I already told you, I am not good with dates and ages, but this is what I think: It was then around the year 1972, and Herman was only in his early fifties or very late forties, I'm not sure. But still, he worried about getting old or dying before he had a chance to have a real family, real love. No one knew Bertha's birthday, but she was somewhere in her seventies or eighties, Juliet was near fifty, or just pass fifty, but her menstrual period had never stopped. Myine was in her early forties. Herman was about ten years older than she was. Cloud was in his middle or late fifties. The child Lola was now at least twenty-three. Graduated high school, and working in a real estate office; she wanted a home of her own. Remember, now, I could be a little wrong, but that's close as I can get. My mama don't remember at all!

Early one afternoon, before the marriage, Herman and Willamena went shopping to get a few more things for the reception she wanted. They were in a large department store and each wanted different things. He wanted to surprise her with a few things, and she wanted a few things for the reception.

He waited for her at an appointed place for a while, watching the busy shoppers around him. After thirty or forty minutes of waiting, he began to look for her. He went to have her paged over the loud-speaking system in the store's office. That was where he found Willamena; she was in the hands of the store detective. She had been caught stealing.

Herman talked to the store manager and was finally able to pay for the stolen items taken from her bags. Later, he told Willamena, "I really care for you; you're nice. But I was reared to believe if you will steal, you will also lie. You won't make good decisions. I don't want that kind of life, or wife. So we have to end our relationship.

"You take care of yourself. Be careful. I'll bring your things to you." That was the end of their relationship. It may seem abrupt, but warnings are warnings, and Herman's experience made him take the warning seriously.

Herman just gave up on having any kind of serious love life. That struck his heart deeply. He was a loving man, a decent man.

He didn't know what to do. He talked to God a lot. But sometimes you don't know when He is answering you. His time is not like our time.

One morning, during all these passing years at about the same time, Myine was sitting on her porch swing thinking. Thinking about how many times she had been happy.

She was happy for Juliet, now. Juliet had Cloud, "but Juliet had always had Cloud all of this time. Even disabled, she has never had to worry about having a man of her own."

Her mind just kept browsing over life, thinking, "Lord, I'm getting old now. Men don't want any forty-something-year-old woman. Pretty soon that's where I'll be." She watched the drifting clouds for a moment, still thinking. "I have nothing. Lola is not always going to be around; with her good education she'll be able to do most anything reasonable she wants to do. Her mother didn't stop her, though she tried. First one in her family to finish high school!

"So I did something good by keeping Lola. But the years I was taking care of her, and working, I should have been courting and getting myself a husband.

"Then Tante sent her daughter, Monee, over here to visit, and the 'visit' turned into a job for years; because Monee left her baby, Poem. Monee left the baby here with me, and went home to marry that older, rich man her mother wanted her to marry.

"Years passed before Monee came and took Poem home. She is in some private school over in France now. I love Poem just like she was my own, but she isn't my own; I still don't have a child of my own. I gave up my life to raise her and Lola. Now . . . my life is gone. I am old.

"I don't have all of my teeth anymore; couldn't afford to keep all our teeth up at the dentist. I've replaced mine now, but they don't look like they are mine. I know I'm grey before my time, I think.

"Lord, there are some mornings I just can't get up from my bed; but I do. I have to. And my feet are always tired and sore. I know I can't limp into some new life. Even Juliet started her affair when she was younger."

She pushed the swing with her foot to start it swinging again. She laid her head back, still watching clouds drift by, and musing over the past.

"Lord, I thought I might have a life with that William Spencer I used to know. He seemed a nice man even though I was always too busy to do all the things he wanted to do. Shame on me, Lord, but I let him be my first beau; I let him make love to me one night.

"I didn't have an orgasm, and that was alright; I thought we had time to get to that. But I think he just wanted a home. When he asked me for some of my money, he had to go!

"Then there was Walter Greene. He seemed like a good man, too. Met him at church. A long time had passed since my last try with William, so I thought You would understand if I tried again. I let him try to make love to me, but still I didn't have an orgasm. I didn't have anything but a dirty sheet! And he wanted me to do all those freakish things I didn't want to do; looking at my mouth, talking about filling every hole in my body with something of his! Not with me, he couldn't!

"But, Lord, those are the only kind of men, those two, that I have known that close. Because I had those two youngsters to look after. And I can't say I really regret having them. I loved Poem, cause she was my blood, even if I didn't give birth to her. And I love Lola; always did love her from the first. They're both mine, but they are gone from me living their own lives, leaving me, alone, with mine.

"I have some good memories, but God, my whole life has belonged to someone else . . . from the time Tonya sold me away from my mother until right now.

"Don't You see? I want my own life . . . and now it is too late. I'm glad I had Lola, and Poem, but I wish I'd had a husband, a child, and an orgasm. God, please, God, think of me. I just want something that is mine. That's why my mother named me Myine: it means mine. And I don't have a thing but a house."

Musing, she watched the lazy clouds a little while longer, then her eyes dropped down to the trees on her land; she saw some of the little, wild animals, birds, squirrels, and such things which she loved. Her spirits lifted and she smiled sadly.

Then her eyes searched in the direction of Juliet's house. Bertha had been sick and dying for years, she just wouldn't let go of life. Myine saw Cloud's old truck nearby on the street; so he was there with Juliet. Juliet still hadn't married Cloud, because of Bertha. "We're just all crazy, I guess."

Myine breathed a heavy sigh, and stood up to go into her house, thinking, "Time is steady passing; I just might as well get used to being alone. I'm not ever going to have anyone of my own. Well, life goes on, anyway it can."

CHAPTER 33

Herman went through the next few years hoping someone would come along with whom he could fall in love, and at last have a home and family. In about a year or two, he met Connie.

Connie was cute, plump, loved to cook and eat, and she was clean. Her two children were grown, but not doing too well in this thing called life. But she seemed always ready, with time for Herman.

He didn't move in with her either. Fear. Caution. But he really liked her pleasant moods; she always made him laugh, and he was comfortable. He visited when the need was upon him. After a few years he was settling in, comfortable with Connie, and thinking he might stay with her. He didn't mess around on her, even though he didn't love her.

Herman was just lonely for someone of his own. He often said to himself, "Mine,

Lord, I want someone who will be mine. Mine alone." As time passed, he began to think, "Lord, I'm too old to be thinking about love anyway. My time has passed. Better take the best I can get."

He was planning to propose they get married, and that he would take some of his money and drive somewhere pretty, and take her on a honeymoon. He would still have plenty of money left to buy a house.

Deep in the nights, and deep in his mind, he thought about what he would be getting into, for life! "She does not do too much in bed; she has two moves at best. And there is not that extra thrill to it, like when you love somebody, but her body is soft and warm . . . and clean. That should be enough for an old man greying at the temples.

"My hair is not only turning grey, it's leaving my head steadily, getting thinner. And I left a few teeth at my dentist last week. I've got this ache in my knee that I use to kneel on all the time; sometimes it pains me all the way to my hip. So, she won't be getting macho man either."

The couple had to take blood tests to get married. Herman was on his way to the doctor's office, when he made a quick turn, and went by to talk it over with Bertha. It was from old habit, when Herman went to talk to Bertha. Bertha hardly knew he was there, and forgot everyone but Juliet almost immediately. Still, Herman thought, "I need to go by there anyway, it's been a while."

He found all of them home; Myine, Juliet and Cloud. They were sinking in grief; Bertha was dying. But, this time, it looked like she might lose her hold on life.

Herman's heart twisted in his chest. "Lord, I never do anything right. I should have kept closer with you all. Cloud knew he could call me, or tell me when I bring him to work."

Cloud said, without blame, "You are always in a hurry, Herman. I thought you were too busy to be worried with . . ."

Herman cut him off. "Too busy? I think of you all as my family!"

Myine spoke. "Then nobody should have to tell you what is happening over here."

Herman raised his head to look in Myine's stern eyes. He said, "You're right, you are right." He put his arms around Juliet, as he took a good look at Myine.

His thoughts were, "Little Myine isn't so little anymore. For real. She is definitely a grown woman. She has been a grown woman for a pretty good while now." He smiled, remembering his old thoughts when he had admired Myine when she was younger. He thought, "She still looks good to me.

"My life has been so full, and busy, I have lost track of time! I've been thinking of her as the kid she was, even though I can't be that much older than she is. I was still a youngster when she was born." Then he really looked at her. "But she doesn't look happy." He smiled shyly because he was ashamed of his thoughts. He was saying softly, but aloud, "Myine, Myine."

He turned his attention to the sorrow of Juliet. But his mind quickly flashed back to Myine. He knew she was teaching small children in the public schools now, and had a few extra students in her mother and grandmother's old classroom. Then his mind flashed back again to thoughts of Bertha, laying there dying.

He was sincere in his sorrow, saying, "What can I do, you all? Whatever you need, I'll do it. What does the doctor say? Does she need medicine?"

Juliet was very sad, and grieving hard in her heart. Cloud kept his arm around her shoulders, or followed her around the little house as she prepared something for Bertha, or he brought her tea, or some food.

Juliet was happy in one piece of her heart; now she could marry Cloud. They were both happy and sad at the same time. Bertha had had a long life. Her life had not been happy very often, but filled with a lot of love. To survive at any time in this world is a job. She had helped her family survive. Juliet loved her mother and truly did not want her to die, although she could hardly wait to marry Cloud.

Juliet had a problem; she was pregnant with Cloud's child. Her mother, Bertha, out of fear would not have wanted Juliet to have the baby at her age, even though she would have smothered her grandchild with love. She did not want Juliet to marry Cloud. Soon she could marry Cloud and have their child. It was hard to grieve, feel miserable, and yet be almost happy at the same time.

But death showed on Bertha's face as she struggled to breathe. She could not fight too hard to live much longer. She was still afraid for her daughter. When she could think coherently, she thought, "My baby will be alone." Too late she thought, "I'm glad Cloud will look over her."

Juliet went back and forth, silently crying, sitting beside her mother soothing her mother's body with her arms, holding her when she could manage it, with her tears dropping on Bertha as she did so.

They all sat and waited with Juliet. Herman felt he was, again, with his family. "Why do I waste so much time looking for something that is not out there for me, and letting things go that are so important to me? I'm always doing things wrong. No wonder I'm lonely."

Finally Bertha drew her last breath. Juliet collapsed as the finality hit her. "My mama, my mama! Oh, Mama. I'm all on my own now." But her friends were there, and the man she loved. But we know what she meant.

Herman finally did leave, after many hours of helping them with the undertaker, and helping Cloud with Juliet. "I'll be back, and sit with you all tonight at the wake. Bertha had a lot of friends."

He drew Myine to him, pressing her body to his. "Cry as you feel. Don't try to be strong for anybody. Tears don't mean you are weak. You've known Bertha as a mother, and a friend all your life." Then he held Juliet the same way. "I know how you all feel."

As he left, he took another good look at Myine, who cried but was really the strength of the little group. She was taking over gently and handling things for Juliet, the clothes, hair arrangements, and many such things, as people came by.

As he was leaving, he hugged them all

again. He looked down into Myine's tear-filled eyes, and his silly heart jerked just a little. He thought of her body again; it had felt good, warm, real, and alive.

Herman left thinking, "Myine is certainly no longer a little girl. I am near fifty, and she was about ten years younger than I am. She is still pretty; even prettier as a grown woman than she was as a young child. Hell! She still isn't old now."

He had made a promise to Myine, Juliet, and Cloud to come by more often. "If I'm not here all the time it's because I don't want to bother you. I get lonely; I'd love to just come sit with you. I just hate to be a bother to you."

When he remembered Connie it was too late to go to the doctor's office for the blood tests, so he called to make another appointment. Something in him had not wanted to keep that appointment. His heart was not in it.

When he did get to keep his appointment, Connie had already been there and taken her test. The nurse took his blood, and then directed him to return to see the doctor the next day.

The next day, the doctor waved him to a chair in his private office. When they were both seated, Herman looked at the doctor expectantly. This was only an approval for the marriage license, after all, and Herman wasn't sure he wanted one anyway. He had been thinking of Connie, and feeling a little guilty about thinking of Myine. He tried to shrug the feelings away, concentrating on Connie, thinking, "love will grow, and I'll be alright. I don't need a lot."

The first question the doctor asked was "How many women do you have sex with?"

Herman was surprised, but not alarmed. "Why do you ask me that question, Dr. Steel?"

"Because I need to know how much work we have to do."

"Work?"

"Yes. You have syphilis . . . and we have to contact the women you have been with, and let them know, so they can be treated before we have a real problem on our hands."

Speechless, Herman shook his head. "I have only made love, slept with one woman . . . for the last three years, sir."

"The woman who was in here day before yesterday? Connie Clay?"

"Yes, Connie."

"Well, her disease is older than yours. Her disease has settled in her body firmly, and widely. We'll give you a few shots. You'll be alright, but you better give her a few months before you go back with her."

Herman stood up. "I'll give her more than that. I'm not going back again. How long would you say she had been infected?"

"A year to six months."

Then Herman knew she had been with someone else. He hadn't been seeing anyone in the last three years except Connie. He thought, "Time has passed so fast." He tried to feel like his heart was broken, but he couldn't. He had really liked her, but he had not loved her the way he wanted to love a wife. "Mine, I want my wife to be mine. My own."

He took whatever few things she had left at his place to her. He had planned to surprise her with the rings at the wedding. He hadn't given them to her yet, so he didn't have to ask for them back. "I wouldn't have wanted to ask her anyway. I would have just given them to her."

He went home, put some Ben Webster with strings on his record player, and sat down to think . . . and think, and think. "My God, what is a man to do in this world? I believe, for me, the masquerade is over. I'm going to forget about marriage, and a family. Hell, I'm too old anyway!"

Distraught, he thought he would lose himself in work. He began taking Cloud more work and hanging around helping him. He looked around for other ways to help Cloud, Juliet, and Myine. One thing he did after Bertha's funeral: he gave the wedding rings to Cloud for Juliet.

They had planned their marriage for years. There wouldn't be a traditional wedding; it would be a mixed ceremony, Native American, Black with a speck of tradition, like a license. A small family gathering.

There was a small marriage ceremony, which a few of Cloud's relatives attended; over time, they had grown to love Juliet. Myine made a beautiful wedding cake. That night Cloud completely moved in with his old love, his new wife, and his future child. They made love as though it were the first time; they really were in love. Cloud was in his late forties, or early fifties. Juliet was somewhere in her fifties. *(That woman still had her monthly periods! You sure can't tell about life! They were making love, and a baby! People worried about her though.)*

CHAPTER 34

During the 1980s Herman was old, but still the best mechanic they had. He was now the head man in Pink's Automobile Service. But his knees had begun to ache, and he got tired of crawling under cars and trucks and moving heavy engines. He said to himself, "I'm old!"

He was tired of so many things, he resigned his job. They tried to keep him, offered him more money because he was so capable, reliable, responsible, and honest. He agreed to be a consultant and to keep cleaning engines and parts for them.

For a while he took a job as a chauffeur for a rich old man who was born in Wideland, went to university in the East, gathered his riches, and fifty years later came back to Wideland, home to retire. He had told Herman, "It's peaceful here, Herman. I'm going to travel a bit to keep an eye on my business, but I'm going to rest here. I just want you to look after the cars and keep an eye on my housekeepers. I'll pay you twice what you made at Pink's. Just keep my automobiles serviced and clean."

Herman was a regular, almost daily, visitor at Cloud's house. Of course, he most always stopped to talk with Myine if she was home. As old as he was, he became extremely shy around Myine; he was in love with her, and too embarrassed to tell her. He was afraid she would laugh at him, reject him in some way.

On the day he told Myine about leaving his job, she was glad for him. "You were not too old for your old job, but this new job is better; less strain on your body."

"Yeah. My new boss travels a lot; always going someplace. He's gone so much he really does not need me. Sometimes I wonder what he does all that time, in all those places he travels to. The good thing is I can take you for rides in something better than a truck! He has several beautiful automobiles, Rolls-Royces and even a Pierce-Arrow. Works of art! He says friends give them to him. Some friends, huh?"

He was looking closely at Myine, as usual. He tried to stand close to her, but she was usually moving about, so he couldn't stand close long. He noticed how there were quite a few more grey curls among her shiny brown hair. He thought, "Her hair is beautiful, always clean and smelling good. Usually she wears braids; I like it when she has it all done up."

She looked up at him, smiling as she said, "I'm glad you were too old to go to all those wars they had in the sixties and seventies. I'm glad you stayed here at home. I liked going to all those marches with you, when I could get away. We even went to Alabama to march with Dr. King. I really, really loved that trip even as frightening as it was."

He looked down into her face, savoring it. "Yeah, with a bad knee!" He laughed lightly. "I enjoyed doing that. And I am not too old. I could go to any war in some capacity if I wanted to; I'm a mechanic, and mechanics are always needed. You retired from teaching at the school, and only teach at home now. That does not mean you are old, does it?"

Myine put a hand on her hip, saying, "Is that all you heard that I said? I never said you were old. I never retired because I was old, I retired because I could. I still have private students. They're mostly older people, Black and white and some Indians, who never learned to read and write.

"Never had a lot of students at home

anyway; don't need a lot. I was really talking to you about the sixties, seventies, and eighties. And now, the nineties. We got Nixon and Reagan out; now we have to get Bush out of the White House before he starves us all to death. Makes us lose our homes the people struggled to get in the first place. 'Trickle down,' my foot! Republicans have their little secrets that are bankrupting people in America. I'm glad I'm not political. I just wait on God to take care of things for me. With mankind, things are only going to get worse!"

Feeling a little better, Herman agreed, "Yea, the seventies and the eighties were really something. Sneaky, foolish, wars, going to the moon, Nixon impeachments. This world is spinning out of control."

She smiled up at him. "Abortion rights, women's rights, some good things. The Black civil rights workers fought us right into a much better world. And I remember all the good music you introduced me to. I never seemed to have time to . . ."

Herman leaned against a near wall. "You don't seem to have time for listening to music with me anymore. Yea, you are always busy; giving your time away."

"What do you mean?"

"Well there was your aunt's daughter,

Monee. You used up almost ten years taking care of her child, Poem. I was glad when she came to get Poem. I liked that name. But, still, you had so many things on you. I think people take advantage of you, Myine. You've never taken time to live your own life. You don't have a child of your own. You don't have a husband or . . ."

Myine stood straight over the hoe she had picked up in the garden. "Let's talk about something else."

Herman didn't want to upset her with an old argument. He looked closer at the work she began doing. It was garden planting time.

She was working on the plot of land Cloud kept cleared for the garden she and Juliet used for their kitchen storeroom, or pantry, or cooler, some people call it. It was larger than in her grandmother Irene's day. Myine loved to work there. They grew almost everything they ate.

Cloud and Juliet had a boy they had named Wings Val Cloud. He was a big boy now, about eight or ten years old. He helped his mother in her garden and helped his father cleaning auto parts. He got paid for it, sometime. They still paid no rent, but Cloud took care of the whole five acres of land in exchange, keeping it clean and the trees pruned and thinned. Just their being there was a blessing to Myine.

Many times all the heads working in the yard were greying. Cloud hadn't replaced some of his teeth, but his smile was just as sunny, bright and happy. He loved his wife and his son. They didn't have another child because the doctor had told Cloud how difficult the birth had been on Juliet.

"One child is enough for us to see ourselves mixed in one piece. And you gave me a son. So there will still be a Cloud dreaming after I am gone," he had told Juliet. She leaned back in her wheelchair and, glad he was happy, agreed with him.

Leaving Myine in the garden after helping her awhile, Herman walked over to Cloud's work place. Besides the concrete platform for the oily parts he worked on, he had also built a five-by-five shed to keep the cleaning solvents, rags, and tools in, away from danger to his wife and son.

Myine went to see Juliet often. They spoke on all kinds of subjects. Myine was glad to have a good friend to talk to. Juliet was still interested in almost everything going on in the world.

One day Juliet asked Myine, "Listen, here, am I looking old? Am I too fat?"

"No, where did you get that from? Not

Cloud, I know."

Juliet laughed a little, "No, it's all these magazines coming out for the last five or six years! With all the 'beautiful people.' Showing all their beautiful asses. I don't blive it! Somebody is doin something wrong to their body. That ain't no natural look!"

Myine laughed. "I heard someone say that when you go to bed with somebody these days, you don't know whether to get in the drawer, after they take everything off, or to get in bed with em. All the good stuff was removable!"

"That's right, Myine! My beautician said wigs sell, even here in Wideland, like hotcakes!"

"Well, we have our own hair, Juliet. We should thank God for that, because some people really need a wig; I'm glad there are wigs for them."

"Well, I'm just glad beauty is in the eye of the beholder. Cause I wouldn't make all these plastic surgery changes even if I had the money. People don't know what may happen to them later on in their life. If God gave it to me, I'm glad to keep it!"

"Some people use plastic surgery, Juliet, for medical reasons. It does more than just make them look better, sometimes it makes them functional, or able to live without being stared at."

"Well, I wasn't being mean, Myine. I'm just telling you what I think. If I could get my legs to work, I would. You know, Cloud has me so I can stand up straight? I can't walk, but I can stand up on my feet!"

"What is he doing to you that you have to stand up?" Myine laughed as she asked.

"He just likes to try to make me exercise, keep my bones strong, and moving! I'm the one kissin and huggin him."

They laughed, and were happy for each other's joys. But Juliet was concerned that there was no one to love Myine like Cloud loved her.

When Herman stopped by to holler through the door at Juliet, Juliet called him in. "What chu doing tonight, Herman? Have you seen that new picture at the movies? Everybody says it is good! You need to take Myine to see it. She likes things like that. All she does is stay at home."

"Well, did you ask her if she wanted to go?"

"No, I hadn't seen you yet, and she already been by here."

Herman didn't want to tell Juliet to use her telephone to call Myine and ask her; that should be his job. But something didn't feel right for him. He didn't want to ask her because he didn't want to hear Myine say no. After all the years he was still hesitant to ask Myine personal, just-the-two-of-us things.

He laughed and said, "What are you today? A matchmaker? Make your man take you!"

"We already saw it. That's why I know you all would like it."

Herman didn't ask Myine. He just passed her front door on the way to his truck, looked at her house as he locked the gate, then got in his truck and went home to put on some more of his lonely life music.

CHAPTER 35

After the day he had helped Myine work in the garden, Herman began to stop by almost every day trying to catch Myine in the yard again. The days he didn't come by he was worried that he was becoming a nuisance. He was the only one who thought that; they were all glad to have his help, and Myine was just glad he was there. They shared the harvest with him, and it even had become a yearly thing.

Herman was, now, going on fifty-eight years old, and didn't look it. He looked worn, but not tired. When he looked old it was because he had been lonely so long. Loneliness can eat away at your body, your nerves. He had been in love with Myine a long time, but thought he was too old to step up to anyone, much more so with My-ine, with his heart in his hands.

Myine loved Herman, but felt she was too old and ugly to be thinking about "love."

Thinking, "a dried-up old woman should stay in her place. I don't want to be frisking around with anybody. I'd look like a fool trying to court at my age."

They were caught in a quandary in life, and didn't have sense enough to see they were both in the same place. Life don't wait for nobody; it was passing, as usual, swiftly, at that age.

But Myine was beautiful to Herman. He loved her new, short, stylish, greying hair and the glow of the golden earrings she wore. He liked that her body was kept supple, slim, and healthy from all the work she did on her land, in her garden. He liked her starched, cotton, wide-skirted dresses with a belt at her waist, in this age of short-shorts and belly-rings and asses hanging out all over the place. You don't have to wonder or dream about what a woman has anymore, they put it all out there for you to see.

Myine didn't have varicose veins on her legs either. "Probably," he thought, "because she never had any children. But they can take those things right out now-a-days. Nobody has to have them. She is forty-eight now, and I am almost fifty-eight. What can I do about this woman? Time is flying right on by us, fast as this world is turning.

"I don't blive she is seeing anyone else;

hell, I'm around there practically every day, and I don't ever see anyone except her regular friends. I wonder does he come late at night?" He shook his head. "No, Cloud or Juliet would know that. So, what's wrong with her?"

He continued on his train of thought. "I wanted a family, but I'll be happy with just a wife. I can't raise no hell in bed, but she does not seem to be doing anything in bed at all.

"I think I've loved Myine ever since she was a little girl, and I asked her to wait for me. She is always sweet. And so bright and pretty. She reminds me of her mother, Rose. And she reminds me of my mother in her ways. Oh, God, I don't want to be a fool; especially not an old fool!"

He laughed at himself. "I don't know why I'm even thinking about it. She isn't thinking about me. But, I haven't been there in a few days, so I'm going by there today anyway. I have to see Cloud about something."

When Herman hadn't shown up for a few days, Myine missed him. She didn't ask Cloud about him, or mention him to Juliet. "She, of all people, does not need to know I'm thinking of him. I don't want her laughing at me. Nobody wants an old lady crying on their shoulders in these days."

This was the planting season so she was working in the garden some part of every day, thinking of things in general as she worked. After awhile, thoughts of Herman came into her mind. "Herman still looks really good for his age. These women I know out here would love to get a man like Herman. He is a good man. Not a lot of fooling around that I know of, and Cloud never would tell me even if he knew. Those old biddies at the church would tell it though.

"People say forty-eight is not old, but I feel old. I don't feel . . . like a woman should. But, Lord, I don't want no more men like the two I almost married. I don't want any more of that mess! I don't usually curse, Lord, but shit on that kind of love. I still don't know what all the fuss is about people making love. I have never felt it. Never! And I want to know!

"And it looks like I'm going to leave this world not knowing. Lord, making love, or sex, can't be the most important thing in life. But, Lord, I want a man. And they are all taken . . . or dead." She struck at a weed with her hoe, but hit a radish plant instead. After she repaired the damage, she began hoeing again.

"You haven't made me live a real hard life

though, Lord, I thank you for that. But I did have some hard times. If I hadn't always answered the call of someone's needs I might have had time to do more courting, and I'd have someone today. And when Juliet tells me how good Cloud makes her feel, down there, I'd know what she was talking about!"

She stopped to wipe her brow with the handkerchief she carried in her pocket, and looked up at the afternoon sun. "Lord, it's getting hot out here. Or maybe it's just me and this menopause I'm having." She turned back to her work, still thinking.

"Herman," she thought a minute. "He used to be too old for me, but . . . not now. When I saw him take his shirt off in this garden the other day . . . Well, he didn't look like any young Adonis, but he wasn't supposed to. What would an Adonis want with me? An old grey-haired lady? And I am not going to dye my hair. I like the grey; it sparkles with the light. It's mine. I just thank God that I have some hair on my head, grey or not.

"And my hair is soft, and smells good, healthy. Some ladies have put so many chemicals and dyes on their head, so that now, they don't hardly have any left; and what they have left is stiff and hard.

"Same way they do their faces. I do give my own self a facial every month or so, and I never did wear all that makeup mess these people on the television say you need to look 'right' or to feel good. Crap! They make money, and you make bad skin.

"You can't believe those models on that TV who probably have never put the product on their smooth, fresh skin! Or they play camera tricks. You can't ever tell. Everybody lies so much in this world today. Everybody! The people in this world are speeding to a miserable end. No one seems to be happy anymore; and other people are getting rich off of it."

Myine stood, and leaned on the hoe handle, thoughtfully. "But when I saw Herman's stomach and his chest . . . Well, his stomach is smooth and you could see the muscles in it, and his chest. All that work he has done all his life, I guess."

She bent over the hoe to work again. "He may not look like a young man, but young men don't look all that good either, now-a-days. Some of them do, in the magazines maybe, but you can never tell; they can be empty, blank, nada inside their heads, beneath all that store-bought beauty. They may even desire other men, and not like you for their self at all.

"Herman has smooth, warm skin on his body, you can tell just by looking at it. And he has just a little pot-belly; gas. He doesn't eat right, I bet. He never talks about his women. I bet he has two or three of these used young women messing around him. Everybody wants 'young.' Young.

"Well, let them. I don't envy the young anything but their health, and the time to make some choices I didn't make when I was able. And, I am healthy, except for all these little aches and pains that come out of nowhere."

She stood up straight, and placed one hand on her back. "Like my back. I used to do things like this gardening all day every day when I was feeding those children, Lola and Poem. Had to do it. I never got pains like this, but maybe that is why I have them now. Well, what's the hell? As my papa used to say."

She bent over to work again, still thinking. "I love Herman's eyes. Eyes like my daddy's, prettier than mine. They look tired though, a little blurry around the edge of his pupils. I think I better take more vitamins than I do already. Go get a massage and a facial, or something. Not going to get any new clothes, though; I'm not going anywhere but to that new church. They

328

don't call it a church, they call it a Hall. I like what they say though. They're saying something! Things I never heard before. I can honestly say it sounds just like the truth to me."

When Herman just happened to come by that very day, Cloud had lain Juliet down on the grassy lawn around their house. She had prepared a nice lunch to have a picnic. She could do all kinds of things in her kitchen, while in her wheelchair.

Cloud had added on to and fixed the house so it was very convenient for her to do anything she might want. Wings Val had his own room, and they had added enough space to their bedroom to put in a queen-size bed. The window spaces were larger, wider, facing away from the big house, into the woods. Juliet loved watching the trees and animal life from her bed.

Juliet's doctor had given her birth control pills because her monthly periods had never stopped, and she took them. They knew they did not need another child. Cloud had told Juliet, "We are blessed to have the one we have, Wings; us, mixed together."

They often made love outside when they knew no one would be coming around their house. He would stretch her out, flat on her back. Juliet loved his patience and understanding. He'd spread her legs enough, then lay his body between them.

They kissed and teased awhile, laughing, together. When she was ready, and trying to pull her knees up, he raised his body and helped her. He smiled down at her as he placed her knees at his sides. She could squeeze his hips with them. Then he lowered himself, slowly, until he entered her warm and waiting body. He loved making love to his woman.

They lived, they loved, and her being crippled did not bother them. Their faith in their God, and the adventure of their life, made them ready when love had come. Their love, and passions, made them indestructible, so far, in the life they had chosen to live. Together.

Herman was on his way to see Cloud, so he happened to see them making love so slow and lazily that day. He didn't mean to watch them, but he did for a moment. It was everything; not just seeing two people make love. It was the blue of the sky, the fluffy white clouds, the light, caressing breeze and the sun shining warmly down on them through the patterns of leaves on the gently swaying trees. Leaves, that made patterns on the gently moving, naked body of Cloud.

All these things made Herman's chest fill up with desire and envy . . . and pain. He turned, leaving before they saw him in his own naked longing.

He had to cross the wide breadth of Myine's land. His throat tightened as he passed the little, old schoolroom so near the main house: Memories. As he reached Myine's house, he stared at her front door, wanting to enter it, speak to her, tell her what he felt; but he didn't.

Still walking on, and thinking, his feelings overwhelmed him. A sob started, deep down in his heart where he was feeling sorry for himself. The sob tried to come out; he fought the sob, fought his feelings.

Finally . . . he was in his car, driving, away. The sob, just one, broke through. He cried out, aloud, "Oh, God! I want a life! I want my woman! You know she's mine! Give her to me, give her to me. Please, Jehovah! She says that is your name; she even showed it to me, right in my own Bible! She says you like to be called by your name because your son said, 'Hallowed be thy name.' So, Jehovah God, please, give me that woman, my woman, please, God, please! Let Myine love me. There is no sense in both of us being alone! I know she must want somebody.

Please, God, give her to me, let me take care
of her. Please."

CHAPTER 36

Herman drove home, took a shower, had a drink, and sat down to think. He didn't shave again, but he put on fresh clothes, a white shirt and a pair of khaki pants. He got back in his truck, and drove back to Myine's house. His heart had calmed down, but the memory of Cloud and Juliet, and his own love throbbing in his breast, made him go back.

Myine was sitting in the swing on her porch. She looked up as he parked his truck. Her heart beat a little faster even as she thought, "I know it's just Herman, but Herman is a man I like." She did not let herself think of it as romantic. She did not want to look like a fool, and be hurt again.

Herman was smiling as he reached the bottom of her steps. "How're you doing, Mz. Myine?"

"Just fine, Mr. Herman. How are you doing on this beautiful day?"

"I could say fine, myself."

After a moment's hesitation, she said, "Come on in."

He started up the steps. His confidence faded as he said, "I'm just stopping by to holler at Cloud."

She smiled, looking directly into his eyes, "I believe they are having a picnic over there. They usually come out on these kind of days."

Herman sat in the swing beside her as he asked, "Aren't you going to the picnic?"

"It's not that kind of picnic. I may go visit her, later, but I always give them a few hours to relax alone, before I butt in."

The thought passed swiftly through his mind, "She has already seen what I saw! She must be made of steel." He said aloud, "Do you think I'd be butting in?"

Myine, nervous, smiled, pushing the swing with her foot, but it did not move because he was too heavy. He noticed, and pushed the swing gently for her, as she answered. "Oh, maybe not, he is always happy to see you. I'm always here with them; they can see me anytime. But you could stay and visit with me a little, first."

Herman was silent a moment, then said, "Well, I'll just walk around there later, since you're going to let me sit here with you a little bit."

"Herman, stop talking silly. You know you are always welcome. I'd love someone to talk to."

Herman leaned back, smiling, giving the swing a solid push. "There is always me, Myine. It's a beautiful day to sit out on a porch with a lovely lady!"

"Oh, Herman! You can sit here with me as long as you don't talk to me like I am crazy. I know you could be a lot of places with someone on a day like this, instead of sitting here with me."

Herman stopped smiling, and looked directly into Myine's eyes. "There is no other place I would rather be, Ms. Myine."

Myine laughed lightly. "Oh, Lord. Now you're going proper on me."

Still looking directly in her eyes, Herman answered, "I'd love to do anything on you. I mean, with you, around you, by you, whatever you let me do."

He saw the blush come into Myine's face, and thought he had overstepped by telling her his truth. He quickly said, "Say, I remember you telling me you would like to have a place to sunbathe some day. Why don't you let me build you a little private space, next to your house?

"I could build it for you from the inside

of your basement coming out. Then you'd have two new rooms. I could build it so you can remove a wall, when you want to, and it would be open to your whole yard. Just when you want to be naked in the sun, the walls would be there. For your privacy."

Myine laughed, happily, and Herman became more comfortable. He couldn't understand why he was nervous; he was used to Myine; he had known her all her life. He made his body move into a more relaxed condition.

He continued speaking, "We can plant flowers; flowers you like. And I'll put in a small Japanese fountain, and a slender, beautiful tree. I can build a platform for a mattress just the size you want it . . . for you."

With Myine's smile glowing on him, he was encouraged. "Let's talk about this, Myine!"

Myine looked at Herman in wonder, asking, "But what will you get out of doing all that for me? I may not even have all that kind of money. What do you get? I know you have . . . other things . . . to do."

Herman thought very quickly of another plan he and Cloud had been talking about. He hadn't planned it this way, but he had to have an answer for Myine right then. He couldn't bring himself to say, "Because I love you." He was disgusted with himself, but to him, there had been no preamble to such words. Their friendship had always been just a friendship.

As his enthusiasm slowly leaked out of his mind, he sat up, stopping the swing. "You know what? I'm going to get my thoughts straight, and if you will allow me, I will come back and discuss them with you. But, I have to tell you this. If you never gave me a dime for doing anything for you, it would be fine with me. Your mother gave me something which I cannot replace, nor name a payment for. I have never forgotten her, or that."

He stood up. "And I'm not trying to pay you back in place of her. I just wanted to do something for you. I . . . I care for you, My-ine. I know you think of me as an old man, an old friend of your family, so I have to do what you let me do."

He started down the steps as she stood up, reaching a hand out toward him. She didn't understand. He turned back to her, saying, "Mighty nice afternoon sitting here with you, Ms. Myine."

She asked in a very gentle voice, "Her-man, stop calling me Ms. Myine, please."

"Alright, Myine. I was just teasing you

anyway. But I enjoyed you sharing your company with me. That's the truth. And I'll be back to talk to you about the sunbathing room and my own ideas. Soon."

Myine just looked after him as he left. Not understanding everything, but thrilled none-theless.

The excitement was gone by the time she went to sleep, but one of her last thoughts was, "I believe I could love that old man. Me, with my old behind."

Lord, chile, seems like these people are just trying to let life pass them by! But, that's the interesting part to me! Some people would have just jumped smack-dab in the middle of anything. But these two people, getting older every day, were letting their nerves, their self-consciousness, their stupid, bashful feelings get in the way of their life.

But, on the other hand, if they had been different kinds of people, their love might not have grown so strong! And good. In my experience you just have to let life, and love, work its own self out.

CHAPTER 37

When Herman reached home he sat down and considered his life, thinking about the future. "I have been working with Cloud for several years now, on Myine's land. Hauling motors, carburetors and other greasy things I pick up at auto shops that they don't have men, nor time, to fix.

"I am quitting my job for Mr. Money as his chauffeur because I don't like working for people who sell bombs, and other ammunition, all over the world; killing and maiming people all over this world. And he seemed like such a nice, retired old man. Since I found that out I am too ashamed to even mention it to anyone."

Herman wiped his brow with the back of his hand. "I have money I will never use, while here I am living in an apartment I only sleep in. And there is no place to store things, or sit an engine while I work on it.

"Cloud does a lot of work with me and

only has a small platform to put a few pieces on, and store his solvents.

"Now, there are two things I need to do; I need to see Myine every day, and make my circumstances better. I think I need to talk to Myine about all that unused land she has. I don't want a wrecking yard. I don't want to mess up that beautiful land she has kept so well all these years; that's her home.

"I just want a storage shed; a big one. I would build it way in the back where she couldn't even see it mongst all her trees. Then Cloud and I could work more comfortably. I'll build it all of wood, like her trees; make it look natural there.

"And if she let me do that, I would put in a road from the street to the shed, so I could drive my truck in for pickups. No one else would be allowed to use that road. No strangers could come in. Only Cloud, and me."

He wiped his brow again, and got up to go in his kitchen to get a cold beer. Still thinking, "She isn't going to let me do it. But, hell, I can ask. I can't see any other way to get close to that woman. She might let me do it; it only increases the value of her land."

Now, Myine had been enjoying Herman being around, being nearby. So, a few days later, when Herman sat down on the porch swing beside her, she was pleased. She had on a freshly starched and ironed pale green dress she particularly liked. "I match my trees." She smiled to herself.

When Herman asked about building a storage building on her land, she thought a moment. She had been expecting him to, at least, start some place he had left off the last time she saw him, like say something kind of personal. He always looked neat in his khaki pants and white shirts.

After thinking a moment, she shrugged inwardly, thinking, "Well, life is life." She said aloud, "I don't want a lot of wrecked cars on this land. This is my home, Herman. I love my trees, the birds, everything. I love the peace and quiet, the mellow feeling I get from just sitting out here. I don't need to see any greasy engines cluttering up my view. Cloud keeps all his work placed neatly away." She liked to look at Herman; he was such a manly man.

Herman leaned back on the swing, and smiled. "I thought of that. All our work is not large. We work on three or four pieces at a time. There will be no pieces or parts waiting around, and, when there are, they will be inside the shed. It will be a good, nice-looking shed, not an eyesore. I'll build it of good wood, except for the room where we will keep cleaning solvents."

He looked at her to see how her thoughts were going; she was looking down, into empty space, so he continued, "There will be no automobiles parked around it, except my truck." She raised her eyes to look into his. In spite of the business in his mind, at the look in her eyes, a thrill shot swiftly through his head and traveled down his back.

He looked away from her, then, slowly, back to her. "I'll put in a narrow driveway for me and Cloud to use."

She gave a little jerk, and faced him. "I don't want a lot of men driving up in here!"

"I don't want them either, Myine. That's why I said Cloud and I will be the only ones to use it." He thought, "I certainly do not want a lot of men coming here where you are."

Myine asked, "Way, way in the back?"

"Out of the way, out of your sight. And I'll make it real nice."

Myine thought of the improvement it might be to her land, then said, "But, how can you improve on nature?" Then she remembered her mother talking about Joseph and Bertha building their house; she had been glad they did, rent or not. Juliet and Cloud still did not pay rent, but they contributed so much to her, she couldn't count the ways. And their house was hers, no matter how much money they put into it.

After a moment, Myine said, "If you build a road, well . . . put it closer to Juliet's house than mine." Herman's whole body gave a sigh of relief. Myine asked him, "When would you want to start . . . all this work?"

"As soon as possible."

"Well, let me see the trees you will have to cut down before you do anything. I love my trees, I don't want to see them go if they don't have to!"

Herman stood up to leave, saying, "I already thought of that, Myine. I know how you are. The shed is going to be twenty by twenty-five feet; just enough for a few heavy parts, and Cloud and me. I don't count those little sheds Cloud put up behind his house; they are too small for what I have planned."

Myine stood also, saying, "Well, Mr. Know-so-much, let me ask you this. Why are you going to spend all that money on my land? I can't offer you any help for something I never even thought of."

"Don't need your help, Myine." He tilted his head as he thought how to answer her.

"I can't say I don't know why, because that would be a lie." He looked directly into her eyes. "I need a place of peace and quiet to work. I like Cloud, and his ways. But, most of all, I want to be close to you. I want to see you every day God gives me."

Myine, taken aback, blushed, and stammered, "I was going to ask you if you wanted a cup of coffee, or a cup of tea, but now, I don't know what to do."

"I want to get started on my work. There are so many things to do. But, if you will let me I'll come back for a cup of coffee, later."

Myine was embarrassed, still blushing, thinking, "How can this man stand up here and make one of my dreams he doesn't know a thing about come true? Is he playing with me?" She said, "Have tea, it's better for you than coffee. Come back, when you have time." Then she hurried into her house; eyes wide, body shaking from nerves, heart not knowing what to do, and a grin on her face she tried to hide with her hands.

Now, I have to clear up a few things. It was about 1991 or '92. Close as mama and I can figure, Herman is about going on sixty-five or sixty-seven, time been flyin, my mama says. Myine is ten years back, younger, so she was fifty-five or fifty-seven. I have already told you I am not good at these number things. What difference does it make anyway? Old is old, young is young, but feeling good . . . can happen anytime!

CHAPTER 38

The work began, and Herman began to come by every day for coffee, or tea. Sometimes Myine fixed lunch for him. But she was never too familiar with him. She was hesitant because she loved him. She teased him, trying to get some more encouraging or flattering words from him. "Going around filling old ladies' heads up with blarney. Make some woman make a fool of her self." She laughed, but she was only half playing.

At this time in his lonely life, Herman was happy. His eyes sparkled, and his heart was soothed every time he walked up her stairs, or saw her coming along the path to the shed-in-progress to see how the work was progressing.

She would comment, "You all are coming right along." Or she would point to a tree, asking, "You all are not going to cut that tree down, are you? That's one of my favorite trees!"

Both Herman and Cloud were dirty and sweaty from the heat and their work. Herman would rub his arm across his brow and say, "No, ma'am. We are not going that far if you don't want us to."

"Well, I don't want you to. This is my private, personal park."

"I'll leave the tree here, so when we sit out here it will still be beautiful to you . . . and me! I like parks!"

Myine and Herman both went around with a lot of sparks going off in their heads and bodies. They were both happy. But, still, neither of them became too familiar. She thought, "Just because I like him, and he is building on my land, I'm not going to be a fool just because he is a man!"

Herman was thinking, "I have to keep things like they are as much as possible; I need her respect for what I want. She is not easy, and I am not easy. I'm fighting for my life, and I think I have a chance of winning, if I don't go too fast." But his hands burned to touch her. He had to tell himself, "She's just a nice older lady, she ain't no hot molly. Keep your hands to yourself. Your day may be coming."

One morning when he stopped to have coffee with her, after she set his cup down, and turned away, he had almost patted her behind. She had been laughing, and the feeling of closeness made him forget it was not his behind yet. He caught himself just in time to stop his eager hand. But she had seen the gesture, and smiled to herself, glad her behind had not sagged down too far yet.

Cloud had made a path as he walked over to the job several times a day; Juliet would ride her wheelchair over to the new building, sitting and talking with them. At times you could hear gleeful laughter ringing out through the trees.

When the building work was all done, Myine was glad all the noise would stop. Lumber, delivery trucks, cement trucks had made a broad path through the wood to the new shed. They knew the woods would take over the land again, and narrow down to the size of their own trucks, once it was not all being used. Cloud and Herman had put in a strong, wide wooden gate. They did not lay gravel, or tar it; it was more like a big path, lined with trees.

Herman kept his word; even though he had spent his own money, there was no traffic, and only one or two people in a month or so came to pick up something Herman or Cloud could not deliver.

Herman had many breakfasts and lunches

and coffee-tea breaks, sitting on the porch with Myine. Cloud always went home; close, but far enough away for them to keep their privacy.

Herman could touch Myine now, in a friendly way, without feeling strange and uncomfortable. He liked to take her hand as he talked to her, or place his hand on her back when he showed her something.

Myine knew she liked being around Herman, but she could not explain to herself the little tingles that went up the arm of the hand he held; or down her back when his arm was nonchalantly around her shoulder. She was thrilled without intending to be thrilled. She was nervous when there was no reason to be nervous. She knew she really loved Herman, as an old family friend, she thought, but she did not dare to dream, to be excited, as she was. About Herman. About Herman, about Herman!

Herman, thinking as usual, said to himself, "I don't need to pay rent for a room I only sleep in. I come here every day, so I might as well sleep here. I'll find some way to give Myine the money for rent."

So, as Herman was leaving one night, he said, "I might need to build a little room for me to rest in sometimes. Nothing big; I won't take up any more land, I'll build it on top of the shed."

The "little room" turned into a small three-room apartment above the shed, the overhang strongly, and correctly, braced, making an alcove surrounded by the trees. Herman placed the steps there, leading to the entryway to the rooms above. It was neat and, after Herman planted a few evergreens, blended in with the woods.

You may think Myine was a bit of a fool for letting them use her land, and never saying a word about rent. But Myine had her own plans. She knew Herman would not use that storage area to work and make money, and not pay her something, "if we are not married," she reasoned, to herself. "Course, if we were married . . . well, that is a thought for another day."

CHAPTER 39

She had already thought about another dream of hers. Traveling. She wanted to see Florence, Italy, as well as Greece and many other places she had discovered in her studies, and long-distance talks with Monee. Monee always called her Aunt Myine; she loved Myine.

Now that Myine knew Tante better, she knew her aunt was controlling and always thinking of herself, even before her daughter's happiness: these were things Myine did not like about Tante, consequently she seldom thought about her, beyond asking about her health. And Tante wasn't really interested in things happening in Wideland.

Besides, Myine was falling deeper in love with Herman. Their new, closer, daily contact with each other was a good thing for both of these lonely people.

As usual, Herman came up with another plan. "You never did get that sunbathing room you wanted, did you?"

"No, I didn't. After I retired working I was just too tired. Too tired to do all that work, and presidents had changed, Reagan was in office, and nobody had any money. Nobody poor, or the middle-class, anyway."

Herman shook his head. "I remember those years. But, you never looked tired."

(Now, you have to remember, time has been passing all the time. They were getting older, like everyone else. They just took a long time to get to what they should'a got to a long time ago.)

"What do you mean, Herman? You know I'm tired; this is 1992, and I am fifty-three years old. Just living through all these crazy presidents, and their new staffs, and self-serving laws, would make anyone tired."

Herman nodded, saying, "I'm sixty-three, but, I don't feel like Methuselah. But still, I guess I'm tired, too. But, you; I'm not saying you look twenty or anything, but who wants to look twenty, the way twenty looks these days. You look healthy, glowing, and really good. Girl, you look sexy to me!"

Myine laughed lightly. "Herman! Stop!"

He reached for her hand, saying, "You do look sexy to me. Very sexy, Ms. Myine."

His touch had given her what felt like a tiny electric shock running up her arm straight to her stomach; it made her snatch her hand away, unintentionally.

She smiled, quickly, so he would take her hand again, saying, "Oh, Herman, you have to tell that stuff to those young women you go out with."

He started to say, "I don't . . ." but decided she shouldn't know he saw no one but her. Instead, he said, "Let's build that new room for you we talked about a long time ago. Right here in the garden by the house. We'll build the room, then build a wall around the small space in the garden, for your privacy. You can plant a small tree, and some flowers in it. And I'll build a platform to put a thin mattress on . . . and you can come outside and lay naked in the sun."

Myine sat down next to him. "Oh, Herman, you know I would love that! And I can let Juliet use it sometimes."

"Myine, Cloud will build Juliet her own." He did not ever want Cloud making love to Juliet right under Myine's nose. "They use all that land over by their house anyway. Your house is at the front gate, where everybody comes in. Yours, I'll fix so only I can see it from the top of the shed."

"Oh, Herman!" She hit him lightly on his shoulder, her body warming as her hand lingered there. "You don't need to see this old tired body full of cellulite."

"That's flesh, too. Your flesh. I want to see everything you have." He stood and leaned over her, saying, "Just make me happy, girl!"

Myine frowned, embarrassed at her own thoughts. Herman quickly said, as he sat back down, "Of course, if you don't want me to . . . Your man wouldn't like that, would he?" He was very still as he waited for her answer.

She stared off into space, then pretended to see a bird to change the subject. "Oh, look!"

Herman took his leave with a soured look on his face. "See you later, Lady."

He thought she had ignored or rejected him.

Myine didn't move, she sat at the table a moment longer. She was thinking of her life: a life disappearing without ever being loved by a man.

You know, you can't help how your mind is built. Being reticent, demure, just plain shy and bashful, can be a handicap; just like it can work to the good for a person, sometimes. There is nothing a person can do about how their mind is made, now is there? I blive that's why God said for us not to judge: We don't usually know a thing for sure. We just like to think we do. Well, that's a sin.

She thought, aloud, "Oh, Lord, I don't want to just screw somebody. No, I'm too old to be talking about screwing. I don't want to just fuck some man, any man. But I am a human woman. I want to be fulfilled. He doesn't even have to make love to me; just hold me, be with me. And maybe, don't leave."

Now! You see that! They are getting too old to breathe, almost, and still, they are too timid, bashful, and embarrassed to just go on and live. I remember a song that asked, "Who Is Gonna Know a Million Years from Today?" I was just out-done when they didn't get together by this time. Even I was married, twice, by that time.

Everybody in town, in church, knew what Herman was doing, but not Myine. Like a lump on a log! She could lose that man! But, still, I knew Herman loved her! And he was not dumb. I saw him move his life right on over to her house on her land! It was the long way around, but the ends had to meet . . . somewhere! I didn't blive Herman was going to let go of that love thing.

CHAPTER 40

When Herman moved his things into his new home above the shed, Myine wondered if she was a fool, being used. But when she really thought of Herman, she knew she was not a fool. He was extremely good to her.

During that day Myine went to visit Juliet. Juliet surprised her by greeting her with "Hello, happy woman!"

Wondering why, Myine said, "No, you're the happy woman."

"Well, aren't you happy too?"

Myine slumped down in a chair. "No, not really. But, I'm glad you and Cloud are happy. Let me ask you something."

"Go right ahead, anytime."

"How did you know Cloud was the one man, the right man, for you?"

Juliet smiled a little private smile. "I was in love with him. And men weren't exactly knocking at my door anyway. But, I didn't need them. I had known Cloud a long time.

I just loved him."

"Yes, but you could have been wrong, Juliet."

"I go by my Bible, Myine. Both your mother and my mother taught me about the Bible and life. Cloud was always honest. You judge a tree by the fruit it bears. He didn't give me no pain, except little boy-girl, men-women pains. They're natural. He was kind to me, always kind. Not only to me, but to Rose, my mama, his mama, and his aunts and cousins.

"He has love built right into him. He just loves; trees, birds, everything. He does not even hunt, and kill things. We mostly eat vegetables that we all grow, less I want a ham hock or something special with my beans. He is the same kind of man you have."

"I don't have a man, Juliet."

Juliet laughed ironic laughter. "Oh, yes, you have a man, you just may not know it. Or you're scared. Herman loves you. Real good."

"How can he love me?"

"Chile, listen to me. You are a good woman. You are kind, and honest, and I know you are faithful, as a woman and as a friend. Your heart is in a place of love. You ain't no blind fool, well . . . You might be a little blind if you can't see how Herman loves you. He licks you all over, eats you up with his eyes. Maybe when you ain't lookin, but I've seen him do it."

Myine moaned in desperation. "Juliet, what can I do? I don't want to lie naked beside some man in this world where youth and beauty are the most important things. I'm old, and my body is breaking down. I have aches and pains I don't tell anyone about. I can't read without my glasses. I even have some false teeth that are worn out; I need new ones. My thighs are changing shapes, and my arms are getting a little flabby. I'm just not a good choice for any man!"

Juliet would not laugh at Myine because she knew how serious this could be to anybody, not only women. She placed her hand on Myine's, and said, "Take all those things you just said you have that you think are so bad; add a flabby stomach, because I had a baby, and almost hanging titties after nursing that baby. And useless legs he has to stand me up on in one place; he has to even open them, most times, when we make love, and then you really got the worst case. And still, still Cloud loves me. And you can add to that, I am older than you."

Myine looked at Juliet a long time.

Both were silent, thinking, wondering.

After another moment, or two, Myine sadly said, "Well, we'll just be two old fools trying to be young, talking about love."

Juliet shook her head as she said, "It does not make you a fool to want love. Love is natural, chile. It would be unnatural not to think of love."

"Oh, Juliet, I ought to go join some senior citizen group and end all this misery in my heart."

"Myine, what you need to do is take Herman and throw him in your bed, and make love to him. Or go get married to him, and get on with your life."

"He hasn't asked me."

"You wait for too much; you are no kid. You talk like someone who hasn't seen some life."

"Juliet, it's been many, many years, since I've even been with a man."

"Then why don't you just cross your legs, and give up on life?"

"Ohhhhhh, Juliet!"

"Then get out, Myine! Go on home. You don't have no problem; you are the problem! Go on, go on over to your own house and cry."

Myine slowly walked home through the woods. But, in about an hour she walked quickly back to Juliet's house. Herman was gathering supplies and tools to start building Myine's sunroom, and he saw her as she was going back to Juliet's.

He motioned to Cloud, saying, "Myine's going back to your house. Wonder what they talk so much about."

Cloud laughed, answering, "Food and sex."

Herman laughed halfheartedly and kept gathering his supplies. He was eager to get started. He had his plans in his head, and down on paper. "I can get this done in two days, if you help me."

Cloud answered, "If we work late, we can get it done in one day and a half. You got everything?"

"Yea, I'm ready."

"You must have some private plans for that sunroom. You awful eager to get on it."

Herman laughed lightly. "This room is coming with its own plans."

As they were walking over to start the sunroom work, they saw Myine headed back to Juliet's house. Herman said, "My lord. They're either cooking a lot, or Juliet's talking about you . . . and sex."

Myine knocked lightly, and opened the

door to Juliet's house. "Hey, Ms. Lady. Juliet?"

"I'm still here; come on in. You forget something?"

"I just have to ask you something."

"Well, let me put some more water on for tea."

Myine sat down, smiling a little. "Let's have a glass of that white wine you're always offering me."

"Oh, my, Myine! It's early, but sometimes I like a glass early."

As Juliet prepared the wine and glasses, Myine sat down in a leather lounge chair meant for Cloud, that he seldom used. He liked sitting or stretching out on the floor. The floors were clean, and comfortable to him.

When they were settled, with glasses in hand, Juliet said, "I like it real cold, so I put ice in my wine."

Myine answered, "I like it cold, too."

Juliet took a deep breath, "Now, my sister-friend, I hope I can answer any questions you have. If I can't you'll be drunk, and won't know the difference anyway."

They laughed a little, then Myine asked, "How do you make love?"

Juliet laughed a little, then said, "Why, it just comes naturally; you do what you feel."

"I mean, how do you look? How do you hold your face? You can't look at him!"

"He is exactly what I look at, Myine. He is my man, and I'm about to make love to him, with him."

Myine sighed, exasperated. "I mean, do you fix your hair? Try to look pretty, and keep everything in place?"

"You do that before you make love, if you have time, and want to. Once you get started, you don't even think about that. At least I don't. You can't make love, if your mind is someplace else!"

"Well, suppose he looks at you while you are making love?"

"Oh, Myine, I see what the matter is. You are scared, and you were always bashful! Don't be bashful, Myine; that man won't be thinking of your hair or your face. Just relax and be yourself."

"I have to be myself, Juliet, but I don't want him to see me in a . . . a nasty way."

"You think he, or any man, will worry bout if you see him in a 'nasty' way?"

Myine thought a minute, then shook her head. "Men are different."

"No they're not, Myine. Not when people are making love; when you make love, you think of the feelings. That's why, maybe, you never had an orgasm. I hear tell that some men can be lousy lovers, but I think you were thinking bout the wrong things while you were trying to make love."

"What do you mean, the wrong things? Tell me the right things, Juliet."

"Number one, it's about making love, it is not a beauty contest. You're not there to be beautiful; that all happens before you get there. Once you get there, you let go, and just be yourself."

"Juliet, I don't know which self to be. How to be . . ."

"Myine, you have to . . . have to relax. I don't mean lay there like a log, but . . . relax. When he gets on top of you, welcome him into your arms, but lay relaxed. Then when he goes to put it in, stay relaxed. But pull your knees up to his hips; but stay relaxed." She gave Myine a sidewise look, and asked "Are you making me tell you these things when you already know?"

"But I don't know, Juliet."

"Okay. When things start happenin, kissin, huggin, pettin, and all that, make your kisses soft, don't tense your lips, don't pucker up; relax your lips, so they will be soft. Now, I don't like all that tongue in your ear stuff! Kiss my ears, soft and sweetlike, and my neck . . ."

"Has he put it in yet?"

"Oh, lots of things can be happening; just remember you have to help yourself to have an orgasm. Don't leave it all up to him to make you . . ."

Myine stared into Juliet's eyes, speechless, drinking in every word.

Juliet stared back into Myine's face, saying, "I can't believe as old as you are, you don't know this already."

Myine shook her head, in a daze. "I don't know though. My mother couldn't teach me."

Juliet snorted softly. "Mamas don't always tell you; you just grow to know. Or, I guess it depends on your man. He has to make you feel . . . make you want to do all the things . . ."

"Okay, Juliet, what else?"

Juliet laughed a little, as she continued, "When he puts, you know what, in, you have to picture what he is doing in your mind, like imagine it, but see it in your mind, the same as he is doing it."

In wonder, Myine repeated, "Picture it in my mind."

"Yes, but pay relaxed attention to everything happening to you down there," she pointed. "Every move he makes, let your body tell you what to do to answer his move. Don't plan it; feel it. Keep on picturing it in your mind til you feel it. If he knows what he is doing, you'll be done forgot about your hair, face, and everything else. Me, I like my knees up and relaxed open; let em fall open more, do they want to, far as they will go to the side."

"Suppose he has a small . . . thing? Not a big one? I've heard men need a big one."

Juliet smiled to her friend. "Chile, don't let people lie, and confuse you. If you love a man, his size won't matter. If you are picturing it in your mind, don't care what size it is, it got to be good. You don't want nobody to hurt you. You just want to relax and enjoy it. Now, some women are built big, but the Lord knew what he was doing when he made men and women. Size don't matter as much as love. If there is love, that is what makes all the difference in the world."

Hesitantly, Myine asked, "Is Cloud . . . ?"

"That ain't none of your business, my sister. And don't you be telling other women bout NOTHING your man can do! That's your business!" Juliet took a sip of her wine, and asked, "Now. Have you made up your mind, at least, to try it?"

Myine's eyes were opened wide in the wonder of life, and she smiled as she answered, "I think I have."

"Stop lying, Myine, You know you're going to do it. You know you love Herman, and I know he loves you, all that work that man does for you!"

"He does that for his own self."

"Well, what's for him, is for you. He cannot wrap the house and yard up, then pick it up and carry it away. He loves you Myine. You will have a good man."

Myine's "Yes" was loaded with smiles, and anticipation.

(And by this time she is at least sixty-two years old! I haven't told you everything, that would take another sixty-two years. You just be glad I wanted to tell you this story, and I wanted to tell it cause people always talking, and writing, about young love; I wanted to let you know there is Old love, too! Love never stops on this earth, cause of the fact God is love. But you got to be in a special place to find it. You got to know what is real about life, and what is false.)

"And you will . . . come through, too, if you do what I told you!" Juliet turned to a small table, reaching for a paper list, saying, "Now, take these things I put together for you. A little perfume, 'Joy': wear only the best for your man. It's expensive; but I make this last me a year or two. That's why you have to pay me back for this.

"Sometimes I order Worth perfume out of

the magazine I have delivered to me. But it is hard to find, sometimes.

"But, I'm'a give you this; Youth Dew by Estée Lauder is good, but use it early in the mornings so by evening time it will be faded enough. Put it in good spots, like between your breast, in your navel, after you wash it. That's enough, cause this stuff is strong, but it smells sexy." She smiled a secret smile for herself.

"By the evening it will fade away, and that's what you want. Then put a little Joy, just a little, behind your ears and on your thighs and neck. You can give me these bottles back in the morning, and you can buy your own. Cause our men buy tools, but these are our tools, and they make enough money. This is all for them anyway.

"I know you got this, your own self; put something pretty on, and soft to his touch. Don't spray nothing on it, it needs to smell like your natural self."

Myine took in every word Juliet said, as if it were holy. "Oh, Juliet, you sound like I'm going out to some big, important affair."

"Myine, this can be the most important time in your life with your man. You want to make him remember it, and all of the times like this, as long as he lives. Love ain't

367

no play thing, but, you are playing for keeps!"

Ardently, breathlessly, Myine said, "Oh, thank you, Juliet! These are the things I wanted, needed to know." She picked up the small bag, as if it were gold. Juliet frowned in wonder. "What I can't understand is how come you didn't already know. Women's born knowing these things; and magazines help a little; but you got to know when they lyin.'"

"I'd wager a friend, or a mother, is the most help, Juliet. And you're the only friend I've ever really had."

"I am your honest-to-God friend, Myine, honest. Your mama and my family were friends from the time I was born. But that ain't all it is: I love you. When I call you 'sister,' I mean it."

They were silent a moment, then Juliet reached for one more thing on the table. "Myine, you might not need this jelly-crème, but I have it, just in case you do. Sometimes, things you don't use, dry up on ya!" They laughed girlish laughter of joy as Myine took the jar and nearly ran out the door.

She headed straight home, smiling as she thought of her friend, Juliet. She saw Herman and Cloud cutting a hole the size of a door on the side of her house. The sight took her aback for a moment.

"Well! Look what you are doing, Herman."

Herman answered, "Yea, just look what I'm doing. Don't worry, Myine, we will have a door here, and a sunroom besides . . . by tonight."

"By tonight?" she asked.

"You don't trust me, Myine?"

Myine relaxed, and smiled. "Yes, I trust you, Herman."

The men laughed, and she ran inside her house.

CHAPTER 41

Herman had all the studs and sheetrock for a twelve-by-eighteen-foot room marked off in the basement. He was also going to set and hinge the door to the outside. Cloud was setting the forms for the walls on the outside that would enclose the ten-by-twelve space for the sun-garden.

They would stucco six-foot Indian adobe walls over the form, with a redwood fence that could be opened to let the rest of the yard and beautiful trees in. It was going to be very nice. The studding and sheetrocking was finished that first evening. They decided to leave the old wooden floors as they were. The outside wall to the private garden had yet to be done.

"We can get that done tomorrow," Herman said, as the two sweaty, tired men left to go to their showers and bed. He added, "I should be going upstairs in this house to take a bath, and go to bed. But, I'll wait."

Cloud smiled, saying, "At the rate you swingin that hammer, I know you ain't waitin long." He turned off on his own path home.

Herman laughed as he answered, "I don't have long. At my age, I could die in twenty minutes, so you are right, brother."

Juliet had Cloud's dinner ready. He showered, ate, and fell into the bed. Myine had fixed Herman a good meal and took it to him at his apartment. He was already snoring on his couch. She set the tray down: a steak, baked potato, and asparagus. Then she woke Herman, who looked dazzle-eyed until he realized where he was and smelled the food. She leaned over and kissed him on the forehead; as he was reaching for her, she said "Good-bye," and left. She was not ready, and she wanted to use all the things Juliet had taught her about.

Herman ate the meal, fell in his bed without a shower, and slept soundly with a smile on his face.

The next day the men started early. By noon they had completed the outside walls, and attached the gate. There were a few things not quite up to par, but nothing that could not be put off for another day.

Myine had been busy all the morning making all the beds, three upstairs. Flipping the mattresses, putting on fresh, fluffy sheets and pillowcases, with pretty spreads. Vacuuming the carpets; just doing everything. She also began setting up for her dinner. Their dinner. A fresh broiled salmon fish with broccoli and rice with chopped parsley, and a tossed green salad.

When the men had been at work for a few hours, or so, Myine put her head out of the window, calling out, "Herman? You are going to eat over here tonight. Alright?"

Herman stepped back, and looked up, with dust and a little paint on his face, and in his eyelashes. Startled, he nodded his head, and said, "Yes, ma'am."

She asked, "When do you think you'll be ready to eat?"

Cloud answered for him, "We're gonna quit here in another hour or two. What time you want him?"

Embarrassed for no good reason, Myine said, "Well . . . in a couple of hours, I guess. Whenever he's ready to eat."

Laughing, Cloud said, "He's ready now."

Myine slammed the window down hard, before she realized they could not read her mind, and did not know what she was planning. "Juliet told him!" Then she was too excited to be angry. She thought, "I don't care, this is my life; our life!"

In a few hours, Herman looked around the room they had built, almost satisfied. Cloud went home. Herman was tired, but he went to the florist, and bought a huge bouquet of mixed, colorful flowers.

"It looks too bare out there right now for Myine to see how it's going to look; so I'll just set a small wooden table out there, with two wood chairs, for the time being, and set the flowers on it." And that's what he did. Then he went home to shower, and try not to fall asleep.

CHAPTER 42

The chairs, table, and flowers were already in the sunroom when Herman rang the doorbell at about 4:30 or 5:00 that evening. Myine opened the door with a bright, eager smile, and held her hand out to him. "Herman, come in, please."

Herman tried to respond with cool dispassion, "Myine, Myine." While he was thinking, "Mine, mine. Oh, Lord, please let this evening go well. I don't want to scare her."

She had on a soft, silken, pale-green dress that buttoned down the front; she looked lovely in it.

He smiled, pleased at her effort. "You dressed for . . . dinner?"

"Oh, Herman, this ole thing? I thought it might lift your spirits. I'm always in . . . some ole pants, or worn-out dress."

"You always look good. Always."

They enjoyed a good dinner, and after,

she gave him a few vitamin pills. "I know you work hard, Herman, and I know you don't always eat right. You need a little extra."

"Oh, I can always use a little extra. Thank you. Say, you want to go downstairs and see how your room will look when we're through?"

Myine stood, ready to go, "Yes. I've been, but I want to go again. I'm so excited, Herman."

"I am, too. I hope you like it."

As they started down the steps to the basement, Myine was in front of him. He put his hands on her hips, and held them there all the way down, saying, "Don't fall." Her hips seemed to roil beneath his tender hands.

She laughed, saying, "Herman, I've been coming down these steps for years." But, she didn't remove his hands, and neither did he.

There was a door to the sunroom, for privacy within the house; he made a little show of opening it. "Open O'sesame!" Then she walked slowly into the room that was empty except for a large, low-shag, sky-blue rug in the middle of the room.

Myine blushed as she said, "I put that here today after you left." They laughed, and he said, "It's pretty. I'm glad you are thinking of your new room!"

"Oh, Herman, I could never come in here without thinking of it as 'your' room. You built it."

He was right on the verge of happy as he said, "Okay then, let's say our room." She was on the verge of happy, also.

He led her to the doorway leading outside, and opened it, showing the little table with a huge bouquet of flowers on it, and two chairs.

She loved everything. Love was in the very air of the rooms. Herman moved the table so it would be in front of the chairs, and put the two chairs closer together, playfully saying, "Have a seat, ma'am." He sighed, saying, "It does not look so good right now, but I'm going to make a little Japanese waterfall. And plant a delicate, slender tree, and some small evergreens. I was thinking of putting a big aquarium tank in that room, so you can get a whole new feel to the house down here."

"Oh, I love it, I love it, Herman." She turned to look at him, "I do, I really do. It's strange how little changes can make such a big difference." She reached for his shoulder, to pull him toward her, then he gently dragged her chair closer to him.

Herman smiled down at her, getting ever so close to crossing that verge of happiness, right into it. "Well, thank you, Myine. Now, let me ask you something. I look at all this work we did in here, and . . . I wonder. Do you think I could have a kiss? A real kiss?"

Myine blushed, for no reason except her shyness, and said, "Oh, don't ask me that, Herman. You don't have to ask that. Of course, you . . ." She leaned over to kiss him, but he stood up. "I don't want a side kiss, I want a kiss. Don't blush, Myine. It's just a kiss."

Myine stood up, stepping closer to Herman, as she lifted her face. He held her face with one hand, while pulling her real close to him with the other. When he raised his face from hers, he didn't step away from her, he held on to her, and asked, "Do you know how long I've wanted to do this?"

Myine stood silent, still looking up at him, her lips closed, but smiling. He smoothed her hair, and murmured sweet sounds in her ear as he pressed her body even closer to his. He raised his head, his eyes searching into her eyes, slowly, steady, slowly, before she closed them. She felt his warm, soft lips on hers. She felt the muscle in her lips let go as she kissed him. Her lips, then, bloomed and softened under his lips; as did her body.

Feelings were rushing through her body, and suddenly she was overwhelmed by a delirious joy as she clung to him. She was filled with such a hunger she had never felt before. "I desire him," she thought to herself, joyously, "I want all of him in all of me."

The sounds of the wind in the trees, a distant roaring in her ears, were mixed inside her head. She seemed to feel the earth spinning beneath her feet. Her heart sang. "Is that my heart?" she asked herself. She opened her eyes and saw the stars, bright as flames; and Herman.

Her knees weakened; he put his arms closer around her and lifted her into the empty room, onto the sky-blue rug on the cement floor, into the darkness; hot, struggling, and full of the voices singing in her heart.

She remembered what Juliet had told her about relaxing, and picturing what he was doing to her, in her mind. The emotional feelings broadened, physical sensations widened, everything expanded the feelings she felt as he entered her body with his. Suddenly, something in her hips made a spreading, tender explosion, and her body and head were filled with the sound of her body singing.

In a moment, he started to say something to her, but she stopped him with her fingers. "No, just let me lie here, and feel the feelings of you and me. Us."

He held her tightly, but tenderly, and murmured in her ear, "That was my hope, forever and ever. For you and me. Us."

She had not needed the jelly-crème this time.

He had moved past the verge of happiness, over the edge, and was deep in the center of his happiness, finding ecstasy, and rapture there. He had brought her with him. He didn't come alone over the verge, and into the depths of love; they journeyed together.

(My My My My)

CHAPTER 43

Now, life being life, and love being love, in no time at all, Herman took Myine to be his wife at the earliest possible time. Myine couldn't stop smiling, and Juliet was smiling, too, throughout all the days, as she baked the wedding cakes, and sewed here and there on things she wanted to give Myine.

Myine wore a simple long white silk dress, and a veil. Her bouquet was made up of purple orchids and pretty branches from the foliage on the land. Herman wanted her to have a grand bouquet, but Myine told him no.

She said, "You must not understand. This way, with the foliage from here, all my family will be with me." That was what she wanted. Herman didn't really mind; he was going to be part of her, part of her family. He smiled to himself, "My family at last!"

It was a small wedding in the front parlor

of the main house: "home." All through that week, every time the couple passed near each other they brushed against each other, touching in any way possible. Smiling all the time.

Herman, naturally, moved from his garage apartment into his new home almost before it was possible, doing everything at once. But, Myine wanted him "home."

After the small family wedding, no one had to leave because everyone who was at the wedding was already home, except the minister.

Of course, Lola was there, beaming. Poem flew over from France a few weeks later to see Myine's new husband. She liked him, but it didn't matter to Myine anyway. Poem looked beautiful in her Parisian clothes. Myine held the young woman, as she said, "Girl, pardon me. Young lady, you look beautiful. I know your grandmother and Monee are proud of you!"

Then they talked of Tante's ill health. "She is old, Aunt Myine. Older than you. But she still dresses every day, in case someone comes to call. I don't think she will be with us much longer. Her health has suffered for a long time now. She thinks it is a secret, but we know. She can hardly get around without a walker, and some help. She always liked secrets."

Poem left, traveling on to New York for some conference in international business affairs. Her mother had wanted her to major in business law and administration, and she had.

She came back to Wideland on her way home, to tell Myine she was coming back to live there awhile. Herman and Myine took her to look at some land, but she wanted the old house right across the street that was for sale, cheap, and sitting on several acres.

Herman told her, "Poem, that house is cheap, but it will cost you a fortune to fix it up for you to live in. A fortune!"

She answered, speaking to Myine, "I don't care. The best time of my life was living here with Aunt Myine, in peace. I miss it. I miss the trees, and the grass, the animals; just everything country. The space! I live in a beautiful city, but you know what I really want?"

She turned to Herman, saying, "I want a cow, a dog, a cat, some chickens like we used to have, and lots of land of my own to walk around on. Like you, Aunt Myine."

She looked thoughtful a moment, then said, "I met a nice man at the conference. It might develop into something. But, even if that does not turn into anything, I still want to come here, home, to live and breathe again."

Herman and Myine left her desires to her own decisions. They gave her the keys to Herman's old garage apartment. "This is your place when you come to get your house ready."

Herman's stepsons, James and Jerome, lived in Philadelphia and San Francisco, respectively. He told them, "This is your apartment when you are in town with your families. You'll be at home here. Myine and I just don't want anyone to live there all the time. It takes away from our space and peace. But we love you, and you'll be welcome."

Even Wings Val used the apartment when he came home on breaks from college. When he was graduated with a computer science master's degree, he was going to be on the road and in the air a great deal traveling for his work. He was still young, but had decided he didn't want to keep living in any large city.

When Poem, who had returned to France for the moment, and with whom he had grown up, called him, she wanted to discuss a few things about her new property. They made a deal. "You help me rebuild my house, and I'll let you build one for yourself on the land." Poem knew she would have many helpers; Herman and Cloud. They may be older men, but they were certainly capable, if only to supervise. Further, she knew someone needed to be living on land, or it would just decay. Land, like a heart, has to be loved to really live.

Herman and Myine watched all the progress around them happily, as long as it was not too close. Cloud and Juliet felt the same way.

So, the next few years passed smoothly, and quickly. Herman and Myine built such a happiness as to compare with any happiness on earth. A happiness that did not depend on money or looks. Using, or being used. They were happy, and content. Of course, everyone who happened to have a chance to be around either of them felt their joy in living.

They had the usual human problems: taxes, health, if they didn't take care of themselves, small debts; nothing they could not handle. They grew all their own food; vegetables and several fruits from their trees. They had a glass of wine with their dinner sometimes. They didn't celebrate Christmas because they discovered Jesus Christ wasn't born December 25, it was a day to profit business stores. But they had eggnog at New Year's celebrations at home.

They didn't have many people in their lives, so it was comparatively simple, quiet, and problem free.

Herman and Myine had sex whenever they felt like it. If they had to wait they waited. But patience and love were woven through their days of marriage. The sex was always good, because it was in their heads and hearts, as well as their bodies.

Herman and Cloud still had their machine shop that could have stayed overloaded if they hadn't refused some jobs. It paid well, more than they needed.

Herman liked to buy things for Myine; perfumes, silk scarves, flowers. He had music he liked to play for her in the evenings when they sat on their porch in the swing, or downstairs in their sun-garden, sitting in the dark. Juliet told Cloud, "Myine is happy, chile!"

When Wings was at home, he began to set up a computer for automobiles for his father, because so many things had changed in the automotive industry, becoming computerized. Halfheartedly, Herman and Cloud waited, and watched, to see how it all worked out. They never did really understand it, and seldom, if ever, used it.

They really felt semi-retired, so new things, to them, did not matter. They felt too tired to bother learning new things, but . . . just in case, they listened to Wings.

What everyone wanted was to see what kind of young woman Wings would bring home; who would share in their life. Well, he took his time. He liked to spend time out on the reservation with his relatives, as well as travel.

He liked trips to New York, or San Francisco. He flew to France to visit Poem once. She gave him the use of her house and a map. They had lunch or dinner together several times. They even cooked a meal at home, together, a few times, laughing and talking about "ole country Wideland!" Even discussed plans for their houses on her land.

Myine went regularly to the Jehovah's Witness Hall on Sundays, and often, Herman went with her. Cloud asked him about it, because Herman had said, "I don't like organized religion. All the people I hear on TV lie a lot, and beg for money. If I want to learn about God, I go to my Bible."

When Cloud asked him about the Hall, Herman sighed, and took a moment to answer. "Well, Cloud, you know I don't like liars. And you know it's not hard to see through most of the people preaching in this world. But . . . these people . . . every time they tell you something they hold that Bible up in your face and make you read it for yourself! It's hard to lie about the Bible that way.

"And another thing, they make you study that Bible; you can't read just one scripture and let it go. You have to study. I know people who say they skip all over the Bible. But, listen. I studied mechanics, and we had to read many books dealing with mechanics to learn all we could about the work.

"Well, it's the same thing. The Bible has sixty-six books in it. The Old Testament, and the New. All these people are talking about Jehovah God, and Jesus; the past, and the future. When they skip around from one chapter to another, they are reading what each one said about their own experience with Jesus and God. So skipping around is necessary for a person to get a full picture of things. Focused on one subject at a time."

Cloud looked thoughtful, because he respected Herman and his mind. Then he asked, "Why do they call Him Jehovah? Isn't it the same God for everybody?"

Herman smiled, "Yea, that's the same thing I asked Myine."

"What'd she say, man?"

"She told me, and showed me in the

Bible, at Psalm 83:18. Don't laugh at me, man. I have remembered a lot of things that were worth less." He laughed, briefly, then continued, "Anyway, He says His name is Jehovah, Myine said, like in the prayer where everybody says, 'Hallowed be thy name'? Well, God is not his name, God is what He IS, it is not his name.

"So at that Psalm 83:18, it says, 'Thou whose name, alone, is Jehovah, is the most high over all the earth.' And, I'll tell you the truth, Cloud, I have heard people called many names out of that Bible; Jesus, Isaiah, Benjamin, and others, but I have never heard of anyone called Jehovah, but Jehovah. Now . . . how did that prophet know that, that long ago? Thousands of years ago?"

Cloud looked at Herman, his best friend, very seriously. They had never written a contract, never did a thing but shake hands on anything. They never argued, or if they did, it was argued like a math problem; solved and forgotten. "And," Cloud thought, "Herman is not a dumb, silly man, by any measure."

He said to Herman, "My people believe that Nature is God."

Herman laughed, lightly and briefly, again. "Man, God created Nature. That's one thing I always liked about you; you are real, and I think your beliefs are real. But, I am learning, 'Don't love the creation as much as you should love the Creator of the creation.' "

Cloud answered, "We believe in a Supreme Creator, man, but my people keep it simple, and real. I can't speak for everyone, but we don't get involved in all this 'Mine is greater than yours' kind of mess. God is God; surely He will decide. He said not to judge, anyway, man."

Herman shook his head, because he understood, saying, "And, another thing I'm noticing, Cloud. All this talk lately, the last few years, on the television . . . about Jesus, and God. The people on television who are always telling you what the causes of your problems are. They like to pick on things like homosexuality, or abortions, or lying. They act like those are the only sins. And they seldom use the word 'lying,' even when they know someone is lying, unless they think that person is inferior to them. The big shots, like presidents and senators, get away clean.

"More important, they never mention, or talk about, Satan; and Satan is all through the Bible from the Garden of Eden to today! As the cause of all problems, even death. It's time to make choices, man. But they try to say Jesus is gay, or married, or something just as unreal.

"You know, Satan is the great propagandist. The first liar! He can really lie, man, and get all kinds of men to lie for him! The big men in these churches? And politics? Satan uses them! Because they are all about money!"

Herman was fired up, passionate. "You know it was the false religious leaders that caused Jesus' death, it was not all the Jewish people. Many of them believed in Jesus. Where do you think 'Christians' came from? The twelve Jewish apostles! The Old Testament cannot be separated from the New Testament. The old foretold the new; the new fulfilled the old. Did you know Jesus was not only their Messiah, he is our Messiah, too!"

Cloud nodded his head, thoughtfully. "But, why do people dislike the Jehovah's Witnesses so much? They're not carrying a gun; they're carrying a Bible."

Herman laughed, lightly, as he nodded his own head, and said, "I asked Myine's teacher that myself. He showed me, in the Bible. I remembered this one: Matthew 24:9. It says, right there, that people would hate God's followers on account of His name. Man, that's the same chapter where you can find out about a lot of things that are happening, even now, and it was written two thousand years ago.

"I want to tell you this also; it says some times hard to deal with would be here on this earth, in that same chapter of Matthew. Things are changing on this earth, man. All over the world. Armageddon is real! People don't pay any attention to it, like they didn't pay any attention to Noah; but the rains came anyway, and so is Armageddon coming. I'm glad I found my wife, Myine, while I was still able to have a life.

"You know, Cloud, I can only say now, my life is full. I have a home, a family, and I have Myine. I have love and peace, and I am learning about God. Man, you can't beat that! I wouldn't have been as lonely before if I had found God earlier, but I use to run from these people talking about God! Satan makes you do that. Every time you listen to Jehovah God, Satan loses you. Satan does not like that! He start giving you problems to take your mind off of God's wisdom."

"I know what you mean, Herm. That's why no one can tell me about Juliet, and her wheelchair. She is all woman to me, and we are lucky to have a good son."

"That's not luck, man, that's a blessing. I

don't mean any harm, man, you know that. But everything you have: your son, a wife you love? Those are blessings!"

"Yea, Herman, I feel blessed. And Juliet and me are thinking of taking our savings, and building a house nearer to the reservation. We saved all the rent we would have paid Myine, and more from this job you gave me. We are getting old, and I am tired; not tired to death, but I know it is near us. We want to be buried out there; another kind of home."

Herman slowly shook his head as he said, "I know it can't be too far off from me either, and I want to leave Myine safe as I can, so I saved. I always have saved my money. I get mad sometimes, because life waited so long to give me a life. A life I could love."

Cloud laughed softly. "Just be glad, man, that life gave you one before it was all over."

"There's more coming, Cloud, at least the Bible says so."

Cloud laughed gently. "Give me mine, man, and Juliet's."

Life is not perfect . . . for anyone. But love makes such a difference in life that sometimes it is the only thing that seems important. It makes life livable.

The world had speeded up so much that mankind could not keep up even with itself. It would soon be the twenty-first century, and so many things were on the horizon that would be different, and difficult, for mankind, harder to bear, from all the years gone before on earth.

Herman and Myine had their love. But, as Herman says, "We are not tearing up our mattress every night, or every week, as some people like to think lovers should. But when we do make love it is of such a quality, it is enough to make us complete in our souls. Lovers just love. The main thing is, we have each other.

"Cloud, you are in your sixties, and Juliet is still in good health, and in her early seventies. You are happy, or at least, content. Good, peaceful, loving stands for a lot. Myine is sixty-three, and I am seventy-three. And I thank God we are happy, because I know human beings seldom had anything to do with our happiness. Happy! Now . . . you know, man, that is something.

"Because, well . . . Life is short, especially if you are happy. And life is wide; especially if you are old, and still have a chance for happiness. But, you have to watch life as you live it, because life is always deep."

Herman sighed, and they both stood up

to leave, going home. Cloud started up his usual path, a little slower than earlier days. Herman bent to rub his bad knee before he started his slow pace on his path home. Saying as he raised up, "Me? I'm not afraid of dying, but . . . I just want to keep living as long as I can keep living." He smiled a sweet, secret smile, as he said, "And Myine keeps making the living worth living."

Cloud, looking back, smiled his own sweet smile, and answered, "Man, that's all a man should want; we are in paradise."

"Thank God," Herman sighed as he waved farewell to Cloud. He looked toward his house, where Myine was waiting for him. Smiling, he said again, "Yes. Thank you, Jehovah God!"

Well . . . that's the story I wanted to tell you. Happened right here in my town. Now, I'm tired, and mama has fallen asleep listening to me tell their story to you. But me? I never get tired of telling it because it's about love: hard-to-find, hard-to-get, hard-to-keep love.

They are old now, but who gets too old to love? Nobody! It is built in us to want love, because God is love. I'm old, but I still love Love, chile. I could tell you a story about that, too. But that's enough for today. We'll just have to talk again sometime, cause I got to go.

Now.

My My My!

ABOUT THE AUTHOR

J. California Cooper is the author of four novels, *Family, In Search of Satisfaction, The Wake of the Wind,* and *Some People, Some Other Place,* and of seven collections of stories: *Homemade Love,* the winner of the 1989 American Book Award; *Wild Stars Seeking Midnight Suns; A Piece of Mine; The Future Has a Past; Some Love, Some Pain, Sometime; The Matter Is Life;* and *Some Soul to Keep.* She is also the author of seventeen plays and has been honored as Black Playwright of the Year. In 1988, she received the James Baldwin Writing Award and the Literary Lion Award from the American Library Association. She lives in California.

5-11